MONKEY Station

Ardath Mayhar
and
Ron Fortier

S0-BNK-156

Cover Art
LINDY GIACOMINI

TSR, Inc.

MONKEY STATION

©Copyright 1989 Ardath Mayhar and Ron Fortier
All Rights Reserved.

This book is protected under the copyright laws of the United States of America. Any reproduction or other unauthorized use of the material or artwork contained herein is prohibited without the express written permission of TSR, Inc.

Distributed to the book trade in the United States by Random House, Inc. and in Canada by Random House of Canada, Ltd.

Distributed in the United Kingdom by TSR UK Ltd.

Distributed to the toy and hobby trade by regional distributors.

DRAGONLANCE is a registered trademark owned by TSR, Inc. FORGOTTEN REALMS is a trademark owned by TSR, Inc. TM designates other trademarks owned by TSR, Inc.

First Printing: June, 1989
Printed in the United States of America.
Library of Congress Catalog Card Number: 88-51729

9 8 7 6 5 4 3 2 1

ISBN: 0-88038-743-2
All characters in this book are fictitious. Any resemblance to actual persons, living or dead, is purely coincidental.

TSR, Inc.
P.O. Box 756
Lake Geneva, WI 53147
U.S.A.

TSR Ltd.
120 Church End, Cherry Hinton
Cambridge CB1 3LB
United Kingdom

MONKEY STATION

©Copyright 1989 Ardath Mayhar and Ron Fortier
All Rights Reserved.

This book is protected under the copyright laws of the United States of America. Any reproduction or other unauthorized use of the material or artwork contained herein is prohibited without the express written permission of TSR, Inc.

Distributed to the book trade in the United States by Random House, Inc. and in Canada by Random House of Canada, Ltd.

Distributed in the United Kingdom by TSR UK Ltd.

Distributed to the toy and hobby trade by regional distributors.

DRAGONLANCE is a registered trademark owned by TSR, Inc. FORGOTTEN REALMS is a trademark owned by TSR, Inc. TM designates other trademarks owned by TSR, Inc.

First Printing: June, 1989
Printed in the United States of America.
Library of Congress Catalog Card Number: 88-51729

9 8 7 6 5 4 3 2 1

ISBN: 0-88038-743-2
All characters in this book are fictitious. Any resemblance to actual persons, living or dead, is purely coincidental.

TSR, Inc.
P.O. Box 756
Lake Geneva, WI 53147
U.S.A.

TSR Ltd.
120 Church End, Cherry Hinton
Cambridge CB1 3LB
United Kingdom

To Ron Fortier, idea man extraordinaire
— Ardath Mayhar

To Ardath M., my Texas godmother
— Ron Fortier

PROLOGUE

Rain pounded on the fan-shaped leaves about him, spraying over his face with the force of the impact, but Tulunga ignored it. About him, the jungle dripped in a thousand voices, and the distant river grew louder as more and more water poured over the rapids.

The old man stood beneath a tree so huge that its crown was lost against the low-hanging blanket of clouds. His back was braced against the rough-barked trunk, and his eyes were closed to the world around him. He was listening to the voice that spoke to him sometimes in the midst of storms.

At the best of times, his face was a mass of deep-cut wrinkles. When he listened to the voice, though, the wrinkles cut deeper still. Rain ran down the channels of his cheeks, off the end of his beaklike nose, dripped from his eyebrows and his chin, and still he listened to the voice.

When he was young, Tulunga had to chew the Vision Plant in order to tap the voice inside him. Although others in his tribe saw pictures forming in their minds after they used the plant, he had always, even as a youngster, heard words. That trait had set him apart from the other would-be seers of his tribe and the nearby groups of Real People.

Now that he was old, the habit of listening was a comfortable thing that needed no stimulation. He could hear the voice while working or sleeping, while walking in the forest or swimming in the stream that flowed between stony cuts to the distant river. Storms brought messages, more often than not, and the storm that assailed him now was filling him with terrible words. He was frightened, for the first time in many years.

When he opened his eyes again, he started off at once through the storm-lashed jungle, ignoring the runnels of water underfoot and the slashes of lightning overhead.

When he reached the huddled straw huts that formed his tiny village in the Amazon Basin, he went at once to the shelter housing the head of the tribal clan. He paused outside at the opening that formed the door, waiting for the elder to know his presence.

"Is it my brother, Tulunga?" came the quavering voice from inside. "Come in and sit beside my fire. We who are old find a chill in our bones when it rains."

If Tulunga was old, Walebe was ancient. The thin

straggle of hair left on his scalp was white, and his face had shrunk to the bone, so that he had no wrinkles left, only a skull covered with parchment.

Tulunga sat cross-legged beside the older man and stared for a moment into the tiny fire blazing in a nest of stones.

"You have come in haste," observed the elder. "I hear your heart beating in your chest, and you are still breathing hard from your run. What have you heard, brother, inside your spirit?"

Tulunga sighed. "I have heard words that make no sense to me. But they frighten me, brother. They hint at terrible things out there beyond the forest edge, in the Dead Lands. Perhaps you can make clearer sense of them than I have tried to do."

Walebe stirred and sat straighter. He turned his bird-like gaze on the seer with full attention. "Perhaps," he said.

"I have heard the voice tell of death in the world out there that the white men talk about. Death for all—or almost all—who walk in the Dead Lands and in the other places beyond the big waters at the river's end. It tells me of things to come that seem impossible. Many of the animals, too, will die. And those that are left will change, and change, and change again. There will be beasts unlike any we know, plants, and even insects, that our children's grandchildren will come to know, but which do not exist now with us."

Walebe sat silently for a few moments. "Ill omens," he said then. "Death, at least, we know and understand.

Our people have been hunted like animals, and we both recall those times not long ago. Times before the missionary came to live near the river.

"He speaks nonsense much of the time, but he has protected our people from the soldiers and the settlers."

Walebe gazed again into the fire. "We should warn him of danger, though we cannot tell him where to watch for it."

Tulunga laughed harshly. "He hates me. He tells me the voice in my spirit comes from that Evil One he knows so well. He will not listen if you say that this was a vision. He does not believe in such matters."

"Then I will send one of the young men with a message. I will say that it has come to my ears, and that is no lie, that there is grave danger in the outside world. That he should be most cautious in his dealings with those from outside the trees. That is all we can do, I think."

Tulunga nodded. Walebe always had a sensible solution to any problem, the younger man thought, and this was no exception. But he had had a premonition that when the danger came upon them, it would be something Walebe could not control and could not prevent.

1

The elevator, of course, managed to stick halfway between AIDS Research and Viruses. It usually did. Harkrider cursed softly, doing his usual number on the buttons. He had wasted more time in this antiquated bit of junk than he cared to think about.

Tonight, naturally, was one of those when the combination of buttons was unusually hard to find—he pushed three combinations, and the computer that ran the thing still didn't catch on.

St. Patrick's Day!

And a hot date with Trudi at one of Atlanta's hottest clubs! And he was stuck in this . . . ah! The thing began moving sluggishly, finally arriving at the institute's twentieth floor.

DNA RESEARCH IN PROGRESS—CLEARANCE

REQUIRED flashed onto the screen overhead. He sighed and lifted his internal clearance card, pressing it against the sensor panel. With a sigh the equal of his own, he thought, the doors of the elevator swished open. He took his satchel of tools and stepped out into the corridor, which was dimly lit and empty of other human life.

There wouldn't be anybody else on the floor, he was certain. There probably weren't three other people in the entire complex. Not on a weekend.

He glanced down the hallway. His call sheet said Lab 2031. Again! What did those eggheads do to those incubators? Tap-dance on top of them?

The door opened to his passkey, letting him into the lab. A hint of Dr. Perkins's perfume still lingered in the air. What a doll that one was! It was a pity she was so wrapped up in her work, not to mention the fact that she considered him nothing more than a lowly technician.

He frowned. He made every bit as much money as she did, on the average. That should have put them on equal footing, but with those dedicated types, money didn't seem to count as much. It was education and the ability to talk about things he couldn't even pronounce. Back home in Mobile, he was as good as anybody. But not here, it seemed.

What was worse, though, was that, education or not, the doctors in 2031 seemed unable to think. He scowled at the incubator with the OUT OF ORDER sign. They had shoved the other pair of incubators right up against it, as if he could work on the damn thing without a bit of elbowroom. The glass was blood warm. Something really grungy was growing in the one between him and his target.

He was going to have to move everything, and double his work time. And Trudi was going to be waiting for him at The Flaming Eye at ten o'clock! This job was going to cut it close, even if things went smoothly, which they seldom ever did.

Harkrider knew Trudi well enough to guess that she wasn't going to wait there alone for very long. Someone was going to move in on her, and if he was very late, that somebody was going to be much more welcome than he was.

He set his satchel on a sink and pushed the gunky incubator over toward the edge of the table. It didn't leave enough room to work, but he wasn't going to waste time moving everything around. Not when a gorgeous red-headed stewardess was on the line.

He tested the electrical plug first, of course. They were always pulling the thing loose and then squawking about its being out of order, when the only problem was that someone had tripped over the cord and unplugged it.

No way was he going to get off that easily, however. Not tonight. He'd known that would be the case. He had a hot date, and a five hundred dollar bonus just begging to be spent where it would do the most good.

He bent over the incubator. No room, dammit. He pushed with his elbow against the other container. It was just too close . . . and even as he thought that, the thing went sliding over the edge and crashed onto the tiled floor.

Green-gray ooze began spreading over the tiles. He tried to step around it, but it slopped onto his shoes as he headed for the cleaning closet for that floor. He'd spilled things before, more than once. He knew just how to deal with this sort of mess without leaving anything to bring the management types down on his back. He got a mop and bucket . . . hot, soapy water was the ticket.

He doused the floor with soapy water and mopped vigorously. Rinsing the mop repeatedly in the sink, he began to make a dent in the mess on the floor, though his shoes were pretty well gunked up, too.

He wondered what the green stuff was . . . but it didn't really matter. The filters between the institute and the sewage plant had been designed specifically to stop anything dangerous before it could get into the sewer system. The river was safe, everyone said so. That business with the viruses last year had been purely a fluke.

Finished cleaning up the remnants of the smashed machine, he slapped a new thermostat onto the out-of-order incubator and plugged the thing in. It began warming just right, and Harkrider sighed with relief.

He looked at his watch. Nine forty-five. If he changed his shirt in the locker room downstairs and put on his new jacket, waiting in the car, he'd just about make it on time.

He stared down at his shoes. He had taken a chance by wearing his good shoes to work. But they didn't look too bad, now. He scrubbed them with a sponge from the sink and rinsed the mess into the drain. Not too bad, he thought. And who'd notice in a dim and crowded night-club?

*   *   *   *   *

The club was, indeed, crowded. Trudi hadn't come in yet herself, he noted with pleasure. He recognized two of her co-hostesses, though, Nita, English and blonde, and Michele, who made him understand why men sighed when they mentioned French women.

Nita's steady, Al, was just entering the bar, and Michele's Fred would be coming soon, Harkrider knew. It looked like a night to remember for the rest of his life.

And it was, although the rest of his life was a lot shorter than he could possibly have guessed.

2

Eric Littlefield stared down, fascinated, as the helicopter skimmed below the cloud layer. Below him lay what looked like a rough green lawn, with an occasional upthrusting treetop showing that it was a jungle, after all.

A webwork of streams wove a lacy pattern among the trees. The sky was cloudy, and the water was the color of freshly cut lead, silvery but with a duller sheen. Eric turned to the pilot. "Is that largest stream the Rio Negro?" he asked.

Steve Porter glanced down to where Eric was pointing. "No, not yet. That's one of the tributaries. You can see that there are a million little rivers and creeks all running into each other. The whole shebang eventually drains into the Amazon, back there behind us. We'll see the black river soon enough!" He grinned and returned to his previous thoughts.

Eric nodded. It had been three years since he had seen his parents. He'd been just sixteen when they were hired to run this experiment in the Amazon jungle, leaving him to finish high school and enroll in college in Texas. He sighed. If it hadn't been for their letters, delivered in big batches about four times a year, he would have lost his feeling of being part of their family at all.

Norman's letters didn't take much space for chitchat. They were full of fascinating stuff about the primates with which he and his wife, Janet, were working.

"The macaque," he had written, "show the most evidence of constructive alteration in both physical and mental capacities since the DNA manipulations were done in France ten years ago. A generation of young ones has reached adulthood, and the differences between these new youngsters and their parents is marked.

"They are increasingly intelligent and cooperative, much like human people. They are also beginning to show a streak of independence and resentment at the intrusion of outsiders into their family areas. That sometimes even includes Janet and me!

"The chimps show little change. The baboons seemed to become more surly, and most of them have died. This may be from the effects of climatic change or from the gene alteration. It's hard to know at this point. All of those kinds left now are getting old, and they have not successfully reproduced a new generation."

That was the sort of letter Eric expected from his father. He wondered why his friends at the University of Texas at El Paso thought he should be bored by the zoological details. He'd always been fascinated by them.

That was, he thought, pretty much natural in someone whose father was a biologist specializing in DNA experimentation, and whose mother was a zoologist, too. Living creatures he found interesting, no matter what those party-oriented clucks back home might say about it.

He glanced toward the horizon, which was lost in a steamy haze of blue-green-gray. Rain forest meant *rain*, he reminded himself.

A crackle of static, mixed with unintelligible words, rippled from the radio. Porter seemed to understand what was said, and he replied, "CRX 103, en route to Monkey Station. Come in, Monkey Station."

Another crackle seemed to be understandable to the pilot, though to Eric it might just as well have been Morse code.

"ETA fourteen hundred hours," Porter said into the mike. Then he turned to Eric.

"There . . . " he pointed toward the thin gray-blue line, " . . . is the Rio Negro. From there, we go west-southwest. They put Monkey Station out in the middle of nowhere so there wouldn't be anybody traveling through or coming in to meddle with or otherwise disrupt the studies your folks are making." He pushed back his mop of dark hair and settled back into his seat.

"Just a bit farther, Eric, and you'll be home." Porter grinned, his dark eyes filled with interest.

Eric frowned. "It's not exactly home to me. I've never been there before in my life. And I'm only going to visit until it's time for the fall term at UT back in El Paso."

The pilot glanced over at him, a line between his bushy eyebrows. "Boy, you'd better believe me when I tell you that your home is where your people are. Since mine died a while ago, I haven't had a place to call home, and it goes hard, even as old as I am. There's no place I know of where there is someone who really cares enough . . ."

Eric turned back to the trees, as he thumbed the button on his pocket radio and listened to a faint, crackly station out of Manaus. It wasn't playing the latest hits, that was for sure. The music had a tricky beat, with a lot of drums. What sounded like a reed flute carried a tune that wandered through the scales as if it had gotten lost in the jungle.

"Native music," said Porter, seeing the puzzled look on Eric's pale face. "They're trying to get all the old stuff they can on recordings. The native tribes are either getting too civilized to keep it in their cultures or else are going so far into the bush that nobody can find them."

Eric had never considered the fact that Monkey Station would be surrounded by a jungle full of native people. He had read, of course, that there were (or had been) headhunters in the Amazon Basin, but his pre-Law studies had taught him little about such things, and he knew even less about any of the other cultures.

What would they be like, those primitive people? Would they be intelligent? He found himself wondering about them intensely. His father had so seldom mentioned any people, even among those of his own staff.

On the other hand, his mother's letters had been full of stories about their co-workers and their doings, but she hadn't mentioned if any of them were natives. He felt, for instance, that he knew Steve Porter before he had ever met him, because of his mother's comments and descriptions.

He almost chuckled before he caught himself. On this trip south, when Porter had told dramatic tales of his love affairs and his amazing exploits flying around the jungle country, Eric had known just how much to credit and how much to disbelieve. His mother had explained that Porter's French-Portuguese-American heritage had given the man a lot of courage and high ambitions, and a love of glamorous stories. Some of them might even be true!

The others she'd mentioned in her letters had gotten mixed up in Eric's memory. He found that he was anxious to meet them. He was, he found, getting impatient to meet the new people, as well as to see his folks again.

"Monkey Station, coming up," said Porter. The chopper made a neat turn and began to descend. Eric found himself looking down on a bald spot in the jungle. In the middle of it were five palm-thatched buildings standing side by side. They were long and narrow. Two more sat at right angles to the first bunch.

"Those two are the mess hall and the dispensary-radio shack," said the pilot. "The others are housing for the staff, with experimental animals temporarily kept close by. And sheds, of course."

Porter circled the clearing, giving Eric a good look at his temporary home. Another clearing, very near the big one, held animal cages, each with a bonnetlike roof of palm thatch.

Another clearing, this one straight and narrow, ran off between the trees. "That's for when the planes come in. Sometimes there are large supply runs with heavy equipment brought in. They take more space than our chopper needs. Our own landing pad is at the other end. Can you see?"

"The whole compound is fenced in," Eric observed.

Porter laughed. "You'd better be glad of that. The jungle is full of critters that would be all over you, night and day, if that fence didn't keep them out. Everything from agoutis to anacondas would pay you visits in the middle of the night. That makes for pretty uncomfortable sleeping. Take it from someone who knows."

Eric could see people emerging from the huts and heading for the landing pad. The chopper came down fast, its rotors kicking up swirls of dust. Through the cloud, he could see someone—two someones!—running toward him.

He knew them at once, of course, even if he had wondered if he might not.

Norman and Janet Littlefield hurried to greet their son.

Eric found his eyes a bit damp, but he managed to wipe them against his shoulder as he leaned into the back of the chopper to get his duffel bag. Shorts, shirts, and sneakers, with one heavy pair of boots, his mother had advised, and that was what he'd brought.

When he looked out from the door, the big rotor was still moving, making a "whick-ee, whick-ee" sound above his head. He didn't wait for Porter to bring the portable steps, just bailed out of the chopper and ran toward his mother, catching her up in his arms, amazed at how small she had become in the past three years.

She's shrunk! was his first thought. Then he realized with delight that he, instead, had grown. At sixteen he had been about five-foot five and slight. Now he was five-foot eleven, a hundred sixty pounds, and could look his father straight in the eyes when he turned to greet him. He felt that he might well catch up to his grandfather, who had stood at six-foot three, according to the family historians.

With one arm still around his mother, Eric felt his free hand caught in that grip which was always so amazingly strong for a middle-sized man. Norman squeezed hard . . . then put his arms around both Janet and his son, and they indulged in a long family hug.

This time, Eric wiped his eyes on his father's shoulder. When they all stepped back, grinning, he noticed that he was suddenly feeling better than he had in a long time. Porter had been right. Home was where your folks were. He knew that now.

"You trying for some sort of record?" asked Norman, staring at the top of his son's head, which seemed, on closer inspection, to have gone a half-inch higher than the top of his own sand-colored crown. "Maybe you want to be a basketball player?"

"I do better at football," Eric said, deadpan. He turned to shake hands with the pilot. "That was a fantastic ride," he told Porter. "I'd like to go with you again, some time."

Porter nodded. "Glad to have you. But right now we need to unload all this stuff and get it under shelter before the afternoon rainstorm." He already had the collapsible steps against the pod of the chopper's hold, and he ran up them to hand out bundles and boxes to those waiting to help.

The Littlefields turned to help. A chain of hands, headed by Norman and his family, grew longer as various members of the Monkey Station staff arrived to help. Soon a long line of cargo was moving from the pad to a waiting Land Rover and a battered pickup, which quickly filled with equipment and supplies.

As the vehicles filled, Eric found himself wondering how the chopper had held so much. No wonder it had felt sluggish sometimes as they flew in.

He grinned at the cute blonde who stood next to him in line. The last package passed from his hands to hers to be stowed safely, and then he turned to her.

She thrust out a tanned hand. "I'm Bonnie," she said.

Her handshake was firm, and her smile was friendly. He felt his heart give a flutter.

He remembered his mother's description: "Bonnie is the general secretary, by title, though she also juggles many other tasks and does them all well. She's about nineteen, seemingly too young for someone with her responsibilities, but she has her B.A. from Mary Baldwin College and is a whiz at almost anything."

Why hadn't Mom mentioned how pretty she was? he wondered. Eric felt himself having his usual problem talking with beautiful women, as he said, "Mom thinks a lot of you. I'm really glad to meet you." He was a bit relieved to turn away to greet others of the group, now approaching to meet him.

A short, fat fellow munching a candy bar sidled up. From his stature and his bright red hair, Eric knew he had to be the doctor—Halloran, his name was.

"Steve, me lad," the man was saying to Porter, "you have been after saving me life again."

"Dr. Halloran, I brought you a boxful of these. This is the sample I brought in my pocket. The rest are in the box marked 5T, along with your cigars. The next box—6T—has all the latest magazines and papers."

Halloran turned and grimaced at Eric. "Welcome," he said, "to the back of beyond. Anyplace without a corner candy shop and a magazine stand is the armpit of creation. I always believed that, and now I know." He shook the young Texan's hand vigorously.

Eric liked the doctor at once. His mother had said in her letters that Halloran seemed to grumble constantly, but it was always good-natured, and he never made trouble. Eric could see for himself the twinkle behind the thick glasses, brightening the faded blue eyes.

"I suspect you'll like it here," said Halloran. "When I was about forty years younger, I surely would have."

Next a tall, dark woman approached, and Eric couldn't think of anyone his mother had mentioned who fit her description. "You have your mother's eyes, though you look a lot more like Norman," she said. "Welcome, Eric. I hope you will like it here."

He wondered again what her function here might be. She was old enough to be one of the technicians—maybe even a biologist—but somehow she didn't look right for that. She looked overly decisive, her sharp brown eyes seeming to miss nothing at all as she surveyed him.

She reminded him unpleasantly of an algebra teacher he had had in high school and disliked strongly. Miss Nash had eyes capable of seeing behind her—or through a stone wall. He felt suddenly ashamed of such a superficial reason for instant hostility and reminded himself to work on correcting that.

Janet said, "This is Lauren Nagle. She has worked with me on several projects, and this time the National Geographic has sent her to write an in-depth study of this one down here. It has been so good to have her here. I don't know how we'll manage without her when she has the study finished. She gets along amazingly well with the Indios, speaks the languages and dialects superbly."

Eric managed a smile. He almost expected her to fix him with her brown eyes and ask if he had done his homework.

"Hello, Miss Nagle," he said. "I'm glad to meet you." He hoped the lie didn't show in his tone. But a glint in those dark eyes made him think she understood him all too well. Just like Miss Nash. . . .

Three young men approached next. Eric thought they had to be Indios, for their hair was long and black, their eyes tarry, their skin a smooth shade of dark coffee. They wore loose shirts and baggy pants of cotton, and they looked cool, even in the steamy heat.

They grinned as he shook their hands, but they said nothing. He wondered if they spoke English.

"Juan, Jesus, and Zachariah, from the village," said his mother. "When we need extra hands, the people of the village are glad to help us. They live off toward the river, three miles through the jungle."

"Zachariah?" asked Eric, wondering at the biblical ring to the name. "That certainly doesn't sound Indian to me."

His father came to stand beside him, putting a hand on his shoulder. "A lot of people in this area have such names. Dr. Nathan Whitlock, the missionary at the village, has been over there for thirty years. He's built a school and a hospital, and for years has been standing between these people and the interests that seem determined to take all their land and destroy their culture—them along with it.

"Back in the Eighties there was a drive to settle city people from the east coast in the jungles. Whitlock went to bat for the tribes in his area, whether or not they had converted to his faith. The Butterfly People, the Cruel People, the Armadillo People, all benefited from his help, though most never knew about it. The tribes that did know about it love and respect the old fellow. They know it pleases him when they give their children names from the Bible."

There came a roar and a blast of gas fumes as the engine of the Land Rover turned over. Then the pick-up backfired, sputtered, and ran at last. Porter turned to the group.

"Well, we're finished for this time." He waved at the empty chopper. "I'd better get going."

"Stay for supper," Janet Littlefield urged him. "Spend the night! We need some fresh gossip from outside."

"Thanks, but I do need to get back. I have a load that needs to go up Rio Branco in a couple of days." Porter looked regretful.

Norman, in his turn, looked innocent. "Too bad. We happen to have a pirarucu that our cook bought from a fisherman this morning. Roasted whole, with sweet potatoes and manioc pancakes on the side."

Porter chuckled. "You just twisted my arm. Old Jefe is the best cook this side of Manaus, and what he can do with fish . . . Of course I'll stay."

"We'll get the supplies under cover. Can't have it raining on them," said Norman. "That will help us work up an appetite for supper."

Porter grunted as they took off up the track after the vehicles. "You are a real con man, you know that, Norman? I thought I was done hauling that load."

But once they reached the compound, he pitched in cheerfully. He even remembered where they had stashed Eric's box of books when they took it off the chopper. Porter rummaged about until he found it and heaved it into Eric's arms.

Bonnie, busily arranging boxes and bundles in the shed, had come out for another load. "What's that?" she asked. She was pink with exertion and prettier than ever.

"Books," he said. "I love to read. I need to do some studying this summer, and I'd like to write, too, some-day. In the meantime, I just read everything I can get my hands on."

Lauren Nagle spoke from behind him, startling him. "Reading is the best thing for a budding writer to do," she said. "What sort of material do you want to write?"

Eric felt uncomfortable. His writing was still very new and tender. But he answered civilly, "Mostly fic-tion, Miss Nagle. Adventure stuff."

She nodded. "By the way, it's Mrs. Nagle. In fact, my husband is the photographer for this assignment. It's nice when we can work as a team, you know."

Eric followed her and his mother toward the cluster of buildings, as they turned away from the storage shed. He was surprised that Lauren was married. He'd have thought those sharp cheekbones and sharper eyes would have put off any man who looked at her.

He decided that he didn't like Lauren Nagle. No matter that she was his mother's friend. There were some people who just rubbed him the wrong way, no matter what.

3

The compound was fascinating, Eric thought. After supper, eaten while rain pattered rhythmically on the metal roof, the group found itself enlivened by Porter's news from Belem and Manaus. Then Norman took his son around, showing him the lab, the storage areas, the portable generator, and a lot of depressed-looking animals in individual cages.

The last building into which they went was the radio shack. "Our link with civilization," said Littlefield. "And we sometimes have some real problems with the radio, too. It breaks down at the worst possible times, and getting parts isn't the easiest thing in the world, down here. But the radio and Steve keep us in touch . . . most of the time."

Eric felt a surge of excitement. "Do you suppose while

I'm here I could call El Paso? I know a couple of guys up there who would really get a kick out of hearing from me, down here."

His father nodded. "Bill can probably manage to patch you through into the phone lines, given some time to make the arrangements. He wasn't at supper, but he'll be back later. He's been fixing Dr. Whitlock's radio, over in the village."

They turned away from the radio shack. It seemed to turn dark very suddenly in the jungle, without even the short twilight Eric knew in Texas.

"Bill is a master at this," his father said. "He sits around sometimes, talking to hams all over the world."

They reached the storage shed, where several native workers were still positioning the fresh supplies. Eric followed his father into the large area beneath the thatched roof and found himself face-to-face with a dark-skinned youth whose even, white teeth gleamed in the artificial light. The young man looked about his own age.

"This is Moses," said Norman. "I suspect that you two will manage to get some fishing and hunting in while you're here."

The Indio grinned widely, showing a large gap in his front teeth. "You are son of the doctors?" he asked. "They look forward for long time for you to come."

Halloran piped up from the other side of the shed, "As you may be able to see, I am the dentist for anybody around here who comes up with a toothache. Moses is my walking advertisement."

Moses grinned even more widely, his black eyes sparkling below the headband holding back his hair. "He fix bad tooth in back, pain go away. He scrape other teeth, make them good, and now no more toothache. I pay in fish. You like to fish, Eric?"

Eric loved to fish! And fishing in a jungle should be really unusual and interesting.

"I do," he said. "But I didn't bring any fishing equipment with me."

The Indio chuckled. "We not use things like Doc use, pole and hook and bait. Use other thing. Moses got plenty. You go fish with me?"

"Not in the dark." That was his mother, who had slipped into the shed without his seeing her. "And not today, even if it were still daylight. You just got here, Eric. And it's time for the evening rainstorm." She took his arm.

"Besides, I'd like to have some time to talk with you. I haven't asked you about college or your aunt and uncle and all my cousins around there. You can just answer all my questions before you go trekking off into the jungle with Moses. There'll be plenty of time for that later."

She fielded his wry glance. "Yes, probably tomorrow."

"Come back to our hut," said his father. "It's time for a rest, anyway, though it isn't late. In this climate you have to learn to slow down and rest regularly. It's very hard on people who aren't acclimated to it. And even those born and raised here take things easy."

Bonnie followed them toward their hut, and Eric was very aware of her nearness, but she peeled off toward her own quarters before they reached their door. Norman grinned at Janet. In the light from the doorway, Eric saw the glance that passed between his parents.

How did parents manage to know your thoughts before you really had time to think them properly? He'd wondered that for years.

It seemed odd to be lying on his cot at eight o'clock in the evening. The rainstorm had come right on schedule, and while it poured down on the thatch, he and his parents caught up on the family news. An awful lot had happened in three years, and they had a lot to talk about.

When the rain stopped, they emerged from their quarters and looked about at the drips from the top of the hut. From the wet jungle, invisible beyond the fence, there came a heart-chilling chorus of squawks and trills and chirpings and rasping cries. The sound tracks of jungle movies, Eric realized, were only a dim approximation of the real thing.

He knew, of course, that most of the sounds were made by harmless birds and insects. He suspected that others might well issue from the jaws of creatures that could swallow him whole as an appetizer.

Eric and his parents found the rest of the staff settled in the large hut devoted to discussions and meals. The tables had been cleared, and everyone could sit around and discuss their daily activities. Don Nagle met the Littlefields at the door.

Eric liked him at once, although he was by no means

the romantic figure Eric had pictured a wildlife photographer as being. The man was well short of average height, with sparse dark hair, and a bit of stomach beginning to protrude above his belt.

His physical lacks, however, were made up for by the warmth of his smile and the firmness of his grip. Eric found himself wondering how such an easygoing person was able to get along with someone like Lauren, who was sharp and abrupt and abrasive.

Bill Smalley had returned from the village, too. He showed traces of his afternoon's work as well as his two-way trek through the jungle. His khakis were grubby, and his glasses looked as if they had been greased. His eyes, however, were shrewd and full of humor.

Norman mentioned Eric's desire to talk with his friends back in Texas, and Bill's bright blue eyes lit up at once. "I think we can manage that," he said.

"I certainly would like to," Eric said. "If it wouldn't be too much trouble."

"Oh, I've got some friends in Texas who are hams. I think I can set it up, and then I'll let you know when to come down to the shack and try for it."

Bill looked past him, and Eric turned to meet Mrs. Smalley. She was a small, round woman, the only member of Monkey Station, if he recalled correctly, whose work did not include the official purpose of the group. She didn't worry about monkeys, but about her husband and the rest of the staff.

Bill looked proud as he said, "This woman has taken

on all the responsibility for seeing the housekeeping
chores are done well and on time. Laundry, cleaning,
cooking—she oversees the lot. Old Jefe thinks she hung
the moon. . . . He gets her to tell him her secret recipes,
even!"

She looked, Eric thought, a bit like a youngish Mrs.
Santa Claus. As she took his hand, he had a sudden
vision of endless snacks of cookies and homemade candy.

A tall fellow, whose slicked-back hair was so far out
of style that it probably was in again, greeted Eric
next. Cold gray eyes examined Eric critically. They
were too close together, and the mouth below the non-
descript nose seemed flat and sharp enough to snip
tin.

"Alberto Gunter," he said, extending a hand that was
so well kept that Eric found himself wondering just what
sort of work he found to do in this primitive place that
could allow him to keep his hands so clean.

Norman came up behind his son and said, "This is Dr.
Gunter, the official representative of the Brazilian gov-
ernment. He is on the faculty of the Brazilian Institute of
Scientific Study."

There was a note in Norman's voice that told Eric his
father didn't care for Gunter any more than he did. He
smiled, however, and shook the offered hand.

Eric found that he couldn't bring himself to say he was
glad to meet the man, but Gunter didn't seem to care
one way or the other.

Later, when the Littlefields had retired to the privacy

of their hut, he asked his father about the peculiar Brazilian.

Norman sighed. "He's from a very wealthy family, which equates with political power down here more than in most places. He isn't really a scientist, degrees or no degrees. He never wonders about how things work.

"He doesn't care a whit for our work here, but he decided that our project was prestigious enough to help make a name for himself. Any breakthrough in DNA experimentation that we make will enhance his chances of becoming head of the institute."

Janet piped up from her bunk beyond the curtain, "Our choice was to take Gunter cheerfully or find another place for the experimental group of primates. This is, climatically, the best place in the world. We can't try the Far East. The political situation is still too unstable there. No, taking everything together, the Amazon jungle with Gunter is better than anyplace else without him."

"So he can get credit for whatever you accomplish without having to get those manicured hands dirty," said Eric.

Janet stuck her head around the curtain and nodded. "Let him. What we learn here, if we're lucky, can benefit our kind for generations to come. This may prove that human DNA splicing can work to eliminate any number of hereditary diseases from the gene pool. Weighed in the balance, Gunter's ambitions are feather light. It's what we do here, not what sort of reputations are made, that matters.''

Eric felt a surge of pride. He'd known his parents did important work, but he hadn't realized just how vital it might be. And, at least for this summer, that he could have a part in it.

4

Harkrider woke early, which was most unusual. He usually slept as long as he could, until the strident burring of the alarm clock drove him from his bed. He kept the thing on a chest of drawers across the room, so he couldn't reach it to fling it against the wall. He had run up a pretty big clock bill by doing just that.

He lay staring at the bar of light under the window blind. It looked very early—too early for a man who had admittedly reveled too long after the holiday weekend. It was two weeks since his fling with the stewardesses, and he had partied again last night with Trudi's successor, a gorgeous brunette. He should have slept like the dead until the clock went off. He didn't have to be at the institute for his shift until three o'clock.

He stared at the luminous dial. The clock face looked

blurred, as if his eyes were not focusing well. There was a stab of pain behind them, and he rolled over and sat up. His gut cramped suddenly, and he knew for the first time that he might be in trouble.

Every joint ached unmercifully when he moved. His stomach began to roll uneasily, and his head pounded sharply in time with his heartbeat. What on earth was wrong?

He reached for the phone and dialed the operator. He couldn't see now, through the pain in his head. There was no point in trying the phone book—he'd never be able to read the fine print.

"Thank you for using Southern States Telephone," said a horridly cheerful voice. "This is Shirley. May I help you?"

He coughed, choked, but finally managed to croak, "Harkrider. 408 Lansing Avenue, Channing. Sick. Very sick. Doctor. . . . " His voice died in his throat, and he dropped the phone.

The operator's voice was a mouse-thin squeak muffled against the bedclothes. Harkrider didn't hear. He was vomiting into his slippers.

It seemed a long, long time before the shriek of an ambulance roused him from his stupor. He was glued to the bed with vomit and sweat and feces, for his bowels were now loosened as well.

"God almighty!" said the paramedic who followed the policeman into the room. "Phew! Get a window open, somebody, while we check him out."

The light blinded Harkrider. He howled like a banshee as even worse pain stabbed into his head through his supersensitive eyeballs. He fought crazily as the paramedics and the police bundled him onto a stretcher and maneuvered him down the narrow stairway. At every landing, faces were crowded in the doorways, watching him go.

He opened his eyes as he was wheeled rapidly along. There was a jabber of voices, a blur of faces. . . . Nurse. Paramedic. Doctor. Orderly. He tried to speak, but a stream of vomit shot out to spray those around the gurney.

"Damn! Call Dr. Lessley to Emergency. Grab that towel. . . . Here. What a mess!"

The gurney whirled around a corner and into a room so bright that Harkrider squeezed his wincing eyes shut again. After that, things took on a surreal speed. People moved about him, needles were thrust into him. Someone was washing him, even as the others worked.

He felt someone near his head. "I never saw anything like this," said a quiet voice into his ear. "Have you been exposed to anyone ill lately? Anything unusual at all?"

He tried to think. If his head would let up for just a moment, he might remember. . . . But it didn't, and he couldn't.

He tried to shake his head, and the motion almost made him faint. But he felt that if he could have one instant of clarity, he did know something relevant. Something that might have caused his illness. . . .

The opportunity never came. Within fifteen minutes, a black wave rolled over him. It drowned out the rest of the world, and Harkrider was dead.

*   *   *   *   *

Eric would never forget his first night in the jungle.

His room was an airy square attached to the back of his parents' hut. The cot was draped with mosquito netting . . . he felt like a bride in a wedding, he told his father later.

There was a single chair and a rack for holding his clothing. A desk filled one corner, and on it he put his present budget of books and notebooks.

The night outside was vibrant with alien sounds, as he thought of the strangely varied group of people he had met. Aside from the staff, there were two African biologists and three dignified Indians, who seemed to be the representatives of the macaque that had been taken from an Indian jungle. It was those monkeys, along with their offspring, that were the main concern of Dr. Ram Dass and his companions.

As he lay in the dark, a kaleidoscope of strange places and many-colored people played through Eric's mind.

He leaned upon one elbow and peered out of his small, mosquito-netted window. This side of the compound was without the light provided by the tall standards that stood in the middle of the huddle of buildings. He could see nothing. . . he might have been at the bottom of a mine. There was no light, he knew, nearer than the village, and by this time everyone there was probably asleep, their fires out and the missionary's lamps extinguished.

He tried to identify some of the sounds he could hear as he lay back. The long quavering trill he thought must be some sort of bird. A croaking gargle . . . could that be a crocodile? But the river was three miles away! And that hair-raising screech—he gave up and closed his eyes. Time stood still in the jungle that night.

* * * * *

The next few days were abustle with activity. One group was off to check on the primates, leaving the remains of their early breakfast for the later crew to clean up. Jefe, supreme in the kitchen, did not trouble himself with such duties, and Mrs. Smalley had found and trained a cadre of small, naked children to take care of that and other necessary but undemanding tasks around the station.

This morning, Janet had gone with the early shift, and Eric found himself dawdling over scrambled eggs and strips of unidentified meat, while his father checked over notes for his day's work.

"These are really good eggs," Eric mumbled around a mouthful. "They have more flavor than any I've ever tasted."

"Turtle eggs," said his father, barely glancing up from his papers. "Moses hunts out the nests along the river and brings us a supply regularly. Tame chickens tend to die or be eaten by hungry predators, and the wildfowl down here is *really* wild."

Eric swallowed carefully. Turtle eggs? He ran his

tongue around the inside of his mouth cautiously. He tasted nothing but something delicious.

Norman looked up and grinned. Before Eric could speak, there came a step at the door and Moses entered, carrying a small net, bow and arrows, and a short spear.

"We go fish today?" he asked, his dark eyes eager.

"Is there anything else I should do, Dad?" asked Eric. He felt excitement at the thought of going out into the forest from which such blood-curdling sounds had come in the night.

His father looked disappointed. "I thought you might want to come out and meet our macaques. They are becoming so like people to your mother and me that I feel I should introduce you to them."

Eric nodded. He wanted to see the jungle first with his parents, he decided, so he turned to Moses.

"Will tomorrow do as well?" he asked. "I really do want to go fishing with you, but I've been wanting to see the monkeys for years now."

"You go with father. I keep fishing thing here in storage shed, so when you want, we go." The Indio turned and left so quietly that Eric knew if he hadn't been watching, he never would have known the young man had moved at all.

Norman handed his son a wide-brimmed hat, checked to see that Eric had worn boots, and took his plastic-wrapped parcel of notebooks from a pigeonhole. The last thing he got was a businesslike automatic pistol, which he attached to his belt.

Eric, remembering his parents' views on hunting, felt

his eyes widen. Norman grinned at him. "That is jungle out there," he said to his son. "No police on the corners. No corners, in fact. Nobody to call if you get into trouble. You have to take care of any problem yourself, the best way you can manage. You take the rifle . . . it isn't quite as dangerous for a less-experienced hand. You haven't forgotten how to shoot, have you?"

"Of course not! Those were some of the best times we had, before you and Mom left. Going out on Uncle Ben's ranch and shooting at bottles . . . why I can still knock nine out of ten off a fence at a hundred yards, with a rifle."

"Good. You'll need the skill, if you're unlucky. This is no zoo, Eric. This is real life with a vengeance. You may stay the entire summer and never even see a poisonous snake. But then we may go out this morning and meet a jaguar in a nasty mood and have to shoot to save our own lives. Keep that in mind all the time.

"Moses is going to teach you a great deal. You watch him, when you start fishing and hunting with him. He has roamed the forest all his life. He knows the drill." Norman put on his own hat, cocking it to one side in his usual style, and gestured toward the gate in the compound fence.

Eric felt a surge of excitement as they stepped beyond the barrier, which was chain-link metal and eight feet tall. What did it hold out in the night, when the heavy gate was secured? He might find a hint, even by day.

The path was narrow, snaking through the thick growth, around the complicated knees of a tree so tall that its top was lost above the intervening growth. Vines of all sorts wove a complex canopy above the track, and multitudes of birds flitted there among bright-winged insects and an occasional band of small monkeys.

As he noticed a pair of apes playing tag through a web of vines, he saw a larger, fatter shape that seemed slung beneath a branch. Eric touched his father's shoulder and pointed.

"Three-toed sloth. Young, too . . . not half grown. You'll see a lot of wonderful things if you keep an eye on the treetops, but if you step on a fer-de-lance or a bushmaster, you'll be dead before you can enjoy the sight of them. Keep your eyes on the ground when you walk. When you want to look up, stop. That's an excellent rule in the rain forest."

Norman turned back to the trail, and Eric set his gaze on the broad back before him and followed.

After about a half-hour walk, they came to the small clearing where his mother was at work. Eric had managed to see quite a lot, even watching closely where he stepped. He was filled with interest as they came through a wall of greenery into a semicircle of space along a bank of a ravine. He could hear the sound of water moving along the bottom of the cut; here was another of the many streams carrying off the daily rainfall to fatten the rivers.

Janet Littlefield sat in the clearing on a folding stool. A gray-brown shape was sitting on an outcrop of stone some yards away, watching with interest as she wrote in the notebook perched on her knee. When she looked up to greet her family, the macaque stood and stretched, scratched one hip meditatively, and moved closer, as if it, too, wanted to greet the newcomers.

Above the clearing leaned a tremendous tree whose stilt-roots spread across at least a third of the space in the clearing. Eight macaque sat along the tree's huge branches, watching the show below them. It was hard to see them clearly—Eric was looking across the brilliantly sunlit glade into deep shadow. He thought he could see much smaller animals playing along the vines and limbs among the adults.

He followed his father to stand beside Janet. She was in shadow, and now, looking upward, he could see that the monkeys in the tree were not doing the things he usually associated with primate behavior. Where was the meticulous grooming of each other's fur? Only the tiniest of them were doing that. The adults were staring down at him as intently as he was looking up. They seemed to be studying him.

He looked at his father. Norman nodded. "Up there are the offspring of those whose genes were modified. The older generation tends to stay deeper in the forest. They'll come out, but they have adapted well to this new jungle. They no longer depend on us for food, and they seem to feel we are no longer necessary to them.

"Every one up there is a young adult, and there are five infants. There are twenty more macaque scattered around in this area, most of them members of the altered generation. The survival rate of macaque in this group is something like four times greater than that of unaltered groups in their native jungles."

"Intelligence," said Janet. "That's the major factor, we're certain. They are much more efficient at finding food than the older generation, though some of that may be attributed to their being reared in this different rain forest environment."

"The principal difference that we can see is that they call on us when there's a medical emergency," said Norman.

Eric stared at his parents. "You don't mean it! How?"

"One or both of us visit here every day. We make notes on behavior, numbers, condition, and so on. If one of the females has trouble giving birth or if one has been injured or becomes ill, Ko, over there, comes to fetch us. We always bring the medical kit, though we seldom need it." She glanced with respect at the macaque on the rock.

"He has never bothered us with anything minor—something that they can deal with themselves. So when Ko calls, we pay attention."

Eric felt again the fascination his father's letters had roused in him. "Are these new ones different from their parents physically?"

"Perhaps larger. The color range seems much the same. The conformation is changing, however, although we didn't expect any drastic changes this soon. Their personalities are a lot different, too. Watch!"

Janet took from beneath her camp stool a bag, and the rich scent of ripe bananas filled the air. "For you, Ko," she said, holding out a handful of bananas.

The ape looked at her gravely for a moment. Then he

moved to take the gift. Instead of stuffing his mouth full at once, he climbed into the tree to present fruit to the group waiting there, before taking one himself.

The Littlefields watched the macaque, who watched them in turn. When the last of the fruit had been enjoyed to the full, Ko went higher into the tree and scrambled about for quite a long while. When he came down, he held something carefully in one hand, using his long, agile tail to stabilize himself while descending.

He dropped to the ground and came toward the family waiting for him beside the camp stool. He didn't come too near, as if he respected the need of animals for space around themselves, but at the distance of a couple of yards he bent and laid something carefully in a nest of fallen leaves.

When he had backed away and taken up his post on the rock, Janet went to retrieve the return gift. Four bright bird eggs lay there in her palm.

Eric stared at his father, then at Janet. This was not normal monkey behavior . . . not by a long shot! Some amazing change had already taken place in the macaque of Monkey Station!

*   *   *   *   *

Eric had expected the procedures with these primates to be similar to those he recalled from an expedition he had made with his parents when he was very young. Then they had measured and weighed the individual animals involved, keeping strict records on their growth and progress. This time, the only creatures subjected to that process were the few remaining chimps and baboons.

Those were the ones in the cages inside the compound. They were now old for their kind, and for some reason they had not adapted to this alien jungle. Eric loved to watch the Tanzanian zoologist work with them . . . his big, dark hands seemed to comfort the beasts as he gave them their regular once-over. Fenister was quiet, friendly, and immense. He handled even the fractious animals with ease and gentleness.

"We tried to keep records on the macaque," Norman told Eric when they had returned to the compound. "This is the first thing we discovered: they simply are no longer experimental animals. They have their own strong opinions as to what should and will be done to themselves and the other individuals in their tribe.

"They interact with us at their own times and places, not ours. They have, in one generation, taken on something very close to self-determination. That is the major item that we keep emphasizing in our reports to the scientific journals."

Eric kept thinking about that, off and on, as he prepared for his fishing expedition with Moses the next morning. He wondered what the Indios thought about this new sort of animal that had been loosed in their jungle, and he was determined to ask as soon as they were well on their way.

Moses again had his bow and arrows, the short spear, and the small net. The morning was, as usual, warming up fast. The jungle steamed gently, emitting strong scents of flowers, of rotting vegetation, of greenness, and of other, stranger things Eric couldn't find names for.

"Be careful," said Janet, as she checked Eric's attire. "Don't lose your hat. You'll not only get too hot, but if you get into the clear along one of the streams, you'll also get soaked when it begins to rain. And watch out for leeches!" she yelled after him, as he followed Moses through the gate.

"You'd think I was twelve instead of nineteen," Eric grunted, as he and Moses headed off into the thick greenery.

Instead of going along the path leading to the macaques' chosen territory, Moses turned aside within a few yards and darted down a way that didn't seem to be a pathway at all. The undergrowth was only slightly less dense. From time to time, Eric could see a glimpse of the mulchy layer covering the ground. No animal track showed there at all. He noted that this time Moses wore sandals, though he went barefoot in the compound. Probably because of thorns he might step on in the jungle, he thought.

"You go this way often?" he asked his guide, trying to keep his tone perfectly calm.

"This no way," said Moses. "This little game trail. Just go the way I want, you see?"

Eric sighed silently. "As long as you know where you're headed, okay," he replied. "But I'd hate to end up wandering in circles in this forest for the rest of my life."

5

Eric stopped dead in his tracks, staring off to his right, where some long-ago giant of a tree had fallen to leave a patch of sky above an area that was quickly trying to replace it. In the sunlight, sliding liquidly along the trunk that was almost overgrown with vines, moved the biggest snake he had ever seen in his life.

"Moses . . ." he whispered, looking up to see if his guide had seen it.

Moses, too, had gone still. He didn't look scared, but he did look cautious, his dark features seeming to have sharpened to focus on the serpent.

He quirked an eyebrow at Eric, which confirmed the need for quiet. Eric was glad of that . . . he didn't think he could move or speak, anyway.

As the pair watched, the reptile slid off the tree trunk

and into the masses of green mossy stuff growing around
the dead tree. Eric was devoutly grateful that the snake
seemed to be going away from them. He had no idea
what he would have done if it had headed toward him;
the growth around him was too thick to run through.

Once the undergrowth had stopped waving sinuously
in the wake of the creature, he found that he had been
holding his breath. He let it out in a rush.

"Just how dangerous is that thing?" he asked Moses.

"Anaconda is very slow," said the Indio. "I see children play with those thing some time, when they go near
village and get into wide place. Before snake can turn
around, child be gone, quick-quick."

Eric found his appreciation for the courage of primitive children raised several notches. He wouldn't have
messed with that behemoth for anything he could think
of.

Again, Moses headed down the trail . . . southward,
Eric thought. With some suddenness, he found himself
staring at an edge of brightness in the trees ahead. The
would-be hunters twisted around an outcrop of rock,
and he found himself standing on the bank of a good-
sized stream, whose rapid waters had worn a smooth bed
into the pale stone of the channel.

Pools lay in washed-out areas along the shallow edges,
and in them Eric could see fish. Small ones, to be sure,
not giants like the pirarucu Jefe had cooked to celebrate
his arrival. These fish glinted pale silver in the strong
light. Moses slipped off his sandals and walked barefoot
onto the rock.

Not to be outdone, Eric did the same, pulling off his hot boots and going stocking-footed after the Indio. Even protected by the socks, his feet felt as if they were frying on the sun-heated stone, but he kept on. If Moses could do it barefoot, he couldn't allow himself to falter.

Across the stream there came a ripple of laughter. Four children emerged from the greenery and stood staring at the two men from the other bank. They, too, held tiny bows and nets and spears.

A stream of unintelligible words was yelled back and forth between Moses and his younger friends. The children waved shyly at Eric. He felt a bit shy himself, as he lifted his hand to wave back.

They didn't waste any more time on civilities, however. Moses turned to his fishing as if his life depended on it. It came to Eric with sudden clarity that in this place, the young man's life probably did depend on such activities. Those children over there weren't playing. They were having a good time, without a doubt, but they were catching fish that were necessary for their families' food.

It was a feeling totally different from any Eric had ever had. Life in Texas was not always easy. The heat was pretty bad sometimes, and crime was becoming a real problem in El Paso. But he had never been in any situation in which the survival of his family depended upon what they could catch to eat with their own hands.

He stood near Moses and watched intently as the Indio moved smoothly over the hot stone, his black eyes focused on the fish moving lazily in the pools. Suddenly, he tensed. The little arrow shot downward, and one of the silver shapes began to flop.

Moses gestured for the net as he stepped into the water and retrieved his arrow, with the fish skewered on the end. Eric handed him the net, and he put the fish into it and tied it to his sashlike belt.

When Moses handed the bow to Eric, the Texan shook his head regretfully. "I couldn't hit the side of a barn with that thing. But I might be able to do some good with the little spear. Could I try that?"

He found that his physical education classes in high school and college had not been entirely wasted. He had learned to throw the javelin, and this was much like that, though he had to learn to judge the deflection caused by the water.

He set his feet carefully on the hot stone, and watched the shiny fish shapes dart through the shallow pool. A larger one, orange and black, bulldozed its way through a cluster of the small silver ones. Eric felt his breath come short as he cast his javelin, feeling the twine that secured it to his wrist jerk sharply as the point pierced the target and the fish lunged, trying to escape the pain of its wound.

Moses had been perfectly still as Eric had stalked his prey. Now he hopped up and down like a boy, grinning.

"Good! Very good! You catch fish first try. I call you Fish-Spear, now. All my people call you so, too. When you have real name, that is good thing. People feel you are one of us."

Eric was startled for a moment. It seemed a very paltry

thing to have done, just spearing one fish. Then he remembered how important getting food was to a primitive society. One who was good at it had to be a valuable member of any tribe.

"Now I take you to special fishing place. Not crowded like this. . . . " Moses nodded toward the group of children, who were drawing a net across a large eddy in the stream, their giggles subdued but noticeable.

The Indio donned his sandals, allowed Eric to retrieve his boots, and led the way up another invisible pathway through the bush, brushing aside shoulder-high ferns and ducking under draperies of vines, some of them decorated with drifts of tiny, fragrant flowers. The young men emerged, in a bit, onto a space that was not thick with undergrowth.

Here the ground was shaded by tremendous trees, stifling most other growth. Thick tendrils of vine curled up the huge boles, carrying the leafy parts up into the light and air at the tops of the forest giants. A few bright fungi and tiny sprigs of unidentifiable growth were all that Eric could see underfoot.

Suddenly an alarming cry rang out, stopping Eric in his tracks. One voice, howling with terrible volume, seemed to conjure up a chorus of others. The darkness of the deep forest was pierced by the cries, and Eric touched Moses on the shoulder.

"What on earth is that?"

Moses' expression, in the dim light, seemed puzzled. "What?"

"That awful noise, up there in the trees."

The Indio began to laugh. "It only howlers," he said. "The howler monkey, he make terrible noise, but he never come down where he might get hurt. You look up, very far. See?"

Eric felt that he really needed to lie flat on the ground in order to look high enough, but at last he saw a group of dark shapes among the distant branches. He could see the animals' long tails, and their bulky heads, as they moved restlessly through the treetops. Among them were smaller shapes, keeping a good distance, yet following the larger troop.

"And those?" he asked.

"Spider monkey. Make very good pet—small sister have spider monkey." Moses gestured for him to follow again, somewhat impatient with this delay to observe creatures that were entirely too familiar to him to be interesting.

They came at last to a wall of greenery, through which Moses slid with ease. Eric, watching closely, darted after him and found himself standing on a narrow strip of rock edging a deep ravine. The place was in deep shadow, for the huge trees in the adjoining jungle on both sides of the cut almost roofed out the sky.

A series of outcrops made a sort of stair that dropped down the side of the ravine to the water's edge. Eric felt a strange sense of excitement, as if he had found some secret of the forest that few were ever privileged to know. He realized that Moses was moving quietly, almost reverently, as he approached the deep pool below them.

"What is this place?" whispered Eric. "It seems so . . .

so . . . I can't find a way to say it."

Moses nodded. "Is my secret place. Nobody ever come here, except, sometimes, old man from the Butterfly People. I see him, he see me, we never speak. This place very quiet."

Eric nodded. He had no need to say anything more, as Moses led him down to the pool and gestured downward.

The water was deep and dark. The current, however, was swift, for bits of debris carried into the pool from the tall waterfall at its upper end were whirled out of sight rapidly. From time to time the sleek body of a fish leaped into the air after one of the insects that fluttered about the half-submerged boulders thrusting wet shoulders out of the rush.

Eric almost cried out. A cluster of butterflies, their scarlet, gold, and black markings vivid, sat on a dark stone. They looked, he thought, like a tiny flower garden, growing out of the boulder's top.

Moses smiled, as if he, too, found the combination of place and inhabitants beautiful, in some way too deep for words. Then he gestured toward the narrow shelf of stone that formed a path along the water's edge, perhaps a foot above the rushing current, leading toward the falls.

Eric, his heart in his throat, followed the slick, wet path on Moses' heels. Only the fact that Moses seemed to consider this the equivalent of walking in the middle of a broad sidewalk kept Eric from stopping and going back to firmer footing.

The path curved upward, and the footing grew even more slippery with the spray from the waterfall, which pounded onto a line of even larger boulders than those downstream. Eric placed his booted feet with care, feeling certain that a slip now would mean his instant death among the boiling waters and the boulders.

Moses was climbing more steeply ahead of him. They seemed to be cutting up toward the area behind the waterfall. So it proved. Moses grinned back at him briefly and turned a sharp corner behind a rocky outcrop. Eric, following, found himself behind the veil of water pouring over a lip of stone ten yards yards above his head.

The noise was at once exhilarating and frightening. The ground underfoot was partly clay and partly rock, and it was greased by millennia of water and moss. The crease in which the young men stood went entirely across the width of the falls, cutting into the hillside deeply behind them.

Moses gestured again, this time because speaking would have been useless. The resounding crack and roar of the flood pouring onto the boulders made hearing impossible.

The cave behind the waterfall was dark. The only light seemed to be refracted through the tumbling strands of water, and it was strange and greenish, making wavering ripples over the rock and the two men's bodies. In that tenuous illumination, nothing seemed impossible, so when Moses disappeared into a cranny at the back of the space, Eric was not really surprised.

He followed again, trusting his guide, and found himself in a long tunnel that seemed to crook sharply up ahead. Strangely, it was fairly well lighted. There was a bit of light coming down from above, where some cranny evidently led out into a clearing in the forest on that level.

The tunnel widened, however, before reaching the bend, and there some bubble in the ancient rock had formed a tiny room. Moses moved to one side and fumbled with something. There came a scritching noise, and light bloomed from a torch he had lit.

"How you like my secret?" asked Moses. "Nobody know this here. Not in my tribe, anyway. Maybe old Tulunga know, but he never come here, never tell anyone."

Now Eric could see that there was a bundle of dried stuff—ferns, he thought—piled against one curving wall. A bed, no doubt. A couple of metal food cans were used, he felt sure, for cooking, when there was a need for that.

A neat array of weapons and fishing equipment was piled behind a boulder. Eric could see a serviceable spear—not a fishing spear but one meant for war, he knew. A bigger bow with a selection of arrows kept company with a roll of the bark netting that seemed to be that most favored by Moses' people. Bundles of what looked like weapons lay neatly along the wall.

Now the pounding of the falls was a dim mutter in the distance. He could hear himself think, at last.

"Do you come here and camp?" he asked, awed at the

thought of having such a remarkable place of refuge.

Moses looked puzzled. "How you mean, camp?"

Eric realized that every day amounted to camping out for this forest-reared fellow. "Back home," he explained, "we live mostly in towns, with a lot of other people and their houses and buildings of all kinds, and roads and cars . . ." He sighed, and tried to make the concept clear to Moses.

"There's no forest, unless you travel a long way. And then sometimes you take a tent or a camper and spend a while living there, enjoying being out of doors." He felt that he hadn't done a particularly good job with his explanation, but it was the best he could do at the moment. He decided to get his aunt to send him some magazines from home with pictures of the cities and the road networks and the swarms of cars and trucks going about their antlike ways.

Moses might not have any mental pictures of a city, but he understood, evidently, that anyone who lived where there was no forest would necessarily go and seek one out. He nodded with understanding.

"Very bad place," he said. "Here we go out of door, walk ten step, we in jungle. Best place to be, you think?"

For a moment, Eric found his heart agreeing fully with his companion. It was, indeed, a wonderful place to be. This cave, the falls, the amazing forest through which they had come, were all matters that he knew he would have been poorer for had he not seen.

But something inside him said, You want more than

this. You want to go to college and learn Law. You want to make a name for yourself, like your parents. You want to do something important with your life. You want to come back here as often as you can, of course, now that you know what sort of place it is. But still, would you be content to live as Moses does, just concerned with survival?

To Moses he said, "This is a wonderful place. I wouldn't have missed it for the world. I want to stay here as long as I can, but I have to go back to school, too."

The Indio nodded again. "You like home, too. Even if no forest. Is true—my village is best place in forest, though many place be just like it."

Eric was delighted with his quick understanding. Intelligence, he was learning, was not a matter of book learning but of quick wit and the ability to deal with the unexpected.

"Do you suppose we could come here and stay for a few days?" Eric asked. "I could get some more canned goods and some blankets, and we could fish in the stream and explore the forest up on top. . . . I think it would be wonderful fun."

Moses looked doubtful. "There is work," he said. "My family need some thing from traders on river. Need money to buy. Your people need you to help them, too. But maybe we find a time. We see."

Eric sighed. He could see that he needed to do some growing up, no matter how mature he might feel. Moses was already responsible for his family. He would be getting married soon. . . . Janet had told Eric that the natives chose mates at what seemed to whites to be very early ages.

Now Moses stooped and took up a strangely shaped net. "We go up. I show you how to catch other fish."

They moved out of the little room and along the tunnel to the bend, where the cavern branched in three directions. Moses turned sharply to his right, thrusting the torch ahead of him and thus burning away thick swaths of spiderweb that smoked and smelled in the still air. The owners of the webs scrambled off their burning bridges and took refuge on the damp stone of the walls, their tiny eyes glowing red and green in the torchlight.

Moses called softly, his voice, distorted, echoing from the distances ahead. He stamped his sandaled feet sharply on the rocky floor of the cave.

"For scare away snake," he said in explanation.

Eric stamped his heavy boots and added his own voice to the din. Every snake he could scare away was that much better, to his way of thinking.

The tunnel smelled strange—of damp and stone and something acrid and something rotten. The torch guttered in the wind of their passing, but when it burned short, Moses had reached another of his stashes of supplies. A pile of already prepared torches waited, and a fresh one lighted their way to the end of the tunnel.

A glimmer told Eric that they were about to emerge into daylight again. He wondered what amazing place he would see next, but he never would have expected what he found when Moses led him out of the darkness into a blaze of sunlight.

All around them was an uneven expanse of rock that looked as if it must have flowed, molten, from a furnace. The sun beat against the pale surface in a blast of heat and glare, and Eric was glad of the shelter of his hat.

"This is the Dead Place," said Moses. "Down there . . . " he pointed off to their left ". . . you see tops of big tree? That is forest we came through. Down there you see tops of tree that grow on top of cave and waterfall hill. Now you come."

He turned and hurried over the burning rock toward a patch of growth on its other side. Eric found himself almost running, for the heat was baking through the thick soles of his boots. He wondered how the thin sandals kept Moses from scorching his feet.

They dashed, breathless, into the shadow of a clump of palmlike trees, whose roots were buried in thick ferns and vines. It seemed like a sort of paradise after the hellish heat of the bare expanse behind them. Beyond the shadowy spot, Eric could hear water gurgling cheerfully.

Moses was grinning again. He gestured onward, and Eric moved after him down a tiny path that seemed to be a game trail. This wound back and forth, going deeper into bigger growths of trees and shrubs, until it hooked abruptly and ended at a wide, shallow space where clear water rushed over worn ripples of rock.

Here again there were water-filled pools along the edges of the stream, and these were filled with frantic fish.

"Rain, he make water rise," said Moses. "All fish go out wide in stream. Then rain, he stop. Water go down pretty fast to regular, leave fish stranded out in little pool that get smaller and smaller all the time."

He pointed toward the one they were approaching. "See . . . little fish jump up in air. That mean bigger fish try to eat him. Come watch. You will see."

Eric stood on the cool rock in the shadow of overhanging trees and vines, and sure enough it was like looking down into an aquarium. Myriad fish, bright yellow and black and silver and striped, milled in the shrinking basin, and from time to time one of the smaller ones would make a desperate leap to escape the jaws of one larger than itself.

Moses knelt beside the pool and held his net ready. It was tied onto an oval hoop, which held the lips of the net open. When a good-sized fish leaped high, its scarlet and black markings flashing in the light, he scooped deftly and caught it.

Eric was assigned to threading a cord through the gills of the catch and letting the string down into another pool, which held fewer denizens. Before they finished, he and Moses had a good catch of palm-sized fish.

"We eat before we start back," said Moses.

Building a tiny fire and cooking their catch was, Eric found, an anticlimax after the other things Moses had shown him. But he felt that he would need many days for thinking about all the wonders he had discovered in this single day.

Perhaps it was a good thing that his parents were going to need his help around the compound. If he found as many new things every day of the summer as he had today, he would probably burst with it all before it was time to go back home.

He followed Moses down a rubbly way that led them off the small escarpment on which they had fished and eaten. This put them into another part of the forest entirely, where bright birds squawked raucously and brilliant butterflies soared in the shadowy aisles among the trees.

By the time they reached the compound again, Eric felt dizzy with the many plants and creatures he had seen. Moses asked him, "We fish again, eh?" and Eric nodded.

"But not terribly soon," he said. "I think you're right. We need to help our people first. Then we'll do our thing."

When Moses grinned back at him, there was a twinkle in his black eyes. Eric felt sure that Moses understood pretty precisely his dilemma. He was one very shrewd fellow, and Eric had a feeling that he was going to learn a great deal from the Indio in days to come.

6

Dr. Araminta Perkins was determined to prove, in her own quiet way, that she was worth any half-dozen of her male peers at the institute. This got her, more often than not, into very hot water. Most of those doing research for the institute were more bureaucrats than scientists.

She had worried quietly for two months after finding the Virus Strain 73 incubator smashed on the day after St. Patrick's Day.

She had been alone when she returned, briefly, to the lab to check on the culture. It was a new one, and she had misgivings about it. She had felt the need to see that everything was going normally with it.

She had found the glass of the vat in bits in the garbage bin. No trace at all was left of the altered strain that she had prepared with such care. She wrote a memo at once and left it on the desk of the subsector's supervisor.

Three weeks ago, her immediate superior, Klaus Marberg, informed her that he had removed her note before the supervisor could find it. When she protested, he had only looked mulish.

"This is a relatively minor accident. Probably, one of the janitors caused it, and we just can't afford any more trouble with the union people. It's hard enough to get cleaning crews as it is.

"Besides, the filters in the drainage system will take care of anything we can put into them. Your viral strain hasn't been tested for dangerous traits, as yet, but it is probably perfectly harmless."

"You have to be joking!" she had told him. "I've done enough preliminary testing to know that this is nothing we want loose in the population.

"We need to learn who broke the vat. He, she, or it needs to be checked carefully for any infection, just in case the virus got into his system. That is far more important than union contracts. Someone might well die because of this, Klaus!"

She'd seen that look before, in the eyes of people determined to keep their own hands spotless, no matter what. But she wasn't happy, and she grew progressively less so every day.

She remembered Harkrider, the swing shift repair technician. He'd died suddenly, just weeks after St. Patrick's Day. Nobody at the institute knew what killed him, but she recalled with terrible clarity leaving a repair call for one of her pieces of equipment about a week before the incubator was broken.

Now, bending over one of her precious vats, she felt not only worried, but also quite ill herself. It was nothing specific, just an ache in her joints and a faint headache. But it grew worse, and that worried her.

Strain 73 might well have caused such symptoms, if it took up residence in a human body instead of a Petri dish.

* * * * *

Word came through for a shutdown of all the labs for the annual overhaul of the filtration system. Except for a few of the most crucial experiments, everything was discontinued, and everyone was ordered out of the institute until cleanup was completed. Only the most stringent measures were sufficient for dealing with the sorts of deadly bugs that might be hung up in the filters.

Dr. Perkins was more than glad to take a few days off. She was feeling worse and worse, and she thought that Marberg didn't look too well, either. When she asked, he assured her that he was chipper, but she didn't believe him.

She dragged herself home and made hot soup. After a shower and a nap, she found herself feeling no better. A small doubt nagged at her. Had Strain 73 been something really dangerous that hadn't shown up as such? Had she picked up the virus after the spill?

The lab had looked spotless when she walked into it the day after the accident. But if the virus had been spread about, say by a mop, she might have picked up traces of something that no doctor in the world was qualified to handle.

* * * * *

She gave in at last on her third day at home and went to her doctor. The clinic, as usual, was full of people. Two of the patients were people that Perkins knew, and both worked at the local emergency hospital. Elmer Davis was a paramedic who had lived in her neighborhood for five years. Amelia Jenkins was an emergency room nurse. She had bandaged Perkins's knee after a bike accident a couple of years before.

They greeted her languidly, looking as miserable as she felt. A cold certainty began to grow inside her. She rose with some difficulty and made an excuse to the office nurse.

Then she took a cab directly to the home of the director of the institute. When Martha Wattles, the director's wife, answered the doorbell, Perkins greeted her from a fair distance.

"I must see Dr. Wattles at once," she told the woman. "It is of vital importance."

"Come in out of the cold," urged the woman. I'll call him."

"I am afraid I'm coming down with . . . flu," said Perkins. "I don't want to infect your family. If Dr. Wattles would just come out for a moment—make sure he puts on a coat. It is freezing out here. I'm afraid I have an emergency to report."

Dr. Wattles was on the porch in a few minutes, bundled in a tweed coat with fur lining. He looked irritated, but he also looked interested.

"What is so important that it brings you to my door on a day off and in the middle of a cold spell?" he asked her.

She braced herself. "There was a spill in Lab 2031 on St. Patrick's Day. I checked back the next day on my culture, and the vat holding Virus Strain 73 was broken. Everything had been cleaned up and was spotless, but the entire culture was gone, and pieces of the incubator glass were in the trash bin.

"I want to know, and I pray that you can tell me . . . was Harkrider on duty that night? And what did he die of, a few weeks ago? I never found out what his problem was. I don't know what is the matter with me, right now, but I saw two people from Emergency who were waiting for my doctor when I went to her office just now. We have to find out . . ."

Dr. Wattles had gone pale and grim. ". . . if they attended Harkrider on the night he died. Yes, he did work the St. Patrick's Day shift. I recall it well. He objected strenuously. He had his bonus burning a hole in his pocket, and there was a red-headed stewardess waiting for him . . ." He broke off, even paler than before.

Perkins stared at him, the impact of his words shaking her to her heels.

He drew a deep breath, very slowly, as if to calm himself.

"You stay right here. I'm calling Emergency. You'll go into isolation, along with the people in the doctor's office, until we know what we have in hand. A stewardess . . . my God! If he infected her, this stuff could be all over the country by now. My God!"

Perkins waited patiently, and the cold no longer bothered her. She burned with fever.

By the time they took her away to isolation, Dr. Perkins hardly knew what was happening to her. She just knew she had done her best—but she had a terrible feeling that it was too little, and entirely too late.

*   *   *   *   *

The crew members in Atlanta who cleaned the filters for the institute were experienced, tough, and inventive. They used, of course, the suits devised by the Decontam people, in order to protect themselves from any esoteric substances that might have lodged in the drains. Still, they tended to take their work for granted.

This spring seemed to be a particularly difficult one down in the drains. The big conduits seemed to be almost plugged with a green, mossy growth that had just about covered the filter system and hung down like Spanish moss from the overhead curves of the big drainpipes.

"Hey, Gerald!" came the cry from a man sitting at the controls of the automatic rooter that cleaned the pipes. "I'm hung up down here! The machine is caught."

The growth was just too thick and spongy for the

equipment's motor and vanes to handle it. The men had to go inside and rake the stuff off the curvatures of the drains before the rooter could complete its mission. The suits, they knew, kept them safe as they worked.

Later, the men stood obediently under the chemical shower for twenty minutes, waiting for all contamination to be killed and removed from their exteriors.

The gunk they released was pumped into the decon pools, where thousands of units of strong chemicals were stirred into it for a week. At the end of that week, the entire lot was loosed into the sewage system that served that end of the city, then drained into the river.

But along with it went millions of healthy viruses, multiplying madly in the warmer weather. Everyone related to the matter was oblivious to the fact that those viruses should have been as dead as Harkrider . . . and Araminta Perkins.

* * * * *

Arthur Wattles sat in his deep chair, staring at the wall. He could hear his wife's voice, dim with distance, as she comforted their granddaughter in her upstairs room. He knew that it was only a matter of time, now. The child would die, as her mother and father had done. She was the last . . . and then he and Martha would sicken, too, and follow them.

He rose stiffly, feeling the ache in his bones, the beginning of unease in his belly, and switched on the television built into the bar. Still another anchorperson.

The—what—fifth, in as many days?

"From London comes word of continuing spread of the nameless epidemic that has devastated most of the western world within the past two months," said the harried-looking young woman gazing into the camera. "The death of Britain's prime minister yesterday has thrown that country's government into chaos, as most of the ministries have suffered major losses as well. Martial law there is impossible to enforce, because more than two-thirds of the nation's military personnel have died also.

"The USSR has issued a bulletin denying that that country is suffering any losses from the plague. Soviet Premier Mikhail Adrianov stated yesterday on Soviet television that the entire problem is a ruse invented by the Western nations in order to distract public attention from his own country's latest peace plan."

Dr. Wattles sighed and turned off the set. There had been nothing but news of the catastrophe for weeks. He wondered how much longer the television stations would have the manpower to continue broadcasting the news. The world's airlines had cut back flights to essential movements of supplies and medical personnel almost at once. The U.S. government was almost at a standstill, except for emergency procedures. And he had heard a rumor that the military had been decimated already.

He suspected that by now there might well be no military forces left that could hold such a title. The institute—he shuddered at the memory—had been sealed off as soon as he understood the vastness of the problem Harkrider had loosed on the world.

He thought of Araminta Perkins. She had tried her best, as soon as she knew what was happening. It was just the luck of the game that she had been too late. Much too late. By the time he had shut down the institute and quarantined every worker concerned with any phase of its work, she had died.

It was sheer disaster that Harkrider had a date with a stewardess on St. Patrick's Day. From that single encounter, the virus had spread over four continents before anyone knew what had happened. It had taken the three stews much longer to show symptoms than it had Harkrider—he had been exposed to intense concentrations of the culture, whereas they were only exposed to vestiges left on his body.

Wattles could only watch the death, not only of his own family but of the civilization that had been such a source of pride for him. "Pride goeth before a fall," he murmured.

"Arthur!" His wife's call from the top of the stairs was low and full of pain.

Wattles sighed again and rose. He knew before he got to the top of the stairs that the child was in the last, most painful stages of the disease. He could smell uncontrolled feces and he could hear the girl's moans.

It was time.

He went into his own bathroom and took a vial and a syringe from the cabinet. When he entered the room reserved for use by his treasured grandchild, his wife looked up at him with a mixture of pain and hope on her face.

"You can . . . help her?" Martha asked.

Arthur Wattles nodded, as he filled the needle and gently inserted it into the fevered skin of the child's arm. It took a terrible effort to push the plunger down, but the sigh of relief, followed by complete and permanent peace on the girl's face, made it worthwhile.

"Are you ready, Martha?" he asked. "It will come, sooner or later. There's nothing more we can do for anyone. I'm tired. What about you?"

Martha put her arms about her husband's waist and laid her graying head against his chest. "I always hoped we could go together," she said. "But I didn't ever want the whole world to die with us."

"I know. I feel as if it must be my fault, somehow, even though it was many unforeseeable accidents. It will be a comfort just to go . . ." He smiled down at her, although he knew that the smile had to seem terribly strained.

"Now," she said, sitting carefully on the bed. She extended her arm and held it steady for the needle.

"I'll be right there in a minute," Wattles said, as he pushed the plunger for the next-to-last time.

7

Life at Monkey Station proved to be endlessly interesting. Eric worked with his parents, helping with record-keeping and general gofering. Bonnie welcomed his aid, and he found himself sharing her tasks with more enthusiasm than he had ever shown for things such as book-keeping and supply ordering. She was pretty and she was nice, and she seemed to like him as much as he liked her.

He had never felt quite so attracted to any of his girlfriends as he was to Bonnie, and he wasn't even embarrassed when his father teased him about being "smitten by the fair Bonita."

He was, however, equally fascinated by the macaque, many of which seemed to grow more and more human-like every day. He accompanied his mother several times to the macaque clearing, only to find Ko waiting patiently on his rock, scratching himself or examining a leaf or bug or even his own hands, as if he were taking conscious note of all the world around him.

It took Eric a couple of weeks to gain the macaque's confidence. He sat for hours beside Janet, just watching the creature watch him. When he dared to move toward Ko at last it was by slow degrees, moving his camp stool a foot or two over a period of several days. Janet let him offer the gift of fruit that accompanied each day's session, too, and that made the relationship progress much faster than it might have unassisted.

While he was working on gaining Ko's confidence, however, Eric was learning a great deal about the creatures that resulted from the French bioengineering experiment. These were no longer monkeys. Not by anyone's definition. They were in the process of abandoning the classic dominant male pattern of behavior. Each member of this new generation seemed to feel relatively independent and self-reliant, although they all still enjoyed communal rest periods in a treetop, during which they evidently exchanged the news of the day in a gabble of talk.

They had given up the grooming habit almost entirely, even among the very young. They seemed, Eric thought, much more grown-up than any monkeys he had ever seen. It was a shame, really. They were sober and responsible now, instead of carefree and full of mischief. Only the babies still scampered through the branches, playing wild games of tag.

Ko himself looked a bit worried and unhappy most of

the time. Eric wondered if that might not be caused by his increasing curiosity about and interest in everything about him, including the people who visited him daily. What would it feel like to be one moment a happy-go-lucky animal, and the next moment to become aware of all the dangers and responsibilities that accompanied living in the world?

The thought made him shudder.

"Do you think the macaque are going to end up as a real people?" he asked his father one evening, as they sat in the communal hut, going over the day's paperwork.

Norman frowned at the report he was completing. "I doubt that they would ever become people as we know them. They have too different a background. When our species became sapient, it was gradually, step by step, and with no outside interference. That made us develop a certain way.

"The macaque, on the other hand, have had evolution speeded up incredibly in the space of a generation. They have outside help and oversight. It is perfectly true that the act of observation alters the thing that is observed. That doesn't happen only in quantum mechanics; it is also true in zoology. Living creatures interact with each other, knowingly or unknowingly, and that interaction changes both sides of the equation."

"So if they become completely sapient, it will be a different sort from ours," mused Eric. The thought excited him.

"It will be like meeting an alien species, I suspect," said his mother from across the table. "At least, for others who haven't been in contact with them from the first, as we have. We're extremely lucky, you know, to have been chosen for this project. A great many others applied for the job."

* * * * *

Eric thought of that exchange often as the days passed. Even when he was following Moses about the forest, checking the traps they'd set or fishing, he kept mulling over the idea of having a new species that had never before existed.

One morning, as he held a net of wriggling eels at arm's length while balancing on a log over a small stream, he mentioned those ideas to Moses.

The Indio waited until they were safely on the other side of the stream before answering. "Tulunga already know that. Many rains ago, he and Walebe send messenger to Dr. Whitlock. Warn him about danger, outside where you come from. Tell him new thing come, new animal, new bird, new everything but man. Man dead, he say."

Eric felt a jolt inside himself. "What did Dr. Whitlock think about that?" he asked. Surely a missionary wouldn't pay heed to the warning of a primitive medicine man, or whatever Tulunga was.

"Oh, he say Satan have long arm. Reach even into forest to touch Tulunga and Walebe. Warn us not to believe anything they say. Dr. Whitlock good man, believe what he say, but we know better.

"Tulunga old, old, now. My grandfather, he recall when Tulunga young. He tell his tribe, and his tribe warn others, when soldier come, kill many Indios, take much land. Butterfly People go deep in jungle, hide there for long time. My people not listen. Armadillo People not listen to anybody, back then. Bat People follow others into jungle, and Cruel People always hide far away." The black eyes stared at Eric, but seemed to be looking into the past that Moses' grandfather had described.

"Soldier come. Many white men come, too. Cut forest, make Indios work in fields, kill many who try to run away. They think we are beasts, fit only to work for them. My people learn then to listen to Tulunga. When Whitlock come, we see he good man, though he is white. He stand up before soldier and say we not slaves, but free men. He go even to city to talk for us.

"The plantings, they die in flood. The people, they die from fever and snakebite and sometime arrows of Cruel People. Soon they go away again, but Whitlock stay, and he take care of our people since. But we never forget. If we listen to Tulunga, long, long ago, many would have lived who died."

"But if something terrible were happening out in the world beyond the jungle, we would know. That's what the radio is for. Bill keeps in touch with people all over the world. And nothing has happened. Not . . . not that he has told anyone about." Eric found himself wondering if Bill would, indeed, trouble the staff of Monkey Station with bad news about which they could do nothing.

He found himself worrying quietly, however, and it made him angry with himself. Why should he concern himself with some foolishness that Moses, an illiterate native, albeit a friend, might come up with?

As soon as Eric reached the compound again, however, he went straight to the radio shack.

"Hi, Bill. Anything doing?" he asked. Then he saw Smalley's face.

"What is it?" Eric breathed, feeling a terrible hollow forming in his stomach. "What's happened, Bill?"

"I'd better tell everybody at once. I thought it was just something normal. Nasty, but normal. But now I know . . . well, you'd better go and beat on the gong. Everybody'd better hear this at once. I don't know if I can bring myself to say it twice."

Filled with foreboding, Eric hurried to the cookshack and whacked lustily on the metal bar hung there for calling the staff to emergency conferences. People popped out of huts and hurried into sight along the path leading into the jungle.

It took a half-hour to get everyone together. Those observing the macaque could hear the gong, but even hurrying, it took at least that long to cover the distance back to the compound. When Janet had arrived, followed by Zachariah, who had accompanied her, the group was complete.

Smalley was standing in front of the radio shack, his face gray and drawn. His wife was beside him, holding his hand. She, too, seemed stunned, and Eric suspected that Bill had told her at least some of the terrible news he had heard.

"What is it, Bill?" asked Norman. "Don't keep us in suspense. We can handle anything except needless worry."

Smalley swallowed hard. "What about . . . about needful worry?" he asked. "I just talked to Helmut Kleinhardt in Berlin. There's an epidemic in Europe that has already killed roughly thirty percent of the population. There are more dead bodies than people can bury, and millions more are already sick. Helmut's sick himself. He says the thing is a virus, and the illness starts with a headache, then goes to nausea and diarrhea. He says he has about twelve hours to live, if he doesn't kill himself to save all the suffering."

Gunter stepped forward, his chilly eyes filled with calculation. "That is Europe. And while most of us have roots there, I see no great danger to us on this continent."

"I also talked to Emmett Dalton in Peoria," said Smalley. "He'd been telling me there was some sort of plague loose, and people were beginning to die. He thought it was something short-lived, until I spoke to him just now. The United States is even worse off, now, than the rest of the world. Seems it started there in a research institute in Georgia. The East Coast has been cordoned off. Nobody can come or go. The port cities are dying miserably, with emergency services disabled because of their own losses.

"Worst of all, Emmett says that the plague is beginning to show up strongly in the Midwest. He doesn't expect it to be stopped. Everyone who knew anything about it at all is dead, and there were no tests run before it got loose to learn its attributes or its limits."

Gunter turned pale, his sharklike jaw clamping hard. He turned to Norman.

"We must go at once. I have family in Belem, in Manaus, and in Rio de Janeiro. I must see to them."

"Dr. Gunter, the sickness is already there, in all those cities and smaller ones, too. With international travel as busy as it always was, this thing got all over the globe before anything showed up to prove it existed at all. If you go back, the chances are that you will die. Believe me!" Bill's pleading sounded desperate.

Eric felt a trace of that same desperation tensing his breathing. Sickness that had nothing to do with a virus suddenly boiled in his stomach. If what he heard was true, his aunt and uncle might already be dead, along with the teachers and everyone he knew in school. It didn't bear thinking about. He put his arm around his mother, who leaned her head against his shoulder, as if she were suddenly exhausted.

* * * * *

Although the day was only half over, it felt suddenly as if the sun were setting. Darkness loomed just beyond their horizon, but it was no darkness natural to the world. Eric thought, as he sat silently among the quiet group huddled together in the communal hut, about all the wonderful things that were dying along with the people who made and used them.

Medicine . . . that was the first and most valuable thing that must be dying out there. The ability to transplant hearts and livers, the capacity for inventing drugs that could overcome almost any sickness. Moses had told him that the jungle held a cure for any ill his people had ever known, but Eric felt sure that nothing growing in the wild could heal a cancer or a brain tumor. He sighed unconsciously.

His mother reached to take his hand, and he squeezed her small, strong fingers. They had each other. . . . He looked across the table at his father and tried to smile. That was a failure, and he felt tears very near behind his eyes.

"You think Aunt Grace and Uncle Ned are . . . all right?" Eric asked.

"We can't know," Janet said, her voice terribly sad. "Bill couldn't get through to El Paso . . . or to Boston or Miami or Kansas City. It might be atmospheric conditions, but that seems a remote possibility for so many widely separated places. Don't . . . don't hope too much, Eric."

* * * * *

Things had changed. Ko had grown used to seeing people, feeling them approach through the trees, smelling their distinctive odors every day. There was no real need for the fruit they brought as gifts, but it was good, and the people seemed to take pleasure in giving it. So when the fourth day passed without any of those he knew appearing, Ko decided to investigate.

He knew well the path leading to the compound. He had often gone high into his favorite tree to watch for those who visited every day. He knew where the bare place was in the forest, and he made for it, traveling through the thick tangle of branches and vines with practiced ease, keeping his nose alert for alien scents and his ears ready to catch any untoward sound. When things were strange, there might well be danger.

As he went, he thought of the noises the woman and young man had made on the last day they had visited the clearing. Although Ko didn't realize it yet, he was beginning to make sense of those sounds, and he could tell even more from the tones in which they were uttered. They had not sounded excited or distressed or angry. They had given the usual gifts.

What had happened to them?

He knew, of course, that the forest swarmed with predators of many kinds. His own people suffered occasional losses, for the big snakes loved monkeys and sometimes lay in ambush in the treetops.

Jaguars sometimes took those venturing onto the ground as well, and ocelots could climb far enough into the trees to capture unwary young. There was danger, but there were also many of the people. Could all of those other people have fallen victim to those who hunted the forest?

When he came to the last rank of giant trees beside the compound fence, he went to the very top and stared over the complex of sheds and huts. People walked about, but there was something different about them. The very smell of the place was wrong.

They seemed busy, but the purposeful and energetic air for which the macaque had no name, but which he had recognized as a part of those he knew, was changed. The subtle comfort he had always felt from them was missing. Something, he realized, was very wrong with the Hairless People.

He considered going through the gate into the compound, but something inside him resisted the notion. No, he would go back into the jungle and wait. His people were learning to be patient.

As he fled through the trees, he heard a shrill cry that was not like any he knew. At that moment, he caught the smoke-and-man smell of those who lived in the village beside the river. It seemed to be at some distance northward, and he turned toward its source, moving quickly but quietly. He had learned long before not to rush into anything in this forest.

He passed above a group of the people from the village on the river. They were busy gathering something from vines and bushes, and there seemed to be no trouble there. He moved on, and again that cry shrilled through the trees, much closer now. And another scent brought his neck hair up, bristling.

Ko dropped lower into the middle range of the jungle. He would need to see clearly if he was to learn what was happening below him. There was a small stream ahead—he had visited it more than once with his family, on their explorations of the forest about their own territory.

He froze on a branch, making himself invisible among the thick growth. On the verge of the stream, a child was being tied by men. Ko recognized those men, for he had traveled widely up and down and back and forth for miles around his home. These were the ones the villagers hated and feared. Though he could not know the name they had for them, his own term came very near it, for he, too, called them cruel. They smelled of blood, those painted men.

One of his own people had been caught in a trap set by those dark-skinned ones from deep in the forest. Before the macaque's companions could reach him, the men had caught and killed him, eating him raw and dancing about, waving his skin. Ko had a bad feeling when he thought of the Cruel People. And they now held a small one belonging to the people he knew from the clearing. . . . What could he do?

It never occurred to the macaque that in another time and place it would have seemed impossible for one of his kind to interfere in the perils of another species. Now, he felt a responsibility, and he withdrew as quietly as he could, turning back toward those he had passed before.

They were still at their gathering, their voices murmuring softly through the scented air. Ko paused above them, wondering how to tell them of the danger their child faced back at the stream. These ones did not know his kind; they were used to the scatter-brained monkeys native to their forest. Would they be frightened of one who approached them and tried to communicate with them?

Or would they simply kill him with their spears and arrows?

It never occurred to the macaque that what he did was courageous. It seemed right, and that was what he must do. In this, he surpassed a surprising fraction of those who had made his kind possible.

He swung down from a low branch near one of the old men in the group. As the elder glanced up, startled, Ko put his hands together, softly clapping them. He nodded rapidly, wishing that he could speak the tongue of these people as easily as he did his own language. It would make his task easy.

He grunted gruffly as he approached the old man. As the Indio showed no sign of either fleeing or attacking, Ko reached to touch his arm. Then he turned back toward the place where the child was and moved away through the jungle, turning now and then to make certain the man was following.

He was, but the others were not. Ko stopped and jumped up and down, making the most compelling noise he could manage. He got enough urgency into his squeaks, evidently, for the man called aloud, and the other men in the group dropped their bags and baskets and ran after the odd pair.

It would have been far quicker and easier to go through the treetops, but Ko knew the men could not manage that. So he stumped forward on his short legs, making urgent cries from time to time to keep his followers moving fast.

When they reached the stream, there was nobody

there. That surprised Ko, until he went over the time it had taken him to arrive with help. There was, however, a fish spear and a net, dropped carelessly on the ferns edging the stream. There were also tracks on the sand bar in the middle of the creek, and to those the Indios went at once.

Ko felt great relief. He was too wise in the ways of the forest and its people to feel certain that the child would be found, but he had done what he could. Now his mind was at rest, and he went aloft and sped again toward his own family and his own tribe.

Where the Cruel People hunted, nobody was safe. They came out of their fastnesses seldom, but when they did it was well to hide and be cautious.

8

The staff at Monkey Station had gone about their most necessary duties for several days. Everyone seemed stunned and abstracted, and things got done automatically, if not well. Janet never thought of visiting the macaque; suddenly the importance of the project had evaporated, along with the civilization that had made it possible.

On the evening of the fourth day after the news, a small delegation of Indios arrived at the gate, waiting politely to be invited into the compound. Eric saw them first, and he called his father to greet the visitors.

Norman, seeing that the villagers had something important on their minds, sent at once for Lauren to interpret. His own use of the dialect was serviceable for most things, but not capable of much beyond everyday needs.

When the group had been invited into the communal hut and given cool drinks, the necessary preliminaries took a much shorter time than usual. Formal greetings having been exchanged, the group's leader, who Eric knew was called Kolambe, set aside his glass of beer and looked at Norman with a serious face.

"Those you placed in the forest clearing, Doctor, are not . . . are not as usual with their kind. That is so?" he asked in his own tongue. Lauren interpreted smoothly.

Norman nodded. "They are a different kind, even from what they were in their own country."

"We knew that. You have told those who work here for you. We did not altogether believe. We have found that white men do not always understand those things of the forest until they have lived with them for a very long time. But this is not so. Not with these monkey-people."

Eric pricked up his ears as Norman leaned forward. "And what was it that showed you that?" he asked.

"Some of our people were gathering medicine in the forest. A child went to fish in a stream deeper in the jungle, and those of the Cruel People caught him. We would not have known this, but one of those macaque came to where my people worked. He came down to the ground and tried to speak with them, but he could only grunt and squeak and beat his hands together." The Indio looked as if he expected Norman to doubt this, but Littlefield only nodded.

"When he made Kaloto understand the need to follow, he led my people to the stream, where the child had dropped his net and spear. They found tracks in the sand. Of course, there were no more in the forest, but we have made it our business to learn the ways the Cruel People travel. We caught them, and we took back our child." He looked quizzically at Littlefield.

"If those who walked in our forest do not return to their own, there are many things that can happen to people in the paths of our world. And if Dr. Whitlock never learns that they did not return, we will be made happy thereby."

Eric could see Lauren struggling to retain her composure as she relayed the man's words to her own chief. He found himself wanting to smile for the first time in days.

"I have known that these monkey-people were wise, in their own way," said Norman. "I did not know that they were also able to understand the things that trouble our kind. This makes me happy for you. I am glad that you regained your child. May he live for many years. And I cannot think that Dr. Whitlock need ever learn about this matter at all."

Eric found himself wondering what had brought this dignified man, who must be the chief of the Armadillo People, to the compound. There was not really any need for informing the Monkey Station staff of this event, wonderful though it might seem.

"We would like to learn about these new people in our forest," said the Indio. "We would like to thank them for their help. As they are yours, we ask you for permission to leave gifts of fruit for them. They seem to need little else."

Now that made sense. If you're going to share a jungle

with other sapient kinds, it is just as well to make friends with them. To learn all you can about them. And perhaps to make allies of them, against the coming of common enemies or dangerous times.

"You have my permission," said Norman. "I am pleased that the macaque have helped you. I hope that we can all help each other, in times to come, for we have had very bad news from beyond the forest."

"Ah. It has come, then," said the chief. "Tulunga is never wrong when he hears voices in his spirit."

"Tulunga?" asked Norman. "I do not know the name."

"He is the seer of the Butterfly People, beyond the small river and the great trees. He said, many rains ago, that there would come a great sickness in the world beyond the forest. That people would die until few were left, and that animals and plants and insects would change and change and change again, until our grandchildren would know creatures that we have never seen."

"Moses told me about that," interrupted Eric. "I thought it was nonsense. And that same day, when we came back to the compound, Bill had learned about it from his radio buddy in Berlin."

The chief turned his attention gravely toward Eric as he spoke. When Lauren had interpreted Eric's words, the man nodded.

"Moses is intelligent. He listens to the words of men and to the voices of the creatures in the forest."

Norman sighed deeply. "Kolambe, our world has changed much in the past days and nights. It may be that in the future we must work together to survive, for that sickness will not remain only outside the forest. People will flee up the rivers. And can we bring ourselves to deny them help? Speak to Dr. Whitlock when you return to your village. Ask him to visit me here, for we have terrible news for him."

* * * * *

When the group had gone down the path into the jungle, Eric sat with his parents. They were silent for a long time, thinking about what they had heard. If only their world had not ended so abruptly, what wonderful news they could have sent back to the foundation that had funded the project.

"They are probably all dead," said Norman. Nobody asked who he meant. They knew he spoke of his colleagues back in Boston, the researchers who had worked with the French in the original DNA alterations.

"Perhaps, even so, they know," said Lauren. "I know that it is the popular attitude to scoff at the thought of anything coming after death, but that is a belief made for a secure world where people know both ease and safety. In the world we are facing now, I think we will have to come up with some belief in something beyond our own puny selves. Simply for our own comfort, if nothing else."

Norman opened his mouth to dispute that with her. Eric expected one of the impassioned critiques on the excesses of religion that his father had reasoned out so closely. But he closed his mouth again without speaking. His expression grew thoughtful.

"Of course, you are right," Norman said. "I suddenly realize that I need something to look to, something to call upon that has some explanation of what has happened. I can tell myself that this is an accident, and intellectually I know it to be true. But something inside me needs to know a reason . . . to know that some purpose has been served by this terrible thing. I never thought that I would say such a thing, but you are quite right, Lauren."

* * * * *

As it turned out, Norman decided not to wait for Dr. Whitlock to visit him. The next morning, after tending the pitiful remnants of the baboons and chimps, he and Halloran, Janet, and Bill Smalley set out for the village in the Land Rover and the pickup. Eric asked to go, too, and his father nodded. Eric leaped aboard the pickup as Halloran cranked it, and he saw for the first time the primitive track leading through the jungle to the river village.

The steady rains, falling almost every day, kept the track rutted, though the network of roots underlying it gave the vehicles traction. Eric braced himself in the bed of the pickup as well as he could manage, but even so, he felt as if he had been beaten by the time the truck jounced over the last rut and pulled up in the cleared area of the river landing.

This was not, he saw at once, a town in any sense he had ever thought of one. Palm-thatched huts were tucked into the greenery at the edge of the forest, surrounded by thorny fences. The church dominated the scene, standing far back from the road leading down to the river. It was a small building of dressed lumber, with a squat steeple from which hung a bell, whose rust shone red in the harsh light.

Beside it was a bungalow with wide porches shading every side, and beyond that was a small metal shack that had to be the only store within a thousand miles of jungle. The missionary stood on his porch, watching them as they climbed down from the vehicles and walked toward him.

From what he had been told, Eric knew that Nathan Whitlock had to be at least seventy. But he looked a hearty fifty, his tall physique showing a lot of strength, no matter what his age. He wore his white hair cut close to his scalp, and his khaki shorts and shirt were clean, though unpressed. He had a pair of shears in his hand, and on a stool behind him sat a small Indio child, her hair shorn on one side and still long on the other.

"Come along, Norman," the missionary called. "I've got Susie here just about done. She got burrs tangled so deep in her hair that we're having to cut the whole shebang and start over again. You hold her hands, Delenda, so she won't get them in the way of my scissors."

Now Eric could see a young woman kneeling beside the stool, comforting the tearful child. With a couple of expert snips, Whitlock finished his barbering and lifted the little girl down from the stool. He fumbled in his pocket and took out a round of peppermint, which he tucked into her mouth.

He turned to his guests and led them into the coolness of his sitting room. "What is this Kolambe told me? I was going to come over today, when I had things in hand. It sounded ominous."

Then he realized that Eric had come in from the porch. "And this is Eric, I know. I have been wanting to meet your son. Sit down, young man, and have something cool to drink. Delenda will be here with fruit juice in a minute."

Norman waited until they were all sipping from glasses of cool juice before answering the man's question. He approached the subject with some caution, beginning with a question.

"Did Kolambe mention running into a group of Cochona, yesterday? That seems to be closer than they have come since we've been down here. He came over to tell me about seeing the Cruel People. I was glad of the warning, though I suspect they are already back in their own territory."

"Yes, he said they had seen some trace of them. I don't expect any trouble, though. It has been years since the Cochona troubled us here. But what was it that your man, Smalley, heard on the radio? That is the thing that is worrying me."

Janet reached to take Norman's hand, as her husband replied, "There's a plague, Dr. Whitlock. One to make the plagues of Egypt look tame. It sounds as if the population of the world is going to be reduced by something like ninety percent. Already, the civilization we knew is gone, and now Bill can't get through to any of his regular contacts, not even those at the foundation."

Whitlock turned pale. Eric had never seen that happen with such terrible slowness, as the color beneath the tanned skin leached away, leaving Whitlock's face a strange shade of gray.

"Are you all right, Nathan?" asked Halloran. "Here, let me check your heart." But the missionary shook his head.

"All right. Just give me a minute. I never expected it, you see, even though we were warned, time and again.

"And what of our people?" There was pain in his question. "Our families, our friends, those who have supported us in our work?" There were tears in his eyes now, and Eric found his own eyes damp.

"From what we can tell, it was an accident of sorts in a research facility," Janet said. "I am grateful, somehow, that it wasn't germ warfare. I can live better with an accident, I think."

"What really concerns me is the fact that I was warned. Tulunga sent word to me, through old Walebe, and I disregarded it. I thought that because he is an Indio and a heathen, he could not possibly have the gift of prophecy. But here it is, the thing he saw—or heard. He hears voices in his mind, I understand. I was arrogant and too self-assured, and God has, among everything else, found a way to humble me."

"Nathan, we're all arrogant to some extent. Being a

preacher doesn't make you any different from the rest of us. And we're all in the same boat now. You, and we, and the Indios. Even Gunter, who wants to get a boat and go downriver, no matter what the risk."

Whitlock looked up sharply. "Let him," he said. "Whatever happens, I believe that we will all be better off without having that man present. God forgive me, I find myself judging him, and I will be better pleased to have him out of our vicinity."

Norman looked at Halloran, who nodded slowly. "I feel the same," said the doctor. "Is there a boat he can take? I suspect that others may want to go, too. Fenister said something about trying to get back to Tanzania."

"There will be a boat. One to go downriver," said Whitlock, his eyes seeming to gaze into the future. "And how many to come, carrying human beings who, in turn, carry the seeds of death in their bodies?"

Eric felt something inside him give a violent thump. For some reason, though he thought that he had accepted the terrible news from outside the jungle, he realized that he had not thought of being in danger himself. This place seemed so remote from everything. But the river still ran to the Amazon, and that, in its turn, led through branches and tributaries and its many-armed complex not only to the Atlantic but to many places he had never heard of.

"Quarantine," murmured Norman, his tone doubtful. "But how could we bear to turn away anyone needing our help?"

"Indeed. I certainly could not, and I doubt that any of

your remaining staff could, either," said Whitlock. "Of course, it may not come to that. The plague may wipe out everything in its path, leaving no sick survivors to run away into the jungle."

Halloran ran his fingers through his hair, achieving new heights of disorder. "I doubt it. I read Smalley's transcript of his conversation with his contacts. It was the consensus that this is a genetically manipulated virus, unlike anything humankind has ever met before. It takes some weeks to make itself felt, and even then it requires a couple of days of discomfort, followed by about twelve hours of terrible illness, before death." Eric realized as the doctor spoke that his Irish brogue was an affectation. Now he was speaking as the scientist he was.

"People could believe themselves free of the disease when they set out upriver, and still might be dying by the time they reach us." He turned to Whitlock.

"You said the old shaman warned you about this. What did he say, exactly?"

"The warning came by messenger from the chief of the Butterfly People. It was rather vague, actually. The first warning simply said that there was danger in the outside world. That I should be very cautious in dealing with anyone who came up the river. But there was another warning. I disregarded it, too." Whitlock sighed, suddenly looking his full seventy years.

"Moses came to me. He had talked with Tulunga in the forest, and the old man had told him about the thing his voices had said. Most men would die, he told me. Animals would change until they could not be recognized by anyone who knows them as they are now. Death would come up the river. God forgive me! I could not believe!"

"And what could you have done, Nathan, if you had believed? Do you think any warning from a missionary down here would have been heeded any more than Tulunga's warning was? To those who control the world, you are both considered unbalanced fanatics who believe in nonmaterial matters that science cannot prove." Norman sighed and stared absently at Eric.

In his father's eyes Eric saw pain and worry and, as well, the loss of the illusions with which his own scientific training had indoctrinated him. Eric rose and went to stand between the chairs in which his parents sat. He put an arm around each, and the warmth of their bodies was somehow comforting, even in the damp heat of the day.

There would, everyone agreed, be no more supplies from downriver. Whitlock and the Littlefields listed all supplies on hand that they could call to mind and agreed to make immediate inventories of gasoline, medicines, and other things that could not be replaced from the jungle.

"If we survive this," said Norman, as they took leave of the missionary, "we are in an ideal situation to prosper. The forest, as our Indio friends continually tell us, contains everything a human being needs to live. Drugs to cure all ills—or all natural ills—grow there as vines or plants or bushes.

"There is more food than a million people could eat,

if you know how to recognize it. There are even depilato-
ries and contraceptives. I know. I asked all about the
things I'd read about when I first came down here. I was
shown the plants that provide them." He looked over at
Janet, then at Whitlock.

"I suspect that if you could prove it, the Garden of
Eden must have been a jungle like this. Everything we'd
need, if we hadn't been spoiled rotten by our technology
and our culture that makes everything easy, is right here
within arm's reach."

They left the pickup there, as they decided not to
waste the fuel to get it back to Monkey Station. While
Whitlock had an ancient motorcycle, he had no better
vehicle, and they felt that it might be helpful if he could
have a reliable way to reach them, if there was need. The
radio could convey word from place to place, but it
couldn't send supplies.

When they got back to the compound, they found
Gunter, Fenister, and the two Indians preparing to
leave. They had their luggage piled up together under
one of the sheds, and Gunter had even stripped some of
his equipment out of the laboratory.

"Is there a boat at the village?" demanded the Brazilian, as Norman pulled the Land Rover to a halt and his
crowded passengers got out. "We want to leave in the
morning, as soon as it is light. It's too late to go today.
We will need an Indio to take us downriver, too."

"There is a boat," said Norman. "Whitlock said you
could use his. But neither he nor you will sentence one of
the Indios to death, guiding you. You can make it on

your own, or not go. There are enough of you to manage the boat."

"I hate to see you throw your lives away," said Janet, her voice near the edge of tears. "This is no ordinary epidemic, Alberto. This is something outside our experience, all the way!"

Eric could see the rejection in those cold Germanic eyes that were so incongruous in the swarthy Latin face. The man shrugged irritably.

"You are fools. You will sit here in the jungle and rot, while I will pick up the remnants of our civilization and become the new ruler of Brazil. Perhaps even a greater area. Stay here, and feel safe. I go to meet a greater destiny."

Halloran raised his eyebrows. "Hail to the Chief," he said, his tone wry. "Now we have work to do. Just because the world is coming to an end, that's no reason to neglect our animals. They had nothing whatever to do with it, poor beasts." He turned toward the hut housing the chimps and baboons.

Norman reached for Janet's hand. "It's time we visited our own group again. Ko will be wondering what has become of us. I wish we could explain this to him. He's bright enough to wonder, but not quite advanced enough to understand if we told him the problem."

"Can I come, too?" Eric asked. "I feel like staying together, if you don't mind."

His father reached for him, and Janet dashed into the lab and came out with her clipboard and her camp stool. "They won't recognize me without these," she said, as they turned their steps into the path leading through the jungle to the clearing beside the stream.

* * * * *

Ko had evidently given up waiting. No furred shape occupied his boulder, though the trees at the farther edge of the clearing held a couple of macaque, who seemed to be taking a late afternoon nap.

Eric stared up at the peaceful shapes. "Will they survive?" he asked.

Janet gazed up thoughtfully. "They can survive in this forest without any problem. They are multiplying at a normal rate. They show few signs of susceptibility to the alien bacteria and microbes here. That will be no problem for them.

"But could they survive contact with the plague? That is the big question. They were altered not only for intelligence but also for disease resistance. Both genetic and environmental diseases were considered when the alterations were made. But those who did the work knew nothing of this new virus. They may be resistant to it, and they may not. Let's hope they don't come into contact with any human beings carrying the bug."

Norman turned his face to the sky and called loudly, a shrill, strange call that made Eric's skin prickle into goose pimples. After a while, there came a shaking in the treetops, and Ko appeared, followed by several members of his family.

The macaque did not descend to his regular seat on

the stone. He perched on a low branch and stared at the three humans, as if he might be thinking hard about what their sudden appearance might mean.

"Oh, hell," said Norman. "I may sound like a fool, but I'm going to tell him about it. Don't laugh. I feel stupid enough already, talking to a bunch of macaque as if they were people."

He moved beneath the branch on which Ko waited. There was a space of clean stone set into the ground there, and he sat cross-legged on it, looking up at the macaque to catch his eye.

Eric didn't move. Janet, beside him, seemed frozen in place, too, waiting to see, to hear. . . . To learn? Eric wondered. He strained his ears to hear what his father was saying.

". . . people die," Norman said. "No more will come with food. No more will the flying machines come . . . I think. We will stay here in the forest with the macaque. The Indios will teach us how to live without the outside things we know." He was looking earnestly into Ko's eyes.

Even from that distance, Eric thought the macaque was staring just as earnestly back at his father. Ko's right hand was moving, the fingers curling and uncurling. His toes twitched against the bark of the tree limb. He seemed, strange as it might be, to be concentrating with all his might on Norman Littlefield's words.

9

Eric had accepted the idea that no aircraft would ever again land on the strip at Monkey Station. The "wip-wip-wip" of a chopper's blades brought him out of the hut, excitement building inside him, along with what he knew must be unfounded hope.

What if the past few weeks had been entirely some sort of communal nightmare?

It was Porter's helicopter. "CRX 103" was painted on the side.

His heart thudding with mingled excitement and dread, Eric ran toward the landing pad, where dust was whirling upward as the chopper came to rest. He could hear other running steps behind him, but he was by far the fastest runner among the non-Indio members of the staff. He pounded up just as the door opened and Porter leaped to the ground.

Halloran was panting almost in Eric's ear, and the Littlefields were just arriving at a trot. The doctor yelled, "Be careful, Steve! Are you infected? If you've come in contact with any of the sick—any at all!—you need to keep a good distance."

Porter nodded. "You don't have to warn me, Doc. After what I've seen in the past few days, I wouldn't take any chances, believe me. I kept my distance from everybody, including my girlfriend and the people at the airport. And I got hold of a couple of gallons of carbolic acid—I've all but bathed in the stuff."

"Then I hope it's all right if you come on in. We can't make certain we're safe, no matter what. If we live in constant fear, we might as well be dead. I'm glad to see you, my boy." Halloran was grinning widely.

Reassured, Eric approached, too, along with the rest of the crew. Porter reached to shake his hand. "Don't worry, Eric. I've scrubbed myself and the chopper, too. But it looks as if you won't be going back to Texas," he said. "I got onto a ham operator out of Lampasas. He said there were no more than fifteen people that he knew about still living in his area, and some of them weren't feeling well. He didn't know how long he was going to live himself. He went out and helped a little kid that was crying in the middle of the street. The kid got sick and died, so he figured he was infected."

"So it's in Texas," said Norman. "El Paso is a busy place—I guess my brother and his wife stand a good chance of being . . . " His voice died away.

Porter nodded. "Everyplace with a good-sized airport seems to have been hit hard. Somebody told me there was a rumor that some stews got contaminated and carried it all over the world before they ever knew they were sick. Pilots, baggage handlers, passengers, customs people—they all got infected before anybody knew this thing existed, much less what it could do."

The others were shooting questions at the pilot as they made their way up to the complex. "How about Natal?" asked Norman. "And Belem and Manaus? Gunter and some of the others took off in a launch downstream, just after we got the news. What sort of chance do they stand of finding anything left? Or of surviving, if it comes to that?"

They reached the bath shack, and Porter halted. "I'll answer all your questions—those that I have answers for—when I've had another bath. I've been careful, but I'll feel better once I scrub down again. You got any carbolic, or should I go back and get mine out of the chopper?"

They did have some, of course, and it seemed a very long time while Porter remained in the bath. But when he came out, his dark hair damp, and his skin pink under its olive tint, he looked a lot happier.

"Did you know about an epidemic when you came a few weeks ago?" asked Eric, before his father could repeat his earlier questions.

Porter nodded cautiously. "I knew there was one. It was just a rumor when I got to Manaus. Some people had died in Rio of an unknown bug. Nothing really frightening. People are always dying of unknown bugs. So I picked up your supplies and those for the mission up the Rio Branco and went about my business.

"When I got back to town, it was . . . it was a mess." The man's face looked almost greenish at the memory. "Would you believe dead bodies lying on the tarmac? Would you believe a control tower full of dead people at Belem? I gassed up the chopper from barrels stored in the supply sheds. There was nobody there, and I was careful not to touch anything with an unprotected hand. I found the carbolic in one of those sheds, along with a lot of medical stuff. I didn't dare touch that—no telling where it had been—but I washed off the carboys of carbolic with some of their contents." He sighed gustily.

"I hope, folks, that it was enough. This was the only place I could think of to come. I don't get along all that well with those missionaries up the Branco. They think I'm a real sinner, I guess. I like you people. I think you stand a good chance of making it, if you don't get too many refugees up the river."

"I don't understand," said Norman. "From what we heard and from what you said earlier, this stuff takes a while to kill its victims. Why should there be dead bodies on the tarmac?"

"Oh, they hadn't died of the virus," Porter said. "They'd been killed with machetes. I think somebody had gone crazy, after getting sick. Or maybe it was looters. I flew over the town at housetop level, and I saw only four people on the streets. They looked sick.

"Maybe there were others inside. Maybe a lot of the

people had fled into the forest. I dunno. And I wasn't about to land and go ask the ones I saw."

Bill was turning to stare back at the chopper. "You don't suppose the skin of that bird is still carrying anything, do you? Can viruses travel through the air?"

Halloran grunted. "Pneumonic plague can. There's no guarantee that this stuff can't, but I'd think it's unlikely. And if it can do that . . . well, it can travel the distance to reach us here without hitching a ride on the chopper."

* * * * *

Jefe had cooked lunch, and it was his usual delicious display of food. Eric had been there when his mother explained the disaster to the old Indio. He had nodded, his face expressionless.

"World not out there for me, ever," he said. "Why I worry if it gone?" Then he'd returned to his tasks, and Mrs. Smalley had raised her eyebrows and shrugged, making Janet almost smile for the first time in days.

As they finished the meal, Porter reached into the pack he had brought from his aircraft. "Almost forgot," he said. "I picked this up for Eric in Manaus a couple of weeks ago and hadn't had a chance to give it to him. Now that . . . this has happened, I expect he may need it worse than I ever thought he would."

He took out a package that was wrapped in brown paper and handed it to the young man. Eric tore the paper off, his hands trembling with anticipation. What could the pilot have brought him?

A tooled leather sheath slid into his grip, its well-oiled finish smooth against his skin. He unsnapped the band securing the ivory-colored haft and pulled a long, sharp knife from the sheath.

The grip was of carved bone, wrapped in the middle with leather to give a firmer hold. The blade was incredibly fine steel, with lacy interlocking lines engraved on it, almost like Toledo blades used to have. Eric took the knife into his hand, and it felt somehow natural there.

Janet and Norman stared at each other from either side of their son. Eric knew what was going through their minds, he thought.

The world in which he would live from now on would depend more on his skill with knife and bow and spear than on any mastery of mathematics or science. All their plans for him—all his plans for himself—had been summarily canceled by the ending of their world.

He grinned up at Porter. "Thanks," he managed to say. "I think maybe I'll need this. Need it a lot."

On the other side of the table, Bonnie gave a hysterical gasp, as if she had grasped, for the first time, the entirety of their problem. Her eyes turned toward Eric desperately, and he nodded, trying to show an assurance he did not feel. Lauren Nagle reached across her husband, who was sitting next to Bonnie, and patted her shoulder comfortingly.

"That's a good blade," said Norman. "You be sure to treat it right. Oil it every night—this climate is death on metal. Keep it in the sheath, but wrap it all in oiled rags when you're not using it."

Eric nodded. Looking at Bonnie again, he recalled suddenly that her family and friends were—had been—in Virginia. They were probably dead. He shook away the thought.

If they let themselves get caught up in thoughts of all those they knew who were now gone, they'd never do anything but sit around and grieve. And grief, he knew now, was a luxury that only a safe society could afford. Nothing in their present circumstances was going to allow the staff of Monkey Station to weep and mourn.

Porter's voice broke into his thoughts. "If you have any gas to spare, I need to go upriver a couple of hundred miles. There's a bunch of hunters up there, and they ought to be warned. They've been there several weeks, so they shouldn't have any contamination at all.

"You want me to tell them to come back here?" He looked at Norman questioningly.

"At this point, the more people we can muster, the better it will be. I keep thinking about those Cochona who were in this area recently. If the Butterfly People have someone who can see the future, who's to say that the Cruel People don't have one, too?"

Eric thought about that as he went with Porter to refuel the chopper. Had the Cruel People foreseen this catastrophe for their enemies, the whites? And were they even now plotting to strike against the settlements and the gentler tribes along the river?

Eric waved to Porter, as the chopper rose and circled. But as he walked back to the huddle of huts, he shivered, despite the humid heat of the afternoon.

* * * * *

Ko was thinking harder than he had ever thought in his short life. Those words the man had spoken to him meant something important. Though not couched in the shrieks and grunts and chatterings of his kind, they made a sort of sense, as he mulled over the look on the man's face and the sound of his voice, as well as the subtle scent of fear that had hung about him.

Ko had talked about this with his family. Though they no longer treated him as the dominant male, having changed that pattern of behavior, they did listen to him. He was, after all, the one who was closest to the Hairless People, as well as the one who came nearest to understanding those enigmatic beings.

They all contributed observations. His mate, Keela, had seen Cruel People in their territory. Not the group Ko had seen, but another one, much later and in a different area. They seemed to be lurking about the compound where the Hairless People lived, although they avoided everyone and seemed to be trying to remain unseen.

In the years the macaque had lived in this jungle, which was most of Ko's life, only the Indios who lived along the river and among the big trees farther inland had come into the place reserved for the macaque. They never disturbed his people, and his folk, in turn, paid no heed to them.

Those others, however, were another story. He had seen, in the travels his family had made, the Cruel People in their own place, and they were not a good kind. He had seen members of that tribe kill their own children. He had seen them take the heads of other Indios and carry them away with them.

All this mixed together with the trouble he had seen in the face of the man who'd spoken to him. Something was about to change. Something was about to make the lives of the macaque more dangerous than ever before.

Ko could feel it like a shiver along his bones. His tail curled and uncurled nervously, as he examined this new sensation. What was coming through the jungle, even now, to bring peril to his people?

He was sitting in the top of his favorite tree, thoughtfully eating a locust, when he heard the outcry. He moved instantly, all his attention centered upon the shrieking words of the young macaque who even now fled through the trees toward the stream.

"Men come! Strange men come! They have killed Kep! Run!" It was the voice of Kep's mate, Chee.

The group feeding quietly around the clearing disappeared into the trees at once. They no longer needed anyone to order them to do the sensible thing, which puzzled the old members of the troop a great deal.

Ko knew it was because of something the Hairless People had done, though he had never been able to determine what that might have been. Now he was glad of it. He wanted to observe the approach of these men for himself, and he wanted to do it unseen and unheard.

Not only the macaque were retreating through the treetops. Spider monkeys passed in a hysterical troop, crying and protesting. His own people made no sound, Ko noted.

He went up swiftly to the top tier of the forest, where the limber branches dipped beneath his weight. He moved quickly in the direction from which Chee had come, going lower from time to time to make certain that he had not missed those who now invaded his jungle.

He did not hear them when he came within range. They moved through the thick growth as silently as fish through a stream. They looked very strange to him . . . they were painted with ash on their bodies and faces, leaving stripes of their darker skin showing. That made them very hard to see.

Ko paused in the top of a giant tree, staring down the great bole toward a space in the forest below. He lay flat, staring through a screen of flowers and leaves, and watched those strange men halt and consult one another inaudibly. From time to time, one would look up into the treetops, as if he felt some watcher there. The faces, too, were painted gray, with huge black circles about the eyes.

Ko shivered. These were not a good kind. They meant harm. His own people were now safely dispersed in the tops of the trees, but the direction in which the strangers were going was toward the Hairless People's compound. Those people could not climb. He had seen this long ago.

He made a sudden decision, and though he did not know it, it was only the second time in all the history of his kind that this had occurred.

He waited until the invaders were out of sight, and then he hurled himself across the jungle, treetop to treetop, toward the place where the Hairless People lived. He knew that he could speed through the branches far more quickly than even the swiftest of men could run through the forest below.

*   *   *   *   *

Eric had been cleaning the cages of the sick chimps. The big Tanzanian had been their caretaker, and now that he and the other three staff members were gone, the work fell harder on those who were left. There had been some talk of freeing the animals into the jungle, but at last the Littlefields had agreed that they were too old and too ill to survive in this alien forest.

Eric now was getting a breath of untainted air, standing beside the fence and staring off into the jungle. He had learned, in the past days, to make his mind go blank. That way, there were no painful thoughts to disturb him. But he was roused from his lethargy by a sound from beyond the fence.

The treetops shook as a flying form moved through them. It dropped to the ground on the other side of the wire netting, and Eric recognized it as Ko. He was bigger than most of the other macaque, and his face had a permanently worried expression.

"Ko, old boy, what brings you here?" Eric asked, moving to the fence to stare into the macaque's eyes. What he saw there startled him.

"Dad!" he shouted, turning toward the huts. "Mom! Ko's here, and something's wrong. Come quick!"

Janet and Norman appeared from different directions. As soon as they saw Ko, they headed for the gate. Eric joined them as the pair approached the macaque.

The creature looked up at Norman, and the look in its eyes was full of meaning. The macaque reached to take the man's hand and tugged at it urgently, as if trying to communicate his message through touch. Even as he did that, Ko was moving his mouth, stretching his lips, trying to shape words comprehensible to the human people.

"He's trying to talk," murmured Janet. She knelt beside the little being and touched his lips. "Danger?" she asked slowly. "Danger?"

Painfully, Ko shaped his mouth to match hers. The 'D' sound seemed to be almost impossible for him, but when he spoke, it was comprehensible. "A'n'gr. A'n'gr!" He tugged more sharply at Norman's hand.

"Where?" asked Janet. She pointed toward the macaque clearing.

Ko shook his head. His hand loosed Norman's and rose. He pointed off into the deep forest toward the southwest. Then he swept his hand in an arc, including in the motion a part of the macaque territory.

Janet stared up at Norman. Eric watched them both, his heart thumping uncomfortably. Wasn't it enough that they lived under the threat of the plague? They didn't need more danger of any sort. He found himself wondering what this new peril might be.

Even as he wondered, his father turned pale beneath his tan. "Cochona?" he asked in a whisper. "Already?"

"I'll get Moses," said Eric. He turned and ran across the compound to where the Indio was hauling in wood for the cookfire.

"Moses, you'd better come," he called, as the Indio emerged from the cookshack and headed again for the big pile against the eastern side of the fence.

"You need Moses? I come right away!" He said something over his shoulder to Jefe and came to meet Eric.

"Ko has come up to the compound. He's trying to tell us something. Something about danger. He . . ." Eric looked warily at Moses, fearing the other man might laugh. ". . . he said there was danger. Said it in a word, whether you believe it or not."

Moses nodded. "Those like people, those macaque. My people know for long time. That one, he bring word when Cochona take child, you remember? We watch those monkey-men. We not surprised at anything they do."

"Then come and talk to Dad. He can't think of anything but the Cochona that would be strange enough and dangerous enough to make Ko come to warn us. Maybe you can help figure this out." Eric was already hurrying back toward the gate.

The Littlefields were entering it. Ko was following them, rather shyly but seemingly without fear. Never before had any of the macaque entered the compound except when brought back injured or ill. But nobody was thinking about that, Eric realized.

Moses approached the group rather hesitantly. While he knew the macaque to be more than monkeys, he seemed a bit shy about greeting Ko as a man. He glanced at Eric. Eric nodded.

"I see you," he said to the macaque, in the formal greeting peculiar to his tribe.

Norman had no time for politeness. "Do you think it's possible that the Cochona are moving this way again? That's all I can think of that would disturb Ko this much. The group your people . . . disposed of—might they be hunting for them?"

"Not hunt for lost ones. Cochona never do that. They not care. But Cochona been move for weeks now. We find trace in jungle. Tulunga have dream, too." Moses looked ever more shy, knowing what Norman usually thought about prophetic dreams.

But Norman Littlefield had discarded a lot of preconceptions. "What did he dream? And when did you see him?"

"See him four day ago. Far in forest. Eric know the place. He sit by stream, think hard. He never speak much there, but this time he wait for me. He send word to chief by me. Say much danger come. Not upriver. Come from south. Maybe Cochona.

"He very worried, Tulunga. He tell me three times, though he know I remember. Tulunga . . . Tulunga afraid, I think." Moses seemed awed to think that anything at all could frighten the seer of the Butterfly People.

"It's time to be frightened. I hope to gracious Steve comes back with those hunters. They will be armed. We have some weapons and ammunition here, but if it comes to defending ourselves, there can't be too many of us. We'll be outnumbered, no matter what."

Eric had always wanted to see a real-live battle . . . he had thought. Now he knew that he would put off that dubious pleasure forever, if possible.

They stood in a circle, there in the glaring sunlight, staring at each other. Their silence was broken by the distant sputtering roar of the pickup in the distance. That had to be Whitlock.

Turning toward the road to the village, which joined the track to the macaque clearing some three hundred yards from the gate, Eric saw that it was the native woman, Delenda, who drove the decrepit vehicle. She pulled up just inside the compound, leaving the engine running. That was always a good move, as the thing sometimes was hard to start.

"Dr. Whitlock say please Dr. Halloran come. Sick people come upriver in motor launch. Fifteen . . . four families. They bad sick. Need help." She looked pale, for an Indio, and frightened.

"When did they come?" asked Norman, going to stand beside the pickup. "And what sorts of medical supplies do we need?"

"They come last evening, at sundown. Dr. Whitlock put them in shed where used to store crocodile hide. We keep all villagers away—just he and I go there. I send my child to sister. You not come too close to me," she warned. "Dr. Whitlock say stay far."

"Get disinfectant, antibiotics—broad spectrum—and plenty of painkiller. I'll go with Halloran. If he does go. How about it?" he asked, turning to the doctor, who had just arrived.

Halloran's red hair was wild, as usual, and his rotund shape seemed suddenly a bit deflated. It was plain in his expression that he knew this was his death warrant.

He sighed heavily. "Of course. I swore an oath. And I'd go even if I hadn't. If we let ourselves act like animals just because we're afraid of dying, then we might as well leave the world to the macaque. They'd probably do a better job of things, anyway." He turned toward his own hut and returned almost at once with his medical bag.

Janet had come to stand beside Norman. She reached to touch his arm. "Norman . . . must you?" But she knew his answer, and she said no more.

Eric moved to stand beside his mother. He put an arm around her shoulders, and he felt her shaking against him with internal sobs that she would not allow to escape into tears. He put his other arm around his father and hugged him hard.

Moses and the doctor piled medical supplies in the back of the pickup and, when the load was secured, both Norman and Halloran elected to sit back there with them.

"No use in getting infected any sooner than necessary. It will give us a bit more time," said Halloran. "I never thought I'd say this, but I'm glad Edie didn't live to see this. She died, and I thought I'd go after her, for a while. But now she's spared . . . all of this." He waved his arm in a wide sweep, as if to indicate the entire ruin of the world they knew.

Janet and Eric had held onto bits of Norman as long as they could. When the pickup pulled up and turned, then sped down the rutted track again, Eric felt as if his entire universe had crumbled about him. He just knew, with terrible surety, that he would never see his father alive and well again. And if word came that Norman was ill, he and his mother would go at once.

Death, he knew with sick certainty, was not the worst thing that could happen to a person. Cowardice in the face of human need had to be.

10

The ancient motor launch staggered up the Rio Negro, its engine sputtering fitfully, seeming on the verge of dying, yet managing to keep going in spite of its fluctuating oil pressure and fouled propellers. The people aboard the craft paid little heed to the struggles of the man at the tiller. They lay, most of them, in the shadow of the tattered canopy, and only an occasional moan could be heard from them.

Alberto Gunter stared ahead at the dark waters of the river. Crocodiles slid lazily from the banks as the passage of the boat disturbed them, but he didn't really notice them. Bright parakeets chattered in the branches overhanging the stream, and flights of insects hung over the water, buzzing maddeningly in his ears as he passed through them. Nothing brought any reaction from him.

He was returning in defeat. All his dreams of seizing a reeling country and creating a new empire lay in ruins, amid the dead and dying of Manaus. Fenister had sickened almost at once, after the group reached the city. Gunter found the hospitals full, the doctors and nurses as sick as the patients, and everything filled with the stench of death.

Fenister had died in a shady veranda of a house whose occupants had either died or fled. Gunter had not left him, as all his instincts told him to do. The big Tanzanian had died quickly, his body racked with nausea and diarrhea. He had shrunk to a skeleton within two days, and he was dead on the third.

Ram Dass and his Indian companions, used to the dreadful plagues that India still managed to generate even in the last decade of the twentieth century, seemed unmoved. They also seemed a bit puzzled at Gunter's insistence upon caring for Fenister. In their world, the sick died without comment from anyone when the plague struck.

They had taken up residence in a distant part of the house where Fenister died, leaving Gunter to do everything necessary. It was ironic, the Brazilian thought, that they had sickened and he had not.

He turned to check on his passengers. Of the ten others aboard the overloaded craft, seven were infected with the plague, he was certain. They had not been ill when he allowed them aboard the launch at Manaus, but the two families of Indios had shown signs of the epidemic before the group reached the branching of the Branco.

They had paused twice to bury children on the river-bank. Gunter found that his preconceptions of the Indios—his conviction that they were, somehow, less human than he, with stoic disregard for suffering and death, was flawed. They had, it was true, endured their pain with less outcry than the Indians had, but he had seen in the women's eyes their unbearable loss, as the launch pulled away from the burial places of their infants.

A boy, no more than thirteen or fourteen, Gunter guessed, moved restlessly. He lurched upright, holding the pole that supported the canopy. He looked terrible, his skin stained with old vomit, his hair lank and dead-looking. Without a word, the boy staggered to the low rail and vomited again into the water.

One of the women moaned, "Ekio! Ekio!" but the child didn't turn. With a terrible effort, he heaved himself over the rail and into the waters of the Rio Negro. Gunter cut the engine to an idle and threw overboard a big plastic bottle secured to a line. The child ignored it, letting himself sink slowly, turning in the current.

The biggest of the crocodiles hunched forward and slipped into the water. Others followed, and Gunter found himself watching with fascination and horror as they converged on the boy, who was now well aft of the launch.

There was a boiling in the water. The dark stream turned temporarily crimson. Gunter swallowed bile and gunned the engine again. It wouldn't do to let it die. He might never get it started again.

* * * * *

Ram Dass died in the night. Gunter had tied the boat to a log stuck in a sandbank in midstream, free of some of the swarming insects that teemed on shore. When he heard the unmistakable gurgle of death in the darkness, he rose from his place near the tiller and went to the Indian's side.

He was already dead. There was no reason to disturb any of the others, so Gunter rolled the big fellow onto a sheet of plastic and wrapped him well. Then he let him down onto the sandspit. No grave would last long here, he knew. Animals would dig or floods would disinter the body. This was as good a place as any.

It was easy digging, and before dawn he had completed his task and still had time for a bit of sleep. Gunter found himself wondering what had become of the hard and self-centered man he had been only a few weeks before. He had never soiled his hands with any sort of manual labor. He had not concerned himself with the affairs, the sufferings, or the joys of other people.

Now he felt that there could be nothing more wonderful than to find a large group of healthy people and to take all their interests to heart. He had always disregarded the strictures of the Church, when it came to loving his fellow man. Perhaps it was because there had been altogether too many of them. Now that it seemed that almost nobody would be left alive in all the world, he found a new appreciation for his kind.

There were many who were productive, pleasant, and

intelligent. The Littlefields came to mind at once. He knew he had been autocratic with them, but never by word or deed had they shown their resentment. They had kept on with their work. He felt that they probably were still doing that, if the plague had not reached them.

And if it had? He had a conviction that some, at least, of the Monkey Station crew would be nursing the sick.

He felt through himself still again for any sign of illness. He had never felt better. For some strange reason, he seemed to be immune to the virus, which meant that he might well be suitable for nursing anyone now ill at the village or at Monkey Station.

That would be a new and strange avocation for Alberto Gunter, doctor of science.

*   *   *   *   *

Nathan Whitlock had spent his long life in service to others. Although he tended to be somewhat authoritarian with those whom he considered his parishioners, he felt that he had always done the best he could for them, whatever the circumstances.

Now he found death on his doorstep. He had to care for the suffering families who had arrived at the village in a series of small boats. There was no question of turning them away to die unaided on the river.

But he knew that this was bringing death into his village. His people had to be protected, if possible, from the ravages of the mutated virus. He had done the best he could, making the sheds into an impromptu hospital, calling for volunteers to nurse them, and explaining the dangers to those who stepped forward.

It soon became apparent that his medical supplies, as well as his knowledge, would be insufficient for his needs. He had earned a medical degree in Edinburgh fifty years before. His requirements had always been simple, but now he knew there was a need for sophisticated modern knowledge, even though he felt miserably certain that none of his patients would live. But for the benefit of his own people he wanted done everything possible. If there was the potential for saving even one life, it had to be found. Desperate, he consulted the old healer of the Armadillo People and began using the mixture of bark and herbs that she recommended, along with his other preparations.

He felt certain that Norman Littlefield and the doctor would come at his call. While there had been tension between Monkey Station and his church in the beginning, each feeling that the other represented something inimical to its own projects, it turned out that there was no need for hostility.

Both sides had wanted what was right, and that had allowed them to settle into a comfortable cooperation, beneficial to each. His people, as well as he, had helped the Monkey Station crew when an unknown parasite had threatened the macaque population years before. He still recalled the many monkey bites he had suffered while holding the creatures for treatment.

He was completely unsurprised when the pickup

returned to the village. Halloran jumped out before the vehicle stopped rolling, and Littlefield followed more cautiously. Both men looked grim, but they were there.

"I hated to call for you. I feel as if I have sentenced us all to death, taking in these people. But I simply could not let them go on upriver, dying by inches. And there are two who seem to be totally unaffected by the virus. Estevan Ramirez worked on a plantation below Branco. Every member of his family is sick and likely to die, but he is healthy and strong.

"That didn't surprise me as much as little Lipatu. She is an Indio, somewhere around two years old, and she is the only survivor of her family, Estevan tells me. She was crying on the riverbank at one of the trading settlements near the mouth of the Rio Negro. There wasn't another living soul in the village."

Halloran grunted. He turned to look at Norman. "Sounds hopeful—a little hopeful. More than we thought we'd find, I think. How do the sick ones look, Nathan?"

"Bad and worse. At least two are dying. And old Miramme seems to be getting sick, though she just started helping with them yesterday. I've put her to bed. I thought you might have some newfangled antibiotic that might help her, along with the native junk I've been using, catching it this early in the game."

"We'll give her an injection right now. There's no use in saving this stuff—most of it degenerates with time, and the day will come when we haven't any fuel left for the generators, so refrigeration will no longer be availa-

ble. And if we're all dead, what use will it be, anyway?"
He took his bag into the shed and slid behind the sheet
that separated the sickest from those less affected.

To the doctors' surprise, a broad-spectrum antibiotic
did, indeed, seem to slow the progress of the disease in
Miramme, when it was applied along with a strong, mysterious herb tea the healer had been giving her. Between
the two, they kept her tissues from drying out and the
fever from burning her up. She rallied. Within a day, the
fever and nausea decreased and halted.

The doctors, heartened by the results, tried the combination on every one of the people who had come
upriver. In the more extreme cases, the recipients saw no
effect, and died. But the less severe cases reacted exactly
as Miramme had.

"You have to catch it almost at once," Halloran con-
cluded the following day. "And use it with the tea. Now
we know. And we've got a lot of the medication—we
knew we would be a long way from anyplace for a long
time, down here. Thank God!"

Even as he spoke, a chugging sound echoed between
the green walls of the riverbanks. An ancient launch put-
tered into sight, its bright canvas canopy flapping
around a tear. There were people in the boat. Whitlock
thought the man at the tiller looked familiar—and then
he recognized Gunter.

Whitlock groaned, and Norman turned to him with
anxiety in his eyes. "You all right, Nathan?"

"It isn't the plague. It's that man. I don't quite know
why I have always disliked him so much, but I had hoped

that, if nothing else, this catastrophe would relieve us of his presence. And now here he comes with a boatload of dying people. Just what we needed."

He looked about the hospital shed. Beds for the refugees had been taken by many of his own people. Even those who had had no contact with any of the sick, the nurses, or the area were coming down with the dreaded symptoms.

They all had been given tea and the useful antibiotic, of course, but they were still very ill, feverish and vomiting, racked with diarrhea. Some had begun to rally, but others seemed to be unresponsive. He was worried enough about his own—and now there would be other—living souls in anguish for him to try to help, both physically and spiritually.

"I'm too old," said Whitlock. "I'm too tired for this. I held up well, as long as I was faced with my regular duties, the usual routine. Now I know that I am getting past it." He sat suddenly on an empty cot, watching the launch chug up to the landing and dock.

Gunter leaped out, seemingly quite well and strong, and began to tie the boat to the pier. Halloran was hurrying to meet him, and Zachariah, who had volunteered to help with the sick, followed him with a stretcher.

Norman had turned to go, too, when there came a gasp from the old missionary. Whitlock felt himself going dizzy, his stomach beginning to tie itself into slow knots.

"Norman . . . I think . . . I am going to pass out," he managed to say. Then a tide of darkness descended upon him.

When he came to his senses again, he was lying in a clean cot, looking up through mosquito netting. A dark face came into view and bent over him. There was something familiar about the gray eyes, though they held an expression he had never seen there before.

"Gunter?" Whitlock managed to whisper. "Alberto Gunter?"

"Yes, Dr. Whitlock. I returned, you see, with refugees when I found everyone dying of El Malo at Manaus. My poor friend Fenister . . . he has died, also. And Ram Dass. The other two, Singh and Dalat, are still alive, but I'm afraid it won't be for long. I seem, God help me, to be immune to the infection."

The tone of the voice was different, too. The stiff arrogance had gone from it, and in its place was a more human sound. Even a caring one. Nathan sighed deeply, as the man turned to answer a call from beyond the sheet dividing the shed.

"God," Whitlock said in his usual conversational tone when talking with the deity, "you really didn't have to get rid of the entire world in order to teach me that I'm an opinionated old fool. Surely you could have found something less drastic to do that would have served the same purpose."

Nausea suddenly filled him, and he groaned. Littlefield was there at once with a basin, and he vomited into it for a long time. When he lay back, he felt as if he had lost pounds of his flesh. Even his hands felt lighter, as they lay across his stomach.

He squeezed his eyes shut. "I didn't really mean

that," he amended his prayer. "I know I'm not important enough for that. Help us all. Help us all."

There came a swift pricking at his arm, and he opened his eyes to see Halloran grinning down at him. "You may feel like death itself, Nathan, but you're not getting out of this so easily. You're responding well to the medicines. I think you'll feel better soon."

"Too bad," breathed the missionary. "It would be so much easier to die." And then sleep overtook him.

* * * * *

The days dragged past. Eric, Janet, Bonnie, Lauren, and Don went about the necessary tasks at Monkey Station, but their minds were not on their work. Even the trips through the jungle to meet with Ko and his family could not break through the deep cloud of worry that enveloped them all.

They knew that there would be no word from the village until the plague had run its course. That had gone without saying, for every one of them understood that if they were to survive, they could have no contact with those infected with the new viral strain.

But things did not stay the same. As they moved up the track through the forest, day after day, they found that the very birds and animals were quieter. The spider monkeys in the trees were listless, picking fleas and quarreling in a subdued way very unlike their usual antics. The birds croaked and squawked in hoarse voices, and when they took wing, they flew, sometimes, in lopsided circles.

Janet watched everything, taking notes all the while. Eric waited for several days to make certain it was not his own imagination that made the difference. At last, he forced himself to speak of the strange epidemic that seemed to be overtaking the tenants of the jungle.

"Is it the plague—what Moses calls 'El Malo,' Mom?" he asked, as they emerged into the macaque clearing one morning. "I can't understand why the animals seem sick and the birds can't fly straight anymore. Can you make anything of all this?"

She glanced up into the tree above the stream. Ko no longer waited on the boulder for them. As if his early warning had made him realize that he was suddenly on the same footing as his human associates, he usually dropped from the treetop to their feet and greeted them with the words he had been working to conquer.

"G'd m'rn," came the strange, squeaky voice.

Janet reached to shake the macaque's proffered hand. "Good morning, Ko. Are you well?"

Eric knew she would go through the greeting ritual with the macaque before she would reply to his question, so he settled onto the vacated boulder and just watched. He was astonished when Ko shook his head violently.

Lacking the necessary words, the macaque shook his hands before his body, hopped up and down distractedly, and at last reached to tug Janet along toward a clump of shrubbery.

Eric sprang up and followed. Behind the bushes lay a young macaque female in a nest of vines. Her worried eyes looked feverish, and when Eric touched her leathery hand, it was hot and dry.

Janet bent and examined the sick creature. When she stood straight again, she looked into her son's eyes.

"I think it's the plague. It has to be transmitted through the air, in some way, or else tame animals that run in and out of the village have brought it out into the forest. I've never seen so many different species affected at the same time. Even the same infection should work differently in so many sorts of body chemistries. It has to be the epidemic."

She turned to Ko. "We get medicine. Go with Eric. He bring back medicine for Keela. Quick!

"Get the bottle marked Q 2-11," she said to Eric. "There should be a dozen of them in the refrigerator in the lab. Also get a whole box of disposable needles, and bring Lauren or Bonnie back with you to help with the macaque. The young ones will be hard to handle, I'm afraid."

Eric nodded and sped up the trail, hearing Ko tearing along ahead of him through the treetops. He knew his mother had sent the macaque with him in order to keep Ko from worrying about his young mate.

At top speed, it took only about twenty minutes to reach the compound. Ko was already inside the gate, trying to make himself understood by Bonnie.

She was shaking her head. "I just don't know what you're saying, Ko," she said, as Eric ran up. She looked puzzled. "Eric, do you know what this macaque wants?"

"Q 2-11," he said, his tone terse. "The macaque have the plague among them, Mom thinks. The sick ones are chewing bark and green vines. The animals in the forest are sick, too, and some of the birds. The parrots in particular look really droopy. I didn't think human viruses could affect other kinds of creatures."

Bonnie turned a shade of pale green. "Oh, no!" She ran into the laboratory hut and jerked open the door of the refrigerator.

"Here. You get the medication and the needles—they're in the cupboard over there. I'll find Lauren and Don. I expect we'll all be needed. I'll tell Jefe not to expect us to supper until he sees us. It's a good thing he lives here—if he lived in the village, we'd have to do our own cooking."

Eric hadn't thought about anything except his errand. He was impressed with the way Bonnie got herself organized in an emergency. She wasn't just a pretty blonde. There was a good mind under that taffy-colored hair.

By the time he had the necessary things bundled into a satchel, she had returned with the Nagles. Bill Smalley followed them and stood worriedly as they got ready to go.

"I feel like I should come, too, but I think I have some contact on the radio. I'm going to try again in fifteen minutes. It was very faint, but I think I have a ham out of Mexico City. It's been days since I got anything at all. Another try may give us some fresh news."

"We have enough hands, Bill," said Don Nagle. "You keep trying to get through again. God knows, we need to know something more about what's going on outside. Maybe there's been a breakthrough of some sort in finding a cure for this thing. Surely the medical people are working night and day on it."

Smalley shook his head. "I don't know. I wish I could be sure Eva would be all right . . . she seems to be under the weather, or she'd be there helping you, too."

Eric, glancing upward, caught Lauren's eye. He saw in her the same awful thought that was troubling him. If the plague had reached into the forest, why not into the compound? Birds flew over, monkeys rummaged about every day. The fence was to keep out predators, not the small and harmless inhabitants of the jungle.

They said nothing as the small group hurried through the forest. Ko raced ahead again, heading for his family, and Eric wished that he could take to the trees and save the time it took to walk the rough track.

The path, even though it was used every day, seemed to have overgrown, to some extent, between trips, so rampant was the undergrowth of vine and fern, bromeliad and fungus. He had to watch his step, for reptiles often could be found crossing the strip of pathway. It was because of this that he saw the mark, close to the base of a young tree.

Orange-gray fungus had overgrown the bark, making a sort of ballet skirt effect about the slender bole. One shelf of the stuff had been sheared away and lay on the moss below the tree. He might have thought he had done that himself, in his hurry to reach the compound, but he knew he had not.

That scar was on the side where the forest loomed. He stopped and pointed, saying nothing.

Bonnie knelt and examined the ground about the tree. She crawled forward beneath the low canopy of vine and fern, watching the ground as she went. Eric saw her stop as abruptly as he had done. Then she backed cautiously from the undergrowth and stood to face the rest of them.

"Someone has gone through the forest. Recently. Probably since Eric came from the macaque. There are indentations in the mulch that I could feel with my hands. Moses taught me how to track in the jungle, and I never thought I'd use the skill. Now I'm glad I did. . . . The villagers use the trails.

"I found this, too." She held out her hand. On the palm lay a strip of animal hide, just a tiny wisp that might have been pulled from a loincloth. It was smeared on one side with ash. Eric reached a tentative finger, and he felt the grease of long use on the thing.

"Cochona?" he asked, avoiding her gaze.

"I think that is probably true," said Lauren. "Let's find Janet right away!"

Now they were almost running, taking chances with uneven footing and snakes. Eric felt an awful hollowness in his chest. If anything had happened to his mother . . . the thought made him fly along even faster.

They came out into the clearing in a rush. Ko gave a shriek from his treetop, and Don Nagle turned in time to see an ashy, dark figure cross the path behind them. The photographer had his automatic pistol out in an instant.

Eric reached around his belt and unsnapped the sheath of his knife. He had never thought he might have to use it on people, yet it felt comfortingly businesslike in his hand. Lauren and Bonnie also went armed when they went into the forest without one of the Indios, and they had small automatics in their own hands. Eric found himself surprised. He had thought, somehow, that the women would object to firearms, as his aunt did back in El Paso.

Even as he was thinking this, Lauren called, "Janet!" She waited for a moment and then called again, even more loudly, "Janet, where are you? Are you all right?"

Ko whimpered a remark from overhead. Eric looked up . . . into his mother's eyes.

"I'm here," came the quiet reply. "Veet knew when the Cochona came, and she pulled me up here by force. Back up against the tree. I think Ko is going to do something about this."

Even as she spoke, Ko sped away to the next tree. A short arrow pursued him into the next, and then he was out of sight. Don fired in the direction of the arrow's origin, but Eric knew it had been a shot for effect. Nothing was visible in the rank growth edging the clearing.

The forest grew terribly still after the pistol shot. Even the birds quieted, and the Cochona seemed to have melted into the trees like mist. Were they still there?

Eric glanced aside at Bonnie and raised one eyebrow. She shook her head, her ponytail flopping comically. She turned again to observe the edges of the clearing. The others were doing that, too, taking no chances of being surprised by any move the Cochona might make.

Janet, higher than they in her treetop hiding place, hissed to get their attention. "Get down. Out of the way. There's a line of boulders on the other side of this tree. Slip back behind it. Ko's coming with reinforcements."

Eric waited until the others had begun to move before stirring. He felt Bonnie's hand on his elbow, guiding him backward, although he continued to watch the forest. This was no time to get caught by surprise.

Now he could hear something like wind moving through the trees. But there was no wind to be felt, as he crouched behind his chosen stone. Then he realized that the leaves were whispering, not with breeze but with the motion of many bodies moving through the branches.

As he turned, he heard Lauren give a gasp of astonishment. Above them, Janet exclaimed softly, and Bonnie, at his side, said, "Holy cow!"

It seemed hardly strong enough. The macaque was bringing reinforcements from outlying families. They were not moving randomly through the trees, as did the other primates of the forest, but as they reached the clearing they split into groups, moving to left and right to get above their enemies.

After a moment, arrows hissed into the heavy canopy, but Eric couldn't tell if any of the macaque might have been hit. There then came a rustling in the branches, and a sharp crackling as of breaking wood.

Eric held his breath, waiting to see what strategy this new sort of warrior might have invented for attacking armed men. How could sticks be enough to combat bows and spears? He felt suddenly sick with worry for Ko and his cohorts.

There came a sudden hail of missiles from above. He could see the undergrowth quiver and shake as the barrage struck it. A howl came to his ears, and it was from a human throat.

He rose a bit, trying to see better. Bonnie jerked at his arm, pulling him back down. "You want to get your damn head cut off?" she asked, her tone cross.

Again a rain of projectiles spattered among the plants in the forest. Another yip sounded. And then Ko and his crew descended from the trees and onto the hidden Cochona.

"Now!" shouted Nagle. As one, the Monkey Station crew rose from their hiding places and dashed into battle. Eric had his knife in his hand, ready for action, and the drawn weapons of the rest promised bloodshed to come.

But the Cochona were no fools. When they realized that they were attacked from above and also from the clearing by people with firearms, they disappeared into the trees.

Lauren fired a parting shot, but she aimed above their heads. Then she turned to her husband and said, "That is a habit I'm going to have to break. The next time we meet those gentlemen, they are going to be out for blood, and we'd better understand that, if we're to survive here.

"It's their country, I know, but now it's the only country we have, and we'd better be able to prove up on our claim."

Bonnie had returned to the tree and was helping Janet down from her uncomfortable perch.

"I never thought I'd have to take up tree climbing again this late in life," grumbled the zoologist, as she brushed bark and leaves from her skirt. She turned to the rest.

"Now that the unpleasantness is over, we need to give our macaque their shots," she said.

Eric felt a laugh rising in his throat, but he quelled it sternly, as he went with Bonnie to retrieve the precious satchel of medicine from behind the line of stones. Trust Janet not to lose sight of her purpose, come what may.

11

In the generally peaceable life his family had led for all his lifetime, Ko had never felt such excitement and anger. Those who had come into his own territory and killed one of his people had been driven away, and any earlier generation of the macaque would have been satisfied with that. However, Ko felt that something remained to be done.

He had seen with great quickness that the Cruel People intended harm to the woman who was the friend of his kind. He had known that she would be taken into the trees, even as he moved away to get help.

The attack on the Cochona had been a tremendous experience for all those who took part in it. They had chattered over their battle, even as Janet and her helpers gave them shots and checked their temperatures and bound their wounds.

The thought of attacking Man had never occurred to any of them before. The thought that Man might be an enemy, at least in certain cases, was also a new one, and the macaque kept thinking and talking about these strange notions, though of course the Hairless People could not understand what they said. At last, Ko realized that he needed more information about this situation than he had.

He followed the group of humans as they moved back along the trail toward Monkey Station. When Janet turned and saw him coming along the trail instead of flying through the treetops, she stopped.

"You need?" she asked.

Ko was now understanding more and more of human speech. He nodded and came near, halting when he was within arm's reach of the woman. There was one sound that was easy for his kind, and now he invested it with his meaning.

"Who?" he asked. "En'my. Who?"

"And why, I suspect you are also wondering," she said. "Go on, Eric, with the others," she told her son. "I need to talk with Ko. To explain some things to him. I think that he understood a lot more of what your father told him than we realized."

When the others were out of sight around a bend, she found a stone outcrop that was relatively free of concealment for snakes, and sat on it. Ko came to hunker before her, his face turned up to hers, his eyes even more worried than usual.

She reached to take his sinewy hand. "Those are the Cochona," she said. "They are angry men. They attack even other men, and they kill many animals. Some they kill for food, some for skins, but most just because they are there to be killed. They take the heads of other Indios and make them small. All fear them. You must take great care. Set a watch. They will come back."

Ko considered her words for a long moment. There were many that he did not understand, but he caught enough and could fill in the rest, if he thought carefully. The awkwardness of forming words with his mouth troubled him, and he recalled the way he had been taught as a youngster . . . he could talk with motions of his hands!

Why had he forgotten that? He tapped Janet's knee with one long forefinger and began signing, as his first human contact had taught him. She reached to slow his hands a bit, as if she were not quick at this sort of talk. He obliged, and now his questions poured forth.

"Why man die, outside forest? Why Doctor go away? Why Cochona sudden-sudden come where they never come before?"

Janet shook her head and sighed. Her hands now moved, rather awkwardly and without ease, but she managed to answer what she could.

"Men have died outside the forest because a strange sickness has traveled all over the world. The Doctor went to the village where our Indios live to help to take care of the sick ones there, who have come up the river. And in some way, the Cruel People know that there is no more help for those who now live in this forest. As soon as they knew, they began to come into our parts of the jungle, to steal the child from the Indios, to kill macaque. Today they would have killed me, if your people had not been wise and quick."

This was worse news than Ko had expected. Many of the things about her statements puzzled him, but she had been his friend for as long as he had been an adult. She was good. She helped when his people were sick, she brought treats of fruit, and she felt close to the macaque. Ko knew this with the sure instinct he had not lost when he became more than an animal.

He moved his hands again. "Those will attack the compound. Hairless People are not quick in the forest. Their ears are stopped, their eyes are blind. They do not see traces where others have passed that we can read with ease." He cocked his head, his old-man eyes studying Janet.

"We will watch for you," he continued. "We will watch for Indios. When Cruel People come, we say, and you can take fire-sticks and shoot them."

She put her hand lightly on the furry head. "That . . . would be a good thing, Ko. A very good thing. I will tell the others. I will tell the Doctor, when . . ." her voice choked briefly ". . . when I see him."

She rose and squeezed his hand. Then she went away toward Monkey Station, leaving Ko to climb thoughtfully into a treetop and make his way home. He had a great deal to think about, and once he arrived at the clearing, he had a lot to explain to his people.

Perhaps it was time they had a leader, as the Hairless People had. The Doctor was not the dominant male, but when there was a problem, he led. That was plain to see. Now it seemed that the macaque might need the same sort of system. In a world grown dangerous, it would be, as Janet had said, a good thing.

His people, many families of them, were waiting when he arrived in the clearing. They had, of course, discussed the brief battle thoroughly, and most were still as excited as he had been. He hated to bring them down to earth with such distressing news, but he knew he had to tell them what Janet had said.

He stopped in the top of his favorite tree and shrieked shrilly. Every face turned toward him as he descended among the rest of those gathered there.

"I have things to say," he chattered in macaque. "The world is no longer safe for anyone. There is danger everywhere, and we must consider it . . ."

He talked for a long while, and those about him nodded and scratched and wrinkled their brows as they tried to understand and remember all his words. When the sun went down, he had finished, and very thoughtful families made their ways home to their own places, considering his tale with great care.

*   *   *   *   *

The winds and rains, the fires and droughts of the world did their work, as time passed. Individuals among humankind, lonely survivors of the plague, moved together, searching always for more of their kind, and they found very few.

The plague, however, did not confine its work to humanity. Many kinds of animals suffered. Some died away entirely, like the horse and the hippopotamus. Those that survived, however, showed drastic alterations at once, when the next generation began to be born. The young were much larger, for one thing. Patterns of coloration changed, and if there had been scientists to observe these things, they would have said that radical mutation had taken place.

In the jungles of the south, the sickness had moved through parts of the forest where humans traveled or lived. All sorts of creatures sickened, from parrots to anteaters, but they recovered much more readily than did human beings. Once the recovery was completed, they continued their lives as usual, and few had the wit to realize that their offspring were strangely different. . . .

*   *   *   *   *

Eric couldn't sleep. Usually, he was so exhausted when the day ended that he tumbled into bed and slept deeply, but tomorrow was his twenty-first birthday. In some strange way, it troubled him, and at last he climbed to the top of the radio shack and sat next to the antenna display, leaning back against the metal shape.

The sky was a black immensity, bright with stars.

The compound had been kept free of intruding trees and vines, principally in order to make any attack by the Cochona easier to spot, so he could now view a wide reach of the heavens. The waning moon hung low in the west, and by its light he could see the huts below him.

He thought of his mother, alone in his parents' hut. It still hurt to think of his father, dead now for almost two years, along with many of those who had lived in the village. Apparently, and dreadfully, the medicinal concoction the doctors had devised failed to stave off the inevitable for many of them, including Norman Littlefield.

Moses had taken his family into the forest as soon as it became obvious that few were going to survive the sickness. His sisters and his smallest brother had lived, while both his parents and their other children died.

Eric thought now of that cavern to which Moses had taken him, so very long ago. Was it there he had taken his people?

At least he had saved his kin. Eric had not been able to see his father again, even in death. That hurt a lot. Whitlock had sent word that he had been buried with the day's dead behind the little church in the overburdened graveyard. It would have helped if the grave could have been here in the compound, but the risk of infection had been too great.

Even then, they had been touched by the hand of death, here at Monkey Station. Eva Smalley was dead. It had, indeed, been the plague. Janet and Don Nagle and

Jefe had become ill very soon after Eva died, and Eric had found a new appreciation of Lauren and Bonnie, as they worked together to take care of their sick.

Every one of them had been ill to some extent, but it seemed that they had an unusual number of people with some immunity to the plague, and Q 2-11, plus that strange herbal tea, had had some effect on human beings, as well as on macaque. Only Don and Jefe had died.

The rest felt like death for some weeks but recovered at last. Now Eric felt stronger than ever before in his life, but he knew that it was the hard life he now lived that accounted for that.

Janet had, he sometimes thought, wanted to die and join her husband. They had been a team, not only in their family but in their work. Every time she checked the macaque or entered the laboratory, he could see her thinking of Norman. He appreciated the help that Bonnie and Lauren had given. The two seldom left his mother alone for long. There was always something they had found that needed her attention, and that had kept her from having time to brood or to grieve too much. But he understood her, and he knew that she would never again want to marry, even if there had been anyone suitable.

The most amazing thing throughout their battle with the plague had been the macaque. The injections of antibiotic had evidently lessened the impact of the plague on their systems, as it had done on most of those at Monkey Station and even some of those in the village. Though they had sickened, and some of them had been very ill, all the macaque had survived the plague.

Nathan Whitlock, as old as he was, had survived a stiff bout of El Malo and was now the sturdy support and comforter of those left in his village.

Moses had told Eric that the Indios were used to catastrophes, from floods to epidemics, and this had seemed no worse to most of them than the other things that happened as a matter of course. Indeed, it was far less devastating than the tales they had from their elders about the incursions of whites intent upon enslaving or eliminating them and taking all their forests.

But even Moses had no conception of the emptiness that must lie beyond the forest and the river and the ocean. In his imagination, Eric could see the empty canyons of New York, the dead automobiles littering the streets, the wild dogs and cats struggling to scrounge a living from the stone and steel of the city.

He could see the long stretches of his Texas home, El Paso, abandoned and isolated, the long miles of highway traveled by nothing except roadrunners and armadillos. He thought of his friends at college and his aunt and uncle, but that was too painful, and he pushed the thought aside.

What was important now was survival, nothing more and nothing less. Since Steve Porter had returned with the hunters, who luckily had missed the impact of the plague on the jungle, being too far from any human enclave to be within its range, they had seen no aircraft and no outsider.

Gunter still lived in the village, helping Whitlock with everything from building huts to hunting for meat. The man's turnabout in character told Eric a lot about the horror of what he must have seen downriver. It had literally scared him straight.

Eric sighed and shifted on the metal roof. If the Cochona did not exist, things might look pretty good. The jungle did, indeed, hold everything anyone could want for survival. The Indios had lived here for countless generations, healing their illnesses, providing for their other needs solely from the forest and the river.

Moses knew all that was needed, and he was teaching Eric as quickly as they could manage. Every free part of a day that either could find was spent roaming the forest, locating and identifying the valuable plants. Now Eric felt that he could teach the others enough for survival, if he had the chance.

It was the Cochona that made things iffy.

His mother, of course, still visited her macaque as often as possible. She had noted in her records (and Eric wondered frequently who might ever read them or care about their contents) that the rhesus monkeys had suffered many fatalities. The spider monkeys had been sick, but few bones had been found on the forest floor, and their numbers seemed not to have decreased. The new generations that she could observe seemed to show differences, already, from their parents.

Eric kept coming back to the macaque. He thought of them now as a tribe of people. They watched the forest and warned when the Cochona came. They came to Monkey Station at times with messages from the village, or went to the village with messages from the station.

Eric chuckled as he thought of Nathan Whitlock's reaction to these monkeys that acted like people and even were beginning to speak with some fluency. The old missionary had no time to wrestle with himself and his Bible the issue as to whether or not they had souls. So far, Moses informed him, the problem was waiting for an opportunity to be solved, one way or the other.

He had noticed for himself that the infants born in the year after the plague were much larger even than the DNA-altered macaque who were their parents. Their distinctive markings had disappeared, smoothing into a uniform dark gray or almost black, and their tails were unusually long and agile. They had, his mother told him, been affected by two different sets of gene alterations, that of the original experimenters in France and that of the altered plague virus, which quite evidently acted on the genetic material of those who had survived it.

As an even stranger phenomenon, the birthrate among all the primates they could see had increased dramatically, as if the fertility factor had been augmented, as well. It was a sort of poetic justice, he thought, that death should end in birth.

He saw the moon set, and he straightened. He would regret the lost hours of sleep when the sun rose, he knew. Without supplies brought in from outside, it took all of them working to keep the staff of Monkey Station fed and supplied with their needs. The medications were expiring now, even with refrigeration, which they were powering with a steam generator cobbled together from parts of the old steam launch at the village.

It was time for his kind, he kept thinking, to stop depending on a culture that was gone. It was time to become Indios, instead of living on the edge, half civilized and half native.

It was time he was in bed, if he was to do his work in the morning!

* * * * *

The hunters, as usual, were up before him. Tom Butler was sitting on the bench outside the cookshack, busily plucking a freshly killed red-billed toucan. It still bothered Eric that they ate the showy birds, but he had not been able to refuse the tasty meat, once Cash Lackman, the camp cook among the hunters, dished it up. Already the smoke from the cooking fire was drifting away in the light morning breeze, which was still damp with the rain of the evening before.

Today was his birthday . . . somehow the thought was not as distressing as it had been in the darkness. Things looked worse in the dark, Eric had decided long before he reached the Amazon. Last night had been sad, but today was hot and the sky was clear. Though it would rain again that afternoon, he had learned to enjoy good things while they lasted.

He pitched in to help Cash with breakfast, while the others tended the last pitiful remnant of the unsuccessful primates and did the morning cleaning of huts and compound. After breakfast, each would go his or her own way, attending to the duties they had volunteered to take care of. Bonnie would be going with him into the forest to identify and harvest some of the medicinal plants. Moses was going to show them how to store and to use them, later on.

Eric suspected that his mother intended some sort of celebration that evening, but he tried not to hope too much for it. Last year it had been too soon for any kind of party—they all had still been grieving for those who were lost. Bill Smalley had been so depressed that Eric was not surprised when his heart gave out, just a few months after Eva's death.

Even as he thought, Eric heard a familiar sound. Porter had taken most of their small store of gasoline aboard his chopper a week before, and had gone out to see if there was anything left at Manaus. Eric had feared the pilot would never return, but here he was, landing on the pad in the strong light of morning. He must have landed farther downriver and spent the night, Eric thought, to arrive so early.

He ran, waving his arms, toward the landing strip. Butler didn't pause in his plucking, and none of the others came, so Eric arrived alone as Porter dropped from the chopper and stretched his long limbs.

"Did you find anybody?" Eric called, panting, as he ran up to the pad.

Porter sighed and reached to cuff him gently on the shoulder. "Not anybody you'd want to know," he said.

Halloran, who had accompanied the pilot, came from the other side of the craft shaking his head. "I had thought we might find something or someone who might be of—or even need—help, but those who live there now are mad. Quite mad. What few there are of them.

"We went as far as Natal. Nobody was at the airport in Manaus, so we stole some fuel and kept going. The population must be less than a tenth of what it was. The streets are all but empty, but we saw men attack each other, as well as women and children—worse than animals."

"We were pretty low on fuel by that time, and the airport seemed deserted," said Porter. "I knew just where I could find some drums that were kept for emergencies, hidden in a shed at the end of the east-west runway, so I landed behind the shed and we manhandled the drum onto a dolly. We had the tanks full and our spare cans almost full when somebody tried to kill us."

"So there was somebody there, after all," Eric said.

"You'd better believe it. They spanged slugs off the fuselage, while we scrambled aboard and took off. We circled and saw them set fire to the fuel dump, as if they don't want anybody flying anyplace. Not from Natal. I think Doc's right. They're just plain crazy."

They neared the cookshack, and Porter called out, "Cash, I could certainly use some of your gourmet cooking right about now."

The red-faced fellow appeared in the doorway, his blocky shape taking all the space in the opening. "Steve! You come on in and talk while I finish up. Tom's toucan is roasting for later, but I've got parrot and turtle eggs and thin-sliced anteater, fried to a crisp, and manioc pancakes. Food for a king, my boy!"

The others gathered quickly and the conversation continued over breakfast. At last Janet asked, rather reluctantly, "Did you go near Rio?"

Halloran nodded. "Steve knew a logging camp where there might be gasoline, and sure enough there was a dump there with more than we could use in a year. We took all the chopper would carry and headed for Rio. It was . . . nasty."

Porter stared at his plate, as if he saw again the city that had been a great metropolis. "Rio has been burned. Whether to try to stop the plague or by accident or just for meanness I don't know. The port is full of half-sunk ships and pleasure craft. There's nobody there, unless they hide in the rubble like rats. I'd never have believed that a city of that size could be devastated without a nuclear war or an earthquake or something of the kind."

"We put our reserve in the tank and got back to the dump and then headed for home," said Halloran. "I know how many people get hurt here, every week that goes by. If it's not snakebite, it's infected cuts or something like that. I felt I might be needed, and I didn't want to see any more ruins and crazy people."

"What about you, Steve?" asked Eric. "Will you stay

for good this time?"

The pilot looked uncomfortable. "I think as long as I know where there are logging or construction sites where there will be fuel, I'll keep on looking around. Settling down in one place isn't my sort of thing, as my three ex-wives could tell—could have told you."

"But you will stay for my birthday, won't you? And you will come back?" asked Eric.

Porter grinned. "Of course. I feel like part of the family by now. When I've scrounged up all the gas I can find and checked out all the settlements and missions and towns I used to supply, I'll be back. You can count on it."

"Then that is the best birthday present I can ask for." It was strange, Eric thought, how close he felt to Porter—it must be because he was the first new friend he had made in Amazonia.

* * * * *

As he had suspected, his mother and Bonnie had contrived to make a cake, using manioc flour, ground cacao, and brazil nuts sweetened with honey. The eight people remaining at Monkey Station seemed eager, after so long a period of gloom and effort, to do something cheerful, and even Moses had taken the trouble to remain behind to help celebrate Eric's birthday.

They spent the evening talking—not about the catastrophe but about all the best things they could remember. Other birthdays, Christmas in Maine, which Lauren recalled with affection, almost cooling her hearers with accounts of blizzards and sleigh rides and skating parties on frozen ponds.

Eric found himself laughing more than he had for almost two years. Everyone seemed a bit elevated, though the only alcoholic beverage was the native beer, which was pretty mild. When the party broke up, Eric volunteered to walk partway with Moses, who felt he must return home that night, even though walking through the forest was less than safe after dark.

When he turned back, Eric was still filled with warmth, and he found his way unerringly along the path, his feet familiar with every vine and hummock along the way.

No longer did the shrill sounds, the gruff snarls, and the cackling cacophonies of the jungle frighten him. He thought with amusement of the greenhorn who had come out from Texas and found the night sounds terrifying. Even as he thought, something touched his shoulder, his arm, his hand.

He smiled. The familiar smell of macaque told him that Ko had joined him on his evening ramble. They said nothing but walked along together, the macaque's short legs taking two steps to his one, their fingers locked together.

This was, indeed, a special day, Eric thought, as he came to the fence gate and turned to look down at the macaque by the light of the fire that they kept going all night.

The small bright eyes stared up at him, reddish in the

firelight. The macaque wrinkled his lips away from his teeth in a grimace that was his version of a grin. Then, still without speaking, he leaped into a nearby tangle of vine, and Eric could hear the quiet swish of his passage through the upper layers of the forest.

It was almost midnight when Eric made his way quietly into his half of the hut. His mother was, he thought, long asleep, and he moved quietly through the front room and across the hall to his own sleeping place. There was a bit of light coming through his window from the central watchfire. He stepped to the opening and stared out.

His twenty-first birthday . . . if only his father could have been with him, it would have been a perfect day. Tomorrow, everything would revert to its regular way, but the memory of this celebration would, he thought, cheer them all for a long time to come.

He stripped and washed himself in his basin; no matter how many times a day you bathed in that climate, you still felt sticky, and a sponge bath before going to bed was very cooling. He also slept naked because of the heat. He pulled back the mosquito netting and climbed into bed.

At the touch of a warm body already there, he recoiled. A hand caught his and pulled him back against smooth skin . . . fragrant hair . . . he caught his breath. They had been so weary and so busy and so full of grief for so long, that he had never told anyone how he felt about Bonnie. Not even Bonnie, herself, though he had caught her looking at him out of the corner of her eye from time to time.

"Bonnie?" he asked in a whisper. "Bonnie!"

He had never expected her to return his feelings, though for the past few years he had followed her with his thoughts and his eyes, dreamed of her at night and enjoyed every moment of working with her by day. He had said nothing to her. Now he realized that he had lost many opportunities—but he wouldn't let that worry him right now. He turned to her and buried his face in her hair. His arms went around her, and hers twined around him.

What a birthday present this was! He had no time to think any more than that.

*   *   *   *   *

The following morning, the pair were greeted with smiles by the rest of the adults. Janet, too, seemed pleased, much to Eric's surprise. He had somehow felt that his mother would react like those of his friends back home—"having kittens" at the thought of him taking a mate.

He should have known his own mother better than that, he thought, as he looked across the breakfast table into her shining eyes. She grinned and shook her head.

"You two remind me of Norman and me when we first married. We looked like that, all bright and new and full of ourselves. I thought when your father died that I would have to follow him, no matter what. But now I understand that life has to go on, even alone. You are old enough to need someone to comfort you, to care for you, and to give you the feeling that you have a lot to live for."

The memory of her words followed the pair as they went with Moses into the forest. Eric felt as if he could float to the tops of the trees, where the littlest monkeys chattered and played among the leaves.

They were alive. They were together. And the world had become a good place, for all its dangers.

12

The rains became heavier again, as the season turned, and the Negro, as it usually did, moved out of its banks and into the low-lying jungle, setting logs and debris adrift, isolating the village, which was built on a bluff above the river, and cutting off those at Monkey Station from their fellows in the village.

Though they still attended to the most necessary chores, those in the compound found themselves without enough to do. They read all the books in the small library over and over again. They cleaned and scrubbed, though every day a fresh layer of mold and mildew sprouted on wood and metal.

Eric and Bonnie found themselves quarreling over nothing, and the two hunters became gloomy and depressed. Lauren, too, withdrew inside herself, and

Eric guessed that she was grieving for Don, though the independent woman she was had never openly admitted to that. It was a bad time for them all, and as soon as the water went down a bit, both hunters headed for the village.

The only cheerful person in all that time was Steve Porter, who had returned just before the rains had settled in. He had inspected all the places he wanted to know about, and he had found two secure communities, their numbers depleted but the survivors adapting to changed conditions without a problem. The rest of his locations had been deserted, whether through death or flight he could not tell.

"You don't find dead bodies or even bones in the jungle," he told them when he returned. "So I haven't a clue whether they're dead or not. The Padres didn't like me at all, but I respected them, and I would like to know . . . but there's no point in wondering. I'm back. You're here and safe, and that's that."

When Tom and Cash complained of a lack of companionship, it was Porter who understood that they did not mean social events. "You need wives," he said firmly. "And the village has got a lot more women than men now. You ought to go and make some acquaintances among the Indios. No hanky-panky, though. Doctor Whitlock will be keeping an eye on you, you can be certain."

Tom had blushed and Cash had growled, but once the way was passable again, both took off for Whitlock's little town. When they returned, after several weeks, they were accompanied by lissom young women, neither of them over fifteen or so, who proceeded to make themselves necessary to those at Monkey Station. Eric recalled from reading he had done in college that in times of stress, when women outnumbered men, polygamy was often the solution that people found convenient.

To Eric's astonishment, Bonnie was immediately taken with them, and the three often had their heads together, joined at times by Lauren and Janet. "Women talk," his mother told him, when he asked what it was they found so interesting.

Two weeks passed. Eric was so busy he had forgotten about the mysterious consultations among the women. When Bonnie whispered to him, just before he drifted off to sleep, he didn't think of it as he mumbled a weary reply.

"Eric! I'm sure, now, and it's time you knew, too."

"Knew what?" Suddenly he was wide awake. All his instincts, nowadays, were attuned to danger and sudden death, so it didn't dawn on him for some time that this was good news, not bad.

"I'm pregnant," she said. "I was pretty sure before, but now I'm really certain. That's what I've been talking to your mother and the other women about. Tikoti and Maribi know more than anyone I ever knew. Back home, when you expected a baby, you went to the doctor and then to the hospital, and everything was taken right out of your hands. Here, they have to understand everything and to know how to cope with problems. Those women have been giving your mother and Lauren and me a crash course in prenatal care and obstetrics."

Eric was still in shock at learning he was to be a father. "A baby? Us?" he gasped.

Bonnie giggled. "Did you think that what we've been doing is some sort of game? If it is, babies are the name of it, that's for sure."

He lay back, still stunned. "When?"

"About seven months. And, Eric . . ." she sounded hesitant, "there are several women in the village who have no chance of finding husbands. Tom and Cash are going to take second wives. Whitlock roared and stamped around, Tikoti says, at the idea. But if our kind is going to continue, even as scanty as the population is now, we're going to have to change some pretty basic assumptions, and one of them is that polygamy is somehow immoral."

This sudden replay of his own thinking made Eric turn on his side and stare at his wife's dim-lit face. His mind was a turmoil of conflicting emotions and prejudices.

"You mean . . . you *want* me to take another wife? You're supposed to hate the idea of that!" He rolled out of bed and lit the tallow lamp he had made out of an old cooking pan and fat from game. He had to see her face, read the expression in her eyes, before he could believe this.

The reddish light wavered over her honey-colored hair, shone in her blue eyes . . . and he could see no sign of distress in her at all. She sat up, pushing the mosquito netting aside and joined him at the window.

"There's a whole world out there, Eric, that doesn't

have enough people in it to keep our kind going, maybe. We're a small group, but our genetic heritage is diverse. With the Indios mixed in and adding their own toughness and know-how, we should produce a strong strain of human beings."

"But—but just surviving is enough, it seems to me, without putting some sort of breeding program into effect!" He still felt a bit of shock at the double-whammy she had dealt him.

For the first time, he realized what people meant when they said that women mature faster and earlier than do men. Bonnie looked up at him with the patient expression of a wise-woman instructing an initiate, as she put her hand on his arm.

"Why survive, if it is just for one generation? And if there is to be another generation, why limit its options because of our own desires and preferences? Eric, people have said and written a lot of things about the reasons for existing and for accomplishing great things. But if it were not for babies, who grow into future generations, what would be the use? Everything would die with us! Your mother and Lauren agree . . . they don't want to marry again, for they want the available men to go to the women still young enough to have children."

He studied her face for a long moment. She still looked like a pretty college kid who hadn't a thought deeper than who might ask her to the next dance. But he knew, now, that she could nurse the dying without showing any fear for herself. She could travel through the jungle as easily and quietly as Moses himself. And she had thought more deeply about the situation they were in than he had taken the time to do.

He blew out the smoky flame in the cookpot. Turning, he put his arms about her, holding her close. "I'm glad about the baby," he said. "Really tickled to death. And if you think I ought to find somebody else . . . well, I'll think about it. I just might," he held her away and grinned into her face, lit dimly by the watchfire, "let you choose who it might be."

That will stop that! he thought.

"Moses' sister Tasla," she said at once. "I picked her out months ago!"

Eric sighed as he got back into bed. His father had told him many years before that anyone thinking to understand a woman was fooling himself. About that, as about so many other things, Norman Littlefield had been right on target.

* * * * *

Lauren had held herself in check for two years. The demands of survival, the needs of those about her, had forced her own grief down into a subsurface place where it seldom made itself felt any longer. She had become Janet's right hand, not only in dealing with the needs of those living in the compound, but also in keeping in touch with the macaque, who were learning many things they needed to prosper in their altered state.

The two of them usually visited the old clearing at least twice a week, taking with them anything they thought might be useful to the monkey-people. Now that they could understand one another, the two kinds found many areas of interest to both. The macaque explained a lot of things about the forest that no human being had ever suspected. In turn, the women gave advice on everything from treatment of wounds to the tending of infants.

"Tikoti and Maribi would be the obvious people to do this," Lauren half-grumbled, as they held one of their outdoor clinics. "If they were not so afraid of coming into the jungle. We haven't heard a word about the Cochona in six months or more, now. But those women won't hear of coming out here with us."

Janet swabbed the infected eyes of a tiny macaque, which set up a shrill chittering crying as its mother tried to hold its hands away from its face. "Well, they are both pregnant. They don't want to take any chances, and I don't blame them at all. I don't always feel perfectly safe myself when we are out of earshot of the compound."

Ko was absent today, which was more and more a usual thing. He seemed to stay busy keeping a constant line of communication going between the scattered bands of macaque, who in the past couple of years had multiplied considerably. Now six family-tribes ranged the forest between the compound and the river, and each numbered at least ten members, the largest including twenty-two, including infants.

The family that had gathered to meet their human friends was scattered, only those with immediate problems lingering in the clearing, while the rest hunted leaf buds and insects and birds' eggs in the trees round-about. The women worked all afternoon, disinfecting small cuts and scrapes, showing the females how to give the medications they had brought for their babies, and sympathizing with one of the earlier generation of maca-que, who had arthritis in his hip joints.

With this one they were unable to talk, of course, but he appreciated a gentle massage and a sip of the fiery liq-uor they were now distilling from local fruits. It seemed to ease his pain, and they took quite a long while work-ing with him, feeling pity for this sad remnant of an altered species.

As Janet began packing up the kit they had brought, Lauren looked around the clearing. Only a couple of macaque lingered, as if reluctant to leave them alone.

"Is all well?" she asked Kree, one of the younger females. The macaque was glancing about as if some-thing indefinable might be making her nervous.

"Somet'ing in for'st. You go quick-quick! Somet'ing bad come!" she said.

"What? What do you see?"

"See not'ing. Hear not'ing. But . . . you go!" shrieked Kree, who went flying up into one of the trees and sent a shrilling cry through the jungle.

Every macaque still within sight immediately dropped what it was doing and went upward. Lauren took the kit from Janet with her left hand and drew her revolver with her right. Janet, too, took from her pocket the automatic she habitually carried, and the pair of them slid off into the forest.

They avoided the usual path. They had, after the Cochona attack, worked out several alternate routes back to the compound, but by necessity they went through the same area and in the same direction. Lauren went ahead, ducking low to go under overhanging vines and branches. Behind her, she could hear Janet moving quietly, and she knew the older woman was as alert as she.

Suddenly she paused, putting out a cautionary hand behind her to warn Janet. She had seen a flicker of motion through the tangle on her right, and until they knew what it was, they were better hidden here than they would be farther on.

There was a slight sound . . . no more than a brush of skin against leaves. They would never have heard it if the forest had not gone quiet all around them. They sank silently to hunker on their heels, their heads concealed behind a forest of tall ferns.

Lauren reached through the nearest layer and carefully moved a few fronds. She could see, beyond a stalky clump of buttress roots, a brown-and-ash-colored shape whip from cover to cover. She heard Janet draw one breath and knew she had seen as well.

The other woman's hand fastened onto her arm above the elbow. Lauren was grateful for the contact. They were in the forest with Cochona. Where there was one, there had to be many more, for the Cruel People did not go abroad from their own places in small numbers. She glanced down at her revolver, but it was growing dark already in the shelter of the great trees. She saw only the dull glint of the metal in her hand.

She had six rounds in the chambers and another six in her pocket. She knew Janet had a full clip in her automatic. They carried extra ammunition, though it was growing scarce and could not be replaced. This was, she admitted to herself, a sticky spot. She felt a throb of longing for Don—he was never at a loss for ideas, no matter how bad the dilemma.

Another Cochona moved behind the buttress roots, and she could see that he was armed with a long blowgun, as well as a bow that hung across his back. Probably the arrows were tipped with curare.

Damn!

Janet tapped her arm with a finger. She turned slowly, cautiously, to see her companion wriggling backward, now full length on the ground. Lauren had no idea what she might be about, but she obediently stretched herself along the mulchy soil and followed.

They had slid out of the unobtrusive path made by their own feet over months of sporadic use when Lauren felt the vibration of the ground under her hands. She laid her cheek and ear flat, listening. Even the most soft-footed could not move lightly enough, when there were enough of them, to conceal their passage from such a listening ear.

She hissed softly, no more than a breath, and Janet touched her foot from her position behind her. They were concealed in a tangle formed by a partially fallen younger tree that had been overgrown by many sorts of vines. The light that its fall had left in the canopy had allowed the ground cover to spring to unusual heights, and the space beneath the tree's trunk was fairly clear, forming a sort of cave.

They drew themselves, inch by inch, into the nook and breathed a bit easier when they found that they couldn't see through the surrounding covert. If they could not see out, then the Cochona should not be able to see in, particularly since it was as dark as full night beneath the tumble of leaves and branches and vines.

They did not speak, of course, but sat huddled together, ignoring the insects prying into their ears and stinging their exposed skin. They felt, with fear-augmented senses, the movement of human bodies just beyond their shelter . . . and then Janet stiffened.

Lauren turned her head with agonizing control. Something slid sinuously across her foot . . . it was very long; its scales rasped gently as it moved . . . and she knew it was probably either a fer-de-lance or a bushmaster. This was too large for one of the lesser serpents she knew about.

Janet was breathing raggedly. "My God!" Lauren said softly. "Did it bite you?"

"Shhhhh," Janet hissed. "Yes."

It was an impossible situation. If she could move at once, running at top speed to the compound, there was antivenin in the refrigerator. It should still be good. But if she moved, the Cochona would either kill her or carry her away, either of which would be of no help at all to Janet.

"Damn, damn, damn!" she breathed.

The feet moving past stopped abruptly. The slightly

lighter patch that marked the opening into their covert was darkened, as a head intruded. Lauren said a small prayer.

Then she fired, and the head jolted forward, moved by the weight of the bending body behind it. Hands caught the dead Cochona and dragged it away from the opening. Lauren could feel the body of the snake still touching her boot. She tensed herself, holding her breath.

Vines tore apart, and the serpent moved irritably against her foot. As a hole was made into their shelter, she lurched forward, caught a length of the scaly body in both hands, and hurled the snake with all her might toward the man who was readying his blowpipe.

The Cochona were not very quiet when an angry fer-de-lance alighted among them. There was a chorus of yells and a shriek. Lauren readied her pistol again, and the next head she saw jerked backward with a bullet between its eyes.

"We've had it," she said softly to Janet. "No matter what, I think we have really had it!"

"I know," came the quiet answer. "But we'll take a good many of them with us."

The automatic stuttered in Lauren's ear, and those who had tried entering the hole again scrambled backward. Something "whicked" sharply. Lauren felt a blow against her upper arm. She felt with her left hand and found an arrow protruding from her flesh.

Then the pain came, followed by a strange lack of response in her fingers. She shifted the gun to her other hand and fired off the remaining rounds, aiming through the tangle and hoping she was hitting something. Beside her, Janet, too, was firing deliberately.

She grew limp, her perceptions becoming disoriented. Janet was gasping. Had it been long enough for the venom to begin its work? Time seemed to have slowed dramatically, yet she knew that had to be some phenomenon connected with the poisoned arrow. She groped in her pocket for the extra cartridges, but her hand was no longer manageable. She felt herself slumping, and beside her Janet moaned.

With the last of her consciousness, Lauren heard something incredible. Shots, seemingly very near, cracked through the forest. Who was wasting ammunition in that lavish way?

She had no time to consider the question, however. The world slid away, and a tide of darkness covered her. This, then, was death. Not really bad at all . . . and then she dropped into that dark well forever.

* * * * *

Eric and Moses moved through the forest as quietly as hunting jaguars. They had made a large arc, beginning at the village and curving almost to the river below that, back through the thick jungle toward the compound. Eric had a couple of agouti slung on the cord that held up his tattered breeches, and Moses' net was loaded with small game as well.

All in all, Eric thought, they lived as well now as they

had done before the world ended. Their diet was different, but once they were used to the available food it was just as tasty and far more abundant than it had been when most of it had been flown in to them in Porter's chopper. The steam boiler from the old launch worked well for the most necessary electrical generation, though it was obvious that once all the medications had gone entirely out of date that would no longer be necessary.

He was glad of that. Keeping the voracious boiler supplied with fuel kept several members of the Monkey Station complement busy for hours every day. They would be better occupied learning from the macaque the secrets of forest living, or even just visiting the village or swimming in the stone-cupped hole in the river, where the villagers said it was safe from piranha. He had thought that the Indios were lazy, when he first came to Amazonia. Now he knew that they took life easily and as it came.

There was no need for punching time clocks or for working hard from dawn to dark in order to live. The jungle teemed with game, and edible plants were crushed with almost every step. Why should one make a religion of hard work when there was no need? Even he was learning to take the time to enjoy living.

As the two made their way along their chosen route, Moses stopped suddenly. "Someone come!" he said.

The pair ducked under cover. Now Eric could hear the swish of a large body moving hurriedly through branches. He gave the whistle that identified the Monkey Station staff to the macaque.

The high-pitched shriek with which Ko and his people acknowledged that signal was followed by words. "C'm! Quick-quick! Bad thing in for'st! C'm now!"

Eric scrambled out of the tangle of ferns and vines, followed by Moses. The messenger was Kree, and her baby was hanging desperately onto her back, almost trailing like a kite-tail at times when she moved very fast. Already, she was leaping back, branch to vine to tree trunk on her return journey.

"The macaque clearing," said Eric under his breath, as he sped along the invisible game trail that led in the right direction. He looked back at Moses, his gut congealing with fear.

"Mom!"

And then the two moved indeed, heedless of snakes draped languidly from branches, of predators large and small, even of the obstacles on the forest floor. They either leaped over or plowed through those, their thoughts always ahead of them, and their bodies trying their best to move faster still.

Although the distance from their former position to the macaque clearing wasn't more than a couple of miles, it was not that straightforward when moving through the sort of thick forest they had to travel now. Eric envied Kree, who came and went, unable to remain still while the two human beings crashed their way over the route she could cover so easily.

All the while she was talking, and Eric caught a word from time to time, as she came low to encourage them or to suggest an easier route for them to take. The word that made him push himself to bursting was "Chona," which was the macaque term for those they had called the Cruel People.

They learned the truth of her words all too soon. Kree led them in an arc around the clearing, toward the route from the compound. When she went high into a tree and pointed downward, Eric and Moses went flat and wriggled through the brush as silently as possible.

And there were Cochona, painted as usual with ash in terrifying designs that made them look like the demons they seemed determined to be. They were in a huddle around something, and Eric refused to think what that might be. He took careful aim and fired, cursing the fact that they had made no provision for extra ammunition when they had the chance.

A tall Indio jerked upright and fell backward without a sound. His fellows turned to find where this attack came from, and Moses skewered one with a well-placed arrow. By the time Eric had picked off another, the group had split and disappeared in several directions, seemingly dissolved into the greenery.

"They wait for you to come," whispered Moses. "They kill you if you go there where they look before."

"I have to go, just the same," Eric murmured. "Cover me if you can. And if they kill me, take care of Bonnie and Tasla for me."

Without waiting for an answer, he moved forward as Moses had taught him, disturbing almost nothing in his progress through the deadfall and ferns and vines. Bright fungi was crushed beneath his weight, and lizards of all degrees of ugliness skittered away as he went, but he was focused fully on the hump of greenery around which those men had been standing.

It was worse than anything he could have dreamed of. When he reached the faintly marked trail, he moved along one side of it until he was beside the viny covert. He could see the hole the Cochona had torn in the vines, and though it was now almost entirely dark, his eyes, adapted to the faint light, could see something lying inside the nook.

He moved with agonizing care until he was half in the opening. He felt a hand . . . a warm hand, but strangely lax as he caught it in his own. Long fingers, wide, strong palm . . . Lauren's, he was certain.

"Lauren!" he said in the softest voice he could manage. "Lauren . . . are you all right?"

There was no answer. He felt her shoulder, her arm, beyond her . . . and there was another body, smaller. It, too, was still warm.

"Mom?" His voice broke. "Mom, are you okay?"

"No, dear," she breathed, and only the silence of the jungle after his gunshots allowed him to hear her. "I was . . . bitten by a snake. Probably a fer-de-lance. It was . . . big." She sounded infinitely weary, as if she could barely make her voice audible.

"Eric."

"Yes, Mom?"

"Don't grieve for me. I'll be with your dad. He didn't believe, I know, but now that I am almost there, I know he was wrong. We do go on. Not to heaven—I really don't think that—but someplace where what we are and what we know isn't wasted. You . . . be strong. For your wives and their children. And don't think. . . of my death . . . as a waste. This is a necessary . . . part of living." She gave a great gasp, and he felt her hand clench on his. Tears were streaming down his face, as he felt her body tremble with oncoming death.

"I wish . . ." It was the faintest possible breath. "I wish I could have seen your children . . ." And the hand went limp in his.

Eric felt the blood pounding in his head and his heart. He had never, he now realized, been truly angry in his life, before now. Dad's death had been a part of something huge and unavoidable. Mom's was deliberate, and he wanted to kill the men who had been responsible for it. He would never rest until his people—all of them, white and brown, were safe from the Cruel People.

Something touched his foot, and he jerked about. He could no longer see, but he knew it was Moses. The smell of his friend was now as familiar to him as his was to the Indio.

"Eric," came a breath of a whisper. "We go now. They come back. We move to south. They between us and compound, us and village. We go on way I know. They not find or follow . . . I think."

"I hope," said Eric softly. He moved backward silently and felt Moses' guiding touch on his shoulder.

Without rising, the two slid off into the jungle like a pair of reptiles, avoiding any path and all the clearer spots that Moses seemed to have imprinted in his mind

as a sort of topographical map. Around him, from time
to time, Eric could hear a whisper of motion, and he
knew it was probably Cochona, encircling their prey,
thinking that he was still there, grieving over his dead.

He was still floating on a sea of rage. Anything seemed
possible to him, as his overloaded adrenals sent him after
Moses, matching silence for silence, stealth for stealth,
with the Indio.

They moved for hours, part of the time on their bel-
lies, but after a time rising to their feet. At last, Moses
caught him by the shoulder and hissed into his ear, "Is
time to climb!"

They went up a set of buttress roots that wove intri-
cately upward, ending in a rough tree bole that gave toe-
holds to a careful climber. Eric went up and up, guided
by the slight scuff of Moses' hands and feet against the
bark above him. Once he set his hand on something that
gave a pulsing slither, but he didn't flinch, and when at
last he could not hear Moses moving, he ventured to look
upward.

The sky was clear, and he was near enough to the
upper layer of the jungle to see glimpses of stars through
the layered leaves. They were high—higher than he had
ever climbed in the forest.

"Come up here," said Moses, his quiet voice blending
with the squawks and chatterings filling the night. "We
go on high place now. Be ver' careful. This not safe."

Eric almost laughed. Nothing that had happened
since they heard Kree coming had been even remotely
safe. Dashing through the jungle, attacking the

Cochona, going to check on his people had all been reckless and foolhardy, though he would not have changed his actions if he could.

He had a sudden disquieting thought. Before Moses could indicate what their next move might be, he reached to catch his elbow.

"What about the village? Will the Cochona attack the people there? The compound should be fairly safe, with the fence and the watchfires and all the guns and ammo there, but the village won't expect anything."

"Village always expect Cochona, if they come, if they don't come," said Moses. "You not worry. Doctor old and wise . . . he ready for anything now. But we get clear, we go get more weapon. Then we come back."

"Oh." Eric thought of the large store of weapons in Moses' secret cavern. He was not at all surprised when the Indio took off southward, moving along interlocked branches, dropping down trailing vines to better routes, and moving through the treetops with some ease.

"You've been this way before," he grunted, when they paused side by side to catch their breath.

"Think when Cochona come after big sick . . . might be good to have secret way to secret place. Take many day to figure. Now is good to have. There more Cochona down there someplace, you bet. We travel through jungle, we take bad chance of get caught. You not want to get caught by Cochona. They not nice to prisoner."

That sounded like the understatement of the decade. Eric almost found himself amused as he moved cautiously in the wake of his friend . . . until he thought of his mother and Lauren, dead in the forest. Then he grew grim and his thoughts began to circle slowly round and round the notion of vengeance.

His father had despised the thought of retaliation for real or imagined injuries, he knew. But Norman had lived in a world that allowed such luxuries. This was no such place. If the people in this curve of the river did not hurt those who had injured them—and hurt them badly—every wild Indio with a grudge against whites and those who lived closely with them would take a swipe at them. It seemed sensible to believe that.

13

After the rash of deaths caused by the plague, the village on the river had settled into a new sort of routine. The men, for some reason, had been more vulnerable to the virus than had the women. Even with shots of antibiotic given by the doctors, they had succumbed to the illness in greater numbers than had their wives and daughters and sisters.

That left most of the fishing and hunting to the women now, in addition to their normal tasks of harvesting the crops of jungle and field. The village was usually almost deserted, except for the children who were too small to help their mothers and the oldsters who watched them, being too infirm to walk far or to do much.

Nathan Whitlock lent a hand wherever he could, but

he tried to remain close to the most helpless of his flock, when that was possible. There were always things to do about the village and the church. Rot and damp kept taking their toll, and he was on the roof of his house, hammer in hand and a pile of flattened tin cans providing durable shingles, when he heard something dissonant in the regular jungle sound.

It was late. The women were already coming up from the river with full nets of fish. Those who had hunted were skinning their kills, while the old women stirred pots of food over the fires fueled by the efforts of the oldest of the men left alive.

He crawled backward down the slight slope of the roof and stood on the ladder leaning against the wall. Something was amiss in the jungle. The sounds were moving toward the village through the twilight. He jumped down the last couple of steps and lit with a groan and the popping of aged joints.

The fence that he had urged his people to build around the jungle side of the village was some hundred yards from his door, and he started off in that direction. On the village's other side was the steep bluff above the river, and there was a stout barricade across the path leading down to the water. The last of the fisherwomen always secured it, and he had no fear for his flank as he moved toward the looming wall of jungle.

He could hear something like a voice calling, and he cupped his hands about his mouth and shouted, "Hello!"

Again the sound of the jungle changed, the noise of

birds going quiet in their trees and insects pausing in their skreekings. From the edge of the trees a small figure scampered.

Whitlock, too, kept a watchfire, and by its red light he could see that the one approaching him was one of those monkey-people about whom he had wondered so much and agonized so long. He had decided that the entire concept was a delusion, and he humored the Monkey Station people when they mentioned their prodigies now, and that satisfied him as well as his friends.

But he could see that this was not a man, and it was coming toward him with purpose in its entire being.

"Chona!" said the furred creature. "In for'st! Chona kill man-people. Come this way. Many-many! I warn. Now I go!" The absurd shape wheeled and darted into the trees, where Whitlock could hear the "whish" of its departure over the crackle of the fire and the renewed efforts of the forest creatures.

Whitlock had no time to examine his prejudices. He did not doubt the words spoken by the creature, and he turned and yelled loudly, "This is not a drill! This is not a drill! Arm yourselves and take your stations!"

His early military service had made itself useful at last, which was something he had never expected to happen. His tough little army of women and few men, oldsters, and older children had taken to his training with enthusiasm and aptitude. The ways in which they had fought their own kind, before the advent of the whites, had not been extremely effective against a ferocious enemy. Now he had taught them a few tricks that could stand them all in good stead.

There came an instant response. Those skinning the game took the skinning knives and left their victims on the long table he had built for such work. Others melted into the gloom between the houses, armed with bows and plenty of arrows. Six boys, aged from twelve to fourteen, shinnied up into the trees that shaded the village and took with them their blowguns and the darts tipped with curare with which they hunted for birds in the forest.

The oldest of the women and men took brands from the fire and hid with them in the sheds where the sick had been nursed. They would make a last line of defense, at need, hurling fire among the enemy.

If the Cochona attacked his village, Whitlock knew, they would know they had been in a fight. But he found himself worrying, too. Who had been the man-people killed in the jungle? Eric and Moses were out there, he knew.

And how were they faring in the compound? Even with firearms, they were very few. The fence was climbable by men, if they wanted to badly enough. He sighed. There was nothing he could do now but wait.

*   *   *   *   *

Steve Porter had spent his life avoiding being tied down to anything. His three marriages had foundered on the rock of his itching feet, and he had given up the thought of settling down before he was thirty. The plague had pulled the rug out from under him, in more ways than one.

His beloved chopper sat, unused, on the pad, covered with a tarpaulin. Gasoline was now too scarce to risk another foray into the remnant of the Amazonian world—he had no intention of being stranded in the bush or in one of the hellish towns he had seen from above.

But being trapped at Monkey Station was sheer torture. He did his best to stay out in the forest, hunting with Tom Butler and Cash or with Eric and Moses. He avoided the women as much as possible, feeling that his own unease might rub off on them. And that would be bad, for all the younger ones were expecting babies.

Only with Janet and with Halloran was he at ease, and even then he found himself becoming irritable and snappish from time to time. He wasn't good at the things that needed to be done around Monkey Station, that was the problem, he thought, as he sat cross-legged on his cot. He sat cleaning his pistol and his rifle, which had traveled with him from the headwaters of the Amazon to the Atlantic, from Colombia to Paraguay.

The sound of running feet roused him from a particularly bad mood. He looked up as Halloran pushed through the netting he kept over his door for keeping out insects.

Before he could open his mouth, the doctor said,

"Cochona! Ko came just a minute ago with the news. They . . . Steve, I think they must have killed Janet and Lauren. The macaque is beside himself. It was all I could do to get any intelligible talk out of him at all, but the gist of what there was made me think—think they're gone."

Porter surged to his feet. "Where? And who's going with me?"

"Bonnie and the other women are arming themselves. They'll lock the gate behind us and connect the fence to the generator. Tom rigged up a way to shoot the juice directly into the wire, so anybody or anything touching it will get an almighty shock. Maybe fatal . . . but this is an emergency, and we're not going to be too nit-picky about that. Tom and Cash and you and I will go, armed to the teeth. Does that suit you?" The Irishman's hair seemed to blaze above his flushed face. His eyes had gone the shade of chilled steel, and Porter was glad he was going to be on the right side in this scrap. He wouldn't want to cross Halloran when he was this angry.

"Suits me," he said. He snapped his rifle together and dug out a box of cartridges. His all-purpose jacket hung on the wall, and he filled its capacious pockets with extra ammo, his reproduction bowie knife, and the handgun that had accompanied his travels, resting unobtrusively in that same pocket for years without being used.

Halloran hadn't waited. Porter could hear his Irish lilt outside, as he instructed the women to keep a sharp watch and to activate the electric fence at any sign of trouble. As the pilot left his hut, he heard Bonnie's voice rise sharply.

"What about the macaque? Sometimes they climb over the fence!"

"I'll tell Ko, and he'll tell the rest of them. It's not as if they were animals!" Halloran sounded impatient.

"Ready," Porter called. He put his jacket over his shoulders and jogged to the spot where Halloran had cranked the Land Rover. He had hardly gotten his feet inside, crunched against Butler in the back, when the doctor let out the clutch and the vehicle sputtered twice, caught, and charged off down the track toward the macaque clearing.

Porter looked back as they pulled away. Bonnie and Tikoti were fastening the chain link gate already. He found himself hoping desperately that the electrical hookup would work, if there was a need for it. Then he was busy holding on, as the Rover bucked over the rutted, root-grown track.

"You think—they're all right—at the village?" gasped Cash, twisting to look back from his front seat position beside Halloran. The Rover's bounces punctuated his words, and Porter found himself nodding, though he had meant to shake his head.

Butler, beside him, grunted skeptically. "They haven't the fence. They haven't the generator, and they haven't enough guns. If the Cochona hit 'em, they're going to be in deep trouble. Whitlock may try to hold off killing anybody for too long, too. He hates killing."

Without taking his attention from the road, Halloran said, "Nathan will kill to protect his people. He knows the Cochona from of old. They took the head of his first convert and shrunk it and returned it to him in a basket. He told me that when he gets to the words 'Forgive us our trespasses' in the Lord's Prayer, he always has to stop and wrestle with himself for a bit to find it in his heart to forgive them.

"That old man has not reached his advanced years by being a fool. A fanatic, perhaps, but a fool . . . never!"

The Rover came to a jolting halt. "Ko said they were on the alternate track, just north of this one. We'd best go afoot from here, for they . . . may be hard to find."

Porter climbed down, feeling his knees suddenly turn unreliable. Janet . . . his friend for so many years! Lauren, whom he admired as someone as strong, at least, as he. He might find their mutilated bodies . . . he shuddered and followed Halloran into the forest.

There had been a fight. That was obvious from the torn vegetation and the patches of dried blood on clumps of fern and the ground underfoot.

"Why did Ko wait until today?" he asked. "Why didn't he let us know where they were yesterday? They'd said they might go to the village for the night, or we'd have been searching for them before dark."

"Ko went to the village," said Halloran, his gaze fixed on a lumpish growth ahead of them. "He had to warn them. Kree went into the forest to locate Eric and Moses, and she did, Ko says. They got away to the south. He knew we couldn't do much in the dark, and it wasn't safe to wander around out here with the Cochona in the area, anyway. He says they're all around the village now, so it's safe to search here."

They were talking softly, their eyes busy checking out every bit of cover, their ears marking every sound. As they neared the hummock, Porter stopped. There was a dark stain smeared over a stretch of ferns.

"Someone was badly wounded here," he said. The growth was crushed down, as if a body had lain on top of the space covered by the ferns.

Ahead of him, Halloran said, "And someone . . . died here." His voice was gruff with emotion, and Porter looked up in time to see the doctor drop onto hands and knees and crawl out of sight into that ominous clump of vines.

He didn't go nearer. The doctor was vulnerable now, while he investigated that spot. Porter crouched behind a thick clump of buttress roots and observed the jungle carefully, noting the actions of a tribe of spider monkeys high above them. As long as the nervous creatures were feeding quietly, they should be safe enough, but he intended to take no chances.

"Tom!" came a muffled call from Halloran.

Butler moved up and crouched beside the hole into which Halloran had crawled. Porter listened hard, but only a mutter came to his ears. After a moment, Butler came back down the dim trail. When Porter looked up, the hunter shook his head, his thin face grim and sick.

So they're dead, thought Porter. Both those strong, brave women . . . and with all the other women pregnant, too. This is bad. This is worse than bad.

Butler came back up the path with an armful of something—Porter realized that he was bringing the extra tarps that were kept in the back of the Rover. For the bodies. . . . He felt both sick and angry.

He was even angrier when he helped to move the remains of the two women onto the tarps. Already they were swelling, the humid heat of the jungle working swiftly to reduce any flesh to soil again. The pistols were removed from the dead hands and cleaned for use again. They couldn't spare any weapons, though ammunition was becoming short.

The four men got the bodies into the Rover at last. Then they sat for a moment, staring at each other.

"Where?" asked Porter. "To the compound to see about the women, or to the village to see if they need help?"

Before anyone could reply, Halloran started the engine and backed the Rover to the junction of the broad track leading to the village. "We can bury them in the cemetery," he said. "And Whitlock can say a prayer over them. The women are all right—Ko would have told us if anything threatened the compound. Those demons are all around the people by the river, and we'd better get there quickly."

They tore along over washouts and stony spots, and when they arrived at the thinner jungle from which the

Armadillo People cut their firewood they could see billows of smoke rising in the direction of the village. Halloran stepped down hard on the gas pedal, and the Rover lurched drunkenly from hole to ridge to rut to root as it raced toward the village.

A hail of arrows clattered on the hood and the windshield. Porter knelt on the floorboards and drew his pistol. The rifle lying under his knees hurt, but he ignored that as he aimed as well as he could from the bucking vehicle and fired off a round at a spot where an ash-marked face had appeared briefly.

He didn't hit it. Nobody could hit anything from such an unsteady stance. But then nobody was having any luck at hitting them, either. As the Rover roared up to the improvised gate, the tangles of thorn were pushed aside by eager hands, and they were inside. Then the gate was being replaced by the hands of women and children.

Whitlock was there, his face smudged with smoke and soot, his hair standing wildly erect on his noble skull, and his grin as wide as his face. "Welcome," he shouted. "We were about to get desperate. They fired our fence, but we managed to fill it in with planks and logs and stones from the river. The old folks in the sheds have worked like devils to keep the fires from spreading, too. We thought they'd sit there and wait to be needed. They had torches they were supposed to throw at the Cochona, if they broke into the village, but they didn't wait for that. They came out like youngsters when the blazes started."

Arrows were "whicking" wickedly over the fence into the area before the church. Porter moved up to the wall and peered through the tangled mass. There was a constant sense of motion out there in the edge of the jungle. Glimpses of brown skin and ash patterns came and went too quickly to afford him a shot.

He realized with sudden shame that this was the first time since the end of his explorations that he had felt really good. That made him some sort of monster, didn't it?

14

The cavern was so peaceful, wrapped in the muffling roar of the waterfall, that Eric wondered for a moment how it could be a part of the chaotic world from which he and Moses had just come. The coolness, there in the shadowy recesses, was refreshing, and the two slaked their thirst before checking farther into the system of tunnels to make certain that no evil surprise might wait there for them.

There was, indeed, a surprise. Moses, going first as usual, came to a halt so suddenly that Eric bumped into his back.

"I smell man," said the Indio. "Here. Ver' strong, ver' fresh."

"Who?" asked Eric in a whisper.

"Not Cochona. They smell of blood and ash. This

more like forest and green thing, smoke and rain. Maybe . . ." Even in the dimness, Eric could hear a thoughtful note in his voice as he turned back toward the depths.

They moved silently over the damp stone and clay, going down the dark passages by feel and smell, for Moses did not offer to light one of his stash of torches, and Eric didn't urge him to. They came at last to a forking of the tunnels, and Moses paused there.

"*Ayi-hi ni kole teni?*" he asked, his tone, as quiet as it was, echoing in the labyrinth.

There came a sound like wind through leafy branches, but Eric realized that it was a concerted sigh of many breaths released at once. "*Hi ni Tulunga*," came the reply.

Though he did not understand the dialect, Eric did recognize the name. This was the Tulunga who heard voices telling him what was going to happen. This was the man who had warned of the plague, months before it occurred. He found himself feeling a bit awestricken, as if he might be about to meet someone of tremendous power and importance, instead of an elderly primitive in the middle of the jungle.

A torch was brought from an inner chamber where its light had been somehow hidden, even in the blackness of the cave. By its light, Eric could see about thirty people sitting quietly around the walls of an oval space. In the midst of them stood a tall old man, whose thinness could not disguise the corded strength of his limbs and torso.

Moses held out his hands. "Tulunga!" he said, his voice full of sadness and pain and doubt.

The elder took both the younger man's hands into his withered ones. He spoke for a long time in his musical dialect, and Eric could see Moses reviving as if some spiritual transfusion might be taking place. When the old man went quiet, Moses turned to Eric.

"Tulunga say Butterfly People hide here when he hear voices say Cochona come, very angry, very cruel. Take weapon, take all thing they need, come here, for nobody know about Holy Place but Tulunga and me . . . and you.

"They find weapon I store here. They bring much weapon of their own. I tell Tulunga that Cochona attack Armadillo People soon. Maybe even now. He say they go with us, back to village. They catch Cochona from rear, before they know. Butterfly People very good at be quiet, be invisible in jungle. Can work, you think?"

Eric thought of Nathan Whitlock, possibly trying at that very moment to protect his small group from the cruel Cochona. There were so few people left in the village . . . He thought for an instant of his mother, and pain threatened to conquer him. He pushed it down and nodded to Moses.

"We can go. Do you know a way that won't take us where the Cochona might run into us?"

Moses chattered for a moment to Tulunga, and then both of the Indios nodded gravely. "Have secret way," said Moses. "Messenger go that way, when Walebe send word to Whitlock and Armadillo People."

"I'm with you," Eric said firmly. For a moment, he thought of how he might have felt two short years before, if someone had told him he would follow the lead of an Indio shaman into battle against headhunters. He would have laughed himself sick at the notion. Now he was devoutly grateful that the tough old man had brought his people here to hide. With the Butterfly People on their side, those at the village might stand some sort of chance for survival.

It was, of course, the middle of the night. Outside, the forest was as dark as the caverns where no torch had been lit. But that did not stop the preparations for the attack.

Eric helped Moses ferret out all of his weapons stashes. It seemed that Moses had had some sort of hunch that they might be badly needed, though he hadn't realized that at the time. He had blowguns and poison-tipped darts, bows and many sizes of arrows, from tiny bird-hunting ones to great, heavy man-killers.

There were knives of chipped flint and knives of rusted metal, made with great labor from scrap iron discarded by traders and other whites at the mission. Every one of the twenty-two warriors of the Butterfly People who were going, as well as the two young men, were armed to the teeth.

Eric realized before long that those Indios he had seen in the room where Tulunga waited were only part of the tribe. As they rummaged through the caverns, he and Moses kept coming upon groups of women with infants, small children tended by older siblings, family groups. There must have been more than a hundred of the Butterfly People there in the tangle of tunnels.

They left before dawn, slipping forth from behind the waterfall, moving silently up the path to the big forest in single file, saying nothing. Moses had told Eric to keep close to him, touching his back if possible.

"This way be very hard to find. You hold on, or you be lost."

Eric was more than glad to agree, once they were in the murky depths of the forest. He could not hear anything above the cacophony of bird and animal sounds that dinned through the heavy growth. He kept a desperate clutch on the tail of Moses' sleeveless shirt as they moved carefully through the darkness. In some miraculous manner, the Indios found their way through the feature-less undergrowth, never varying their direction except to avoid some obstacle they could neither climb nor go under.

So gradually that he never knew exactly when he was able to see, the light came filtering through the canopy above, and Eric realized that they must be nearing the river, for he could hear the grumble of the falls above the village. Moses stopped beside Tulunga, who seemed to materialize out of the ferns, and the two communicated silently with nods and gestures and twitches of the fingers.

When they were done, Tulunga gave a whistle that seemed to blend seamlessly with all the other morning birdcalls in the forest. The few brown bodies that Eric could see melted from view at once.

Moses turned and nodded to him before sinking to his knees in a tangle of undergrowth. On hands and knees, the pair of them wriggled along toward the sounds of occasional shouts and single, very deliberate gunshots.

Eric hoped that in all his tearing through the jungle he hadn't damaged his pistol or his ammunition. It seemed as if he might need both very soon. Then Moses rose to his feet behind a big tree trunk and gestured again. Eric nodded and checked his weapons. He wished suddenly that he could use the efficient-looking blowgun that Moses was readying. That would be something whose ammo you could replace yourself.

He made a resolution to learn how, if he survived the next few hours. And then it was too late for thought, for Tulunga whistled again, and a rain of arrows struck from many areas, disappearing from Eric's sight into the cover between the deeper jungle and the thorny wall around the village.

*   *   *   *   *

The Cochona were not fools. Used to jungle fighting of the most desperate and primitive sort, they realized immediately that they were caught in a crossfire, and every one of the ash-painted warriors eeled away from his former position, trying for the forest on either side. But the village was set in a wide loop of the river, and the forest was restricted by the riverbanks on either hand, though it was thick enough for their purposes in attacking the mission.

Now they found themselves faced with devastating fire from bows and blowguns. Eric found himself firing deliberately as a flicker of brown skin or striped ash paint showed for an instant through the undergrowth. His eyes attuned themselves to their work with more ease than he would have dreamed.

Suddenly, he found himself able to distinguish a brown fungus from a brown hide, a gray patch of lichen from a decoration painted onto a demonic mask of a face. Spurred on by the peril of his situation, he could hear a furtive movement in the vines and bushes and know at once if it was a lizard scurrying for safety or a Cochona trying for the deep jungle behind him.

The thought of his mother was not exactly foremost in his mind, but every time he pulled the trigger and saw a body flop jerkily in the brush, he found himself obscurely comforted. He was avenging her. It couldn't bring her back from the dead, but it seemed to soothe his wounded heart, though, by everything he had ever been taught, vengeance was supposed to be destructive rather than helpful.

Those owl-eyed faces didn't really look human. That was something that helped, he was sure. And the Cochona had never come out of the forest to meet his kind, so to him they were no more or less than any other jungle animals that proved themselves dangerous.

He realized, after a time, that he was a bit delirious.

Nothing seemed real, seemed to have solidity and immediacy. Moses, just ahead and to his right, was the only thing he could depend on in this fluid world where the leaves whispered with the passage of arrows and darts, and gunshots interrupted the quarrels of parrots and toucans in the trees.

Where was Ko? Where were the macaque? Eric found himself profoundly worried in the midst of his automatic watching and firing and watching again. It would be a tragedy if all his parents' work to educate and help the macaque should be lost to savages like the Cochona . . . and even as he thought that, something struck his thigh.

He looked down, expecting to see another branch that had flown back behind Moses' passing body. But an arrow protruded from his leg, the black shaft already turning scarlet where it entered the flesh.

Eric opened his mouth to cry out, but suddenly his muscles didn't cooperate. He couldn't move. Moses halted and turned back, but Eric could not call out to him. . . .

* * * * *

Porter and Gunter were covering the ends of the fence, where they abutted the river. Those would be obvious places for an enemy to try slipping around the barrier. Tom and Cash and Whitlock were strung out along the curve of the fence, anchoring the line of bowmen and -women and those with blowguns.

Porter had been mightily amused at the missionary's shock when his devout parishioners dug out those deadly weapons from the thatch of their roofs and produced fresh poison for the darts. He had thought those things long discarded, it was evident.

Porter squeezed off a round, aiming carefully. There was a quiet thrashing in the growth some distance into the forest, but it soon stopped. Gunter fired shortly after, the sound of his shot seeming much more distant than it should have. The murmur of the river and the sound of the falls muted everything else.

Then something changed. There seemed to be unusual movement in the undergrowth. A flash of brown, too quick for aiming at, wriggled past . . . heading away from, not toward, the village. Porter squinted hard. Something was happening out there beyond the fence.

He watched for a moment. Then he slipped along the barrier toward Whitlock's position. "I think someone else has taken a hand in our war," he said to the old man. "Have you noticed anything strange?"

Whitlock nodded. "There is another force out there. They are firing on the Cochona, who are pulling back. They are not white . . . or at least not all are white. I've only heard one firearm, but arrows are cutting down the Cochona we can see.

"Delenda says they are Butterfly People." His voice sounded dubious. "I cannot think how or why they would come to our aid. They are, after all, not believers. But someone is out there, and they are the nearest." He sighed heavily.

"God has not given up on educating me, it is clear. He keeps sending messages that show me to have been wrong about all too many matters. So I will not say that the Butterfly People are not selfless enough to come to the aid of their fellow man, even if he is not of their kind or their faith."

*   *   *   *   *

Now it was clear that the Cochona were thinking of nothing but escape. Some few broke past the ends of the fence and plunged into the river, taking their chances with piranha in the shallows farther downstream. Others were lying still on the ground, obviously dead or dying. Still others were dashing through the forest, taking their chances with the blowguns and arrows of the Butterfly People.

The gun out there had gone silent. A voice rose shrilly in the suddenly quiet air.

"Come quick!" it said. "Eric, he hurt . . . Cochona shoot with arrow. Maybe he die!" The shout ended almost in a wail, and Porter vaulted over the thick layers of thorn bush and wiring forming the fence and ran toward the source of the cry.

He found Moses crouched beside Eric, who lay limp in a clump of thorny vines. Without pausing, Porter scooped up the long shape and said, "Come on, Moses. Halloran's in the compound, and surely he's got something that can stop the work of that poison."

He was vaguely aware of dark-skinned bodies coming out of hiding as he passed them. The gate opened before him, and this time it remained open to let a string of Butterfly People follow him into the village. But Porter was barely aware of them.

Janet was dead. Norman was dead. It seemed unfair that their son should also die here in the jungle, after surviving the plague. It would leave Eric's wives without a husband and his children without a father. Porter found without shame that tears were streaming down his face.

Halloran gestured toward Whitlock's house, and Porter hurried up the steps and into the shadowy room that Delenda indicated. When he laid Eric on the narrow bed, Halloran was right there, his hypodermic already in his hand.

"We can handle this, I think. Moses tells me that there are two commonly used poisons besides curare. I can give a combined shot that should keep him stable until we can decide which was used. Then we can counteract it."

He bent over Eric and cut deeply beside the shaft of the arrow, which still thrust out from the thigh. With a deft motion, he had the head of the thing out. Moses took it from him and ran out onto the veranda.

Tulunga was waiting. Porter watched through the window as the old shaman took the arrowhead and smelled it. He wiped away the blood with a bit of his wispy G-string, and then he tasted the tip delicately, a mere flick of the tongue. He nodded and said something to

Moses.

"Curare," panted the Indio, as he ran back into the room. "Tulunga say, and he know."

"Ah," said Halloran. "Good. That is easier to manage than one of their combination poisons. Steve, will you get Delenda to boil some water? I need to sterilize this wound, and my scalpel is fouled."

Porter was glad to have something to do. As he waited for the water to boil over the cookfire behind Whitlock's house, he found himself trembling with reaction. It had been some sort of day.

* * * * *

When Eric woke from his long sleep, it was a great relief to everyone in the village. Moses had crouched beside his bed, refusing to move, even to eat and sleep. Porter had paced restlessly in and out, and Whitlock had prayed hard in his chapel, once the wounded had been tended and the scars of battle somewhat mended.

The first sign of his waking came when Eric moved a bit, murmuring, "Mom! Mom!" in a distressed voice.

Moses rose at once and put his hand on Eric's.

"Bonnie?" asked the young man. "Tasla?"

"No. Is Moses," came the reply. "You all right. In village with Dr. Whitlock. We bring you here. Is all fine. Compound okay, too. Ko bring word."

Eric sighed. His eyes opened, and he looked around the room as if puzzled by where he might be. "Bonnie

. . . she's all right? You're sure?"

"Sure," said Moses.

Halloran, who had been dozing in the next room, entered and looked into Eric's eyes, pulling back the lids and shining his little light into the pupils. He grinned down as he switched off the light.

"You're going to be fine. And from what I hear, you did a job of getting us help just in the nick of time. The Cochona had us outnumbered by a lot."

Out on the porch, Porter sighed with satisfaction. He had brought that young man into the jungle. If Eric had died there, something would have gone terribly wrong with Porter's whole idea of fate and the world.

15

Things would never be quite the same again, Eric knew. Not only the loss of his mother and Lauren and those others killed by the Cochona assured him of this. Everyone knew that while the Cochona had suffered a humiliating defeat, that had been the effect of the unexpected attack of the Butterfly People, Moses, and Eric against their rear. There were many Cochona.

At least two branches of the tribe lived on the south side of the river, and even more in the fastnesses to the north. Some of these wild tribes had, indeed, been in contact with white men and missionaries. Those that had retreated into the forest had done so in bitterness and anger, stung to the quick by the arrogance of soldiers and planters, missionaries and traders. They would never reconcile themselves with those who had accepted the wise and gentle teachings of Nathan Whitlock.

The little enclave of people in the compound and the village were now surrounded by a hostile world, and they could expect other attacks in the future. The tribe they had defeated would probably be the first to come back, more carefully and more craftily than before, to wipe out their humiliation in blood.

This meant that changes would have to be made. The compound, though protected by its fence and generator, was watered by a stream that led away into the jungle. It could be poisoned easily. Wells were too easily contaminated in the forest to make safe sources of drinking water possible.

"We've got to move to the village," said Halloran, when the Monkey Station group met to make some final decision. "They have the river in an arc around their flanks. They have a safe water supply in the spring that gushes out of the rock behind the church. There is always the possibility of escape by way of the river, if things get entirely too desperate to stay put. It seems to me the only thing we can do."

"But the fence—theirs isn't any good at all, really, for it can be burned. Dead wood will burn, even if it's raining. And the electric lead . . . that has a lot of possibilities," objected Bonnie. She was now more than eight months pregnant, very heavy and uncomfortable. Halloran said she was going to have twins.

"The fence can be moved," said Eric. It was the first time he had felt any desire to take part in the planning. Depression had lain heavy upon him since his mother's

death, and even his wives' concern had not been able to
bring him out of it.

Now, however, he found himself feeling unusually
alert. His father had been a master of improvisation', and
Eric had found that he had some of Norman's flair for
solving problems with sudden bursts of insight.

Porter and Halloran were staring at him. "Moved?
That would be a lot of work. The posts are set in cement.
How could we get them loose, and where could we find
any more to use when we reset them?"

Eric found himself leaning forward, his hands sketch-
ing swift plans in the air. "Look, the footings can be dug
up. We have plenty of hands if some of the Indios help
us. Then all it will take is digging big enough post holes
in the perimeter of the village. We set the big heavy
chunks of cement around the feet of the posts into place,
tamp the holes back full of crushed rock and mud, and
put stones on top of the loosened soil.

"The steam boiler and the generator can be disman-
tled and moved—we moved the boiler here without
much trouble in the first place. There should be
enough gas for the pickup to make several trips back
and forth, carrying the heaviest of the fencing and the
equipment."

Porter frowned thoughtfully. "Yes, there ought to
be more than enough fuel for that, if we can crank that
stubborn jackass of a truck. Set the footings of the
fence posts along the riverbank, drilling some of them
right into the stone of the embankment, and you have
a semicircle of metal fence that can be electrified to

keep anyone or anything from touching it. Sounds good!"

He turned to Tom Butler. "What do you think, Tom? You're the mechanical genius of the outfit, now that Smalley's gone."

The thin hunter leaned his chair back against the wall. His face, with its worried lines, became even more thoughtful. "Sounds as if it can work," he said. "You suppose the Butterfly People might want in on this? They're going to be on the Cochona's hit list, for sure. They just might want to move into the village with us and the Armadillo People. God knows, there's plenty of room, after all the losses we've had."

Eric leaned back, relaxing for the first time in a long while. Bonnie beamed at him across the table, and Tasla, sitting beside him, took his hand and held it under the table. He glanced up at Halloran and found the doctor grinning at him.

"Welcome back, my boy. We've been worried about you while you were off in your place of mourning. What else can you come up with? You seem to have inherited your father's knack for figuring things out."

The young man looked up and down the table, at the two hunters and their four wives, at Halloran and Steve Porter, Bonnie and Tasla. Moses was staying in the village now, caring for his own four wives and their children, so he was not present. In his mind's eye, Eric saw his father and the Smalleys and the Nagles also sitting there, lending their invisible strength to the group they had to leave behind them.

"Okay. I've been thinking, even when I didn't feel like talking. There is a bunch of peccary that ranges through the macaque's habitat. Why don't we try to fence them into one of the peninsulas running out into the river? They're pretty big, some of them, and the forest is thick, with plenty of food for the animals. They swim, of course, but if we put them onto one of those that stands high above the water, they might not jump so far. That way, we'd have a meat supply close at hand, accessible from the river, if necessary, should the Cochona cut us off from hunting in the jungle.

"The macaque might keep an eye on them for us and let us know if the Cochona tried to mess with them. I think that would relieve our minds, because if we can't hunt the forest, we're in big trouble, sooner or later."

The older men looked at each other, and Eric knew they were impressed with his plan. How would they, as well as the women, react to his next one? He could only put it forth and see.

"You know how the children in the village play at battles? Even with Whitlock fussing and carrying on for so many years, they still take their little spears and blowguns and practice all the skills their ancestors developed over generations for dealing with their enemies. Well, when our children are born and big enough, I think we ought to put them right into the middle of those practice battles."

Tasla squeezed his hand. Bonnie looked a bit shocked, but in a bit she, too, nodded agreement.

"We don't have enough ammunition for even one more real pitched battle, that is certain," Eric said. "We need to learn to use the native weapons ourselves, all of us. Something that can be made by hand and supplied with its ammo by hand, out of the jungle, is the best we are going to be able to do. I feel as if we may be able to make some improvements in the weapons Moses and his friends use, too. We have some knowledge of the ways such things developed over the years, how other kinds of primitives have made and used them. . . . If we can't do some good there, I'm ashamed of us."

The atmosphere of the council had livened up a lot. The air of depression and dismay that had attended others seemed to have dissipated, and Eric found his own grief thinning away to a manageable level. If he could find something very hard to do and do it with all his might, he would pull out of this. That was suddenly plain, and his mother's motto: "Hard work can cure anything" came back to comfort him.

"I'll go tomorrow and talk to the people in the village," he volunteered. "Moses will be able to get loose, maybe, and the two of us can visit the Butterfly People. That can take up to two or three days, I suspect. Moses says their village is a very long way from here." He found himself looking forward to the chance of a long trek through the forest.

"Good thinking," said Halloran. "We will be looking into the situation here—there are a lot of things that need to be stored carefully. Books and records must be protected from damp and insects, and the lab equipment can be packed away for future use. I suspect that it will come in handy, in times to come. I can teach you youngsters more about chemistry and biology, and we may be able to learn to refine some of the medicines the Indios get from the jungle and make them more reliable and safe." The doctor bent his red head and stared down at the table.

When he looked up again, he said, "Just because the world out there came to a crashing halt, there is no reason to think that we must do the same. We are alive. We are, thank God, relatively sound and healthy. We have years ahead of us and young ones coming into the world who will need to be taught and cared for.

"We can make our own world here. With the help of the Indios—and maybe even of the macaque—we can live well and intelligently. There is an old fallacy that people have believed about primitive life, which is that primitives have to scrape so hard for survival that there is no time for anything else. In a place such as this, it is full of leisure time, for there is no need to struggle for every bite of food and bit of shelter.

"With the right attitudes, we can improve not only our own lot, but that of the Indios, if they want to share in it." Halloran rose and stood staring out the window, across the compound toward the spot where the useless chopper sat under its tarp.

"We can make a better world, if we try, than the one that destroyed itself . . . out there."

* * * * *

Tulunga was tired. The death of Walebe, just after his people reinforced the Armadillo People against the Cochona, seemed to have cut his strength in half. He had not known until now how much he relied upon the wisdom of the ancient chief.

So unexpected had been the foray against the enemy, that few of his people had suffered so much as a wound. Those, of course, could be dangerous if caused by poisoned darts or arrows. But in addition to the medicines of the white shaman, Halloran, Tulunga knew many of his own, culled from the work of his predecessors and the vast pharmacy of the jungle.

All the injured were now well, for no one had been badly hurt. The Cochona were sent back into the fastness of their deep forest, but Tulunga knew all too well that they would not remain there. They were a bitter and determined people, and when they had licked their wounds, they would emerge again into the jungle where his own people worked and hunted and wandered for pleasure.

The village of the Butterfly People was not defensible. They were shy people, seldom in contact with others of their own kind, and they had made few enemies . . . until now. The old shaman found himself worried, as he sat on a rock thrusting from the bluff above the stream that served the village as water source, bathing place, and fishing spot. Below him, the children were splashing in the rocky pools where piranha never came. Three young girls were stalking silently along the bank with their tiny bows, and even as he watched, one shot into the water and pulled forth a fair-sized fish, whose orange and black markings glinted in the sunlight off the water.

It was a good life that he and his people had known here, but Tulunga found his internal voice warning him of change. "Danger will come," said the voice in his spirit. "The people must go to a safer spot, and you must send out young men to find such a place. There will be no more help from the white people and the Armadillo People. They have lost too many of their number to be of much help, even if they were to come to our aid.

"The world has changed, Tulunga. The old ways must change, too, no matter how well they have suited your people in the past. There must be a stronger spirit among the Butterfly People. They must practice the skills of war, and even the children must learn to fight more fiercely. The world has changed. . . ."

A sudden longing overcame the old man. He needed to find, once more, the peace of the secret ravine, the caverns where he had hidden his people before. Amid the roar of the falls, he seemed to find answers that he found nowhere else. He rose and called down to his nephew, Kaliche.

"I will go into the forest, Nephew. Will you come with me? It is no longer safe for our people to range alone through the jungle. The Cochona are devious and they recover rapidly from their defeats, as we have learned to our cost in years past."

The youth moved lithely up the steep side to join him. He had, his uncle thought, the grace of a deer, his narrow face and his slender body seeming to swim through the reflected light of sun and stream.

"I will go," he said softly as he joined Tulunga. His blowgun was in its sling, and the darts bulged in his pouch. All the Butterfly People now went armed, even so near to their village, for they knew the Cochona of old, and they did not trust them.

The shaman turned and disappeared into the shadows of the forest, moving with the ease and silence of a breeze. Behind him, he knew, his nephew watched everything that moved, every dark shadow, every concealing tree trunk, every clump of vine or fern.

By noon he had come to the ravine below the waterfall. The stillness of the place was almost complete—only a small bird atop a tree beyond the water kept up a continual "Chip-Chee!" of comment, as the two Indios stood staring down into the deep.

Without speaking, Tulunga started down the unobtrusive track leading to the water's edge. Kaliche came behind him, still alert for anything unusual. No Cochona had ever come here, as far as either of them knew, but there was always a first time, and they were taking no chances as they moved swiftly along the waterside and up the path leading behind the falls.

As they went through the mist of water sprayed upward from the stones below, Tulunga paused, his head up, his nostrils widening. As had Moses, weeks ago, he said, "I smell man."

From deeper in the cavern there came a quiet voice. "Tulunga, my friend, we have come to talk with you. It

is good that you have met us halfway." The old man recognized Moses' voice at once, and behind him Kaliche
relaxed.

A torch was lit, and Tulunga saw that both Moses and
Eric had come. Hope sprang into his heart. Perhaps
these young men had come with some plan that might
safeguard his people!

They went into the nearest of the inner chambers
and sat facing each other, as the torch burned red and
painted their features with color and shadow. The old
man noted that Moses seemed well and content, but
the white man was drawn and paler than he had been.

"He has recovered from the poison?" he asked Moses,
gesturing toward Eric. "He does not look well."

"He has been filled with grief," the Indio replied.
"His mother and his friend died at the hands of the
Cochona, and he cannot seem to forget it. He has been
silent and his temper has been ill for a long time. Only
now has he begun to recover from that grief-sickness.
But even as he suffered, he was thinking of the good of
those who live in the forest, your people as well as mine
and his own. We have come with a plan."

It was just what Tulunga had wanted to hear. He
leaned forward, as Moses, frequently clarifying his
understanding of Eric's plan by consulting with his
friend, translated into the dialect the plan worked out
with the Monkey Station staff, Kolambe of the Armadillo People, and Nathan Whitlock.

They talked for a long time, for Tulunga had many
questions, and even Kaliche thought of an objection or a

problem from time to time. But when they were done, and the sun outside the caverns was gone behind the trees, the old shaman felt that his deepest desire had been answered.

"This will be a safe place for my people. We will be near enough to this place to visit it, when I feel the need, and the forest will be at hand. But the Cochona cannot come upon us secretly, and we will be reinforced by the knowledge and the craft of the white men. It is very good."

Moses translated his words for Eric, and the young man smiled and leaned forward to take Tulunga's hands in his own. "We are all human beings," he said. "It will be necessary for us to be cruel, sometimes, to our enemies. We must learn to fight fiercely and to harden our hearts, when necessary. But we will be friends among ourselves, the Armadillo People, the Butterfly People, the macaque, and the people from the compound."

Moses translated as he spoke, and Tulunga felt a deep satisfaction at the words. "We will become a new people now, protected by a metal fence and the white man's magic from those who would attack us. Instead of the Butterfly People and the Armadillo People, we should take a new name that describes us all."

Kaliche raised his head, the torchlight glinting in his dark eyes. "The Metal People," he said. "We can all become the Metal People, hard and cold to our enemies, yet offering shelter and life to our friends."

The three others glanced about at each other. When

Eric understood what had been said, he nodded decisively, and all of them smiled.

"The Metal People it shall be," said Eric. "And the macaque will be our friends, to shelter in our village at need. Is that a thing that you can approve?"

Tulunga thought for a moment, after Moses had translated. "Those are the monkey-men in the forest near the river. They have traveled through our jungle, and we have seen them watching us, as if they were thinking about the way in which we live and the things that we do. They have been known to help the Armadillo People. I have heard the talk of that." He looked aside at his nephew, his expression questioning.

Kaliche was staring into the torch fire, his brow wrinkled with thought. When he looked aside at his uncle, his eyes were wide, the look of dream in them. Tulunga knew with sudden joy that this young one, of all those he had watched and considered, might have the gift that he was so near to laying aside. Kaliche might well carry on his work for his people.

"They say," said the young man in a dazed tone, "that this is good. The monkey-men are wise and kind. The village is safe. This is the good thing for us to do now."

Tulunga sighed deeply. He took from his neck the amulet that he had been given by his own uncle. It was strung on a bit of blackened thong, and its thin oval was polished dark and gleaming by contact with his own flesh and that of his ancestors. The thong seemed to cling to his fingers as he held it out to Kaliche.

"The Metal People are a new people. They have been given a new shaman. Kaliche, take this as a token of your work and your place. Keep it as long as it serves your needs, and if a time comes when the voices tell you to pass it on to others, give it freely."

The young man extended his hand and took the amulet into trembling fingers. His eyes were still wide and dazed, his expression bewildered, for his gift had come upon him in his manhood, and he had had no time to become used to it.

Eric, watching with shining eyes, understood what was happening without any translation. He nodded as Kaliche put the thong around his neck. And when Moses told him the old shaman's words, he seemed to take on color and life again.

"The world that was would not accept this as a true thing, " he said. "My own father would not have considered it, before his world ended. But I have seen the things Tulunga's voices have predicted coming true. The fact that he is here now, when we would have had to travel for another half day to reach him, shows me that such things are real and vital, and all our peoples together will profit by the presence of this new shaman."

Moses spoke to the others in a quiet tone, but his face was glowing with pleasure. He had, Tulunga suspected, felt that his friend was unconsciously persuaded that the ways of the Indios were inferior to the ways of the white man.

In some ways, that might have been true, in the past.

But now it was different, and Eric recognized that and was ready to compromise his prejudices in order to help all their peoples to survive.

16

Ko had grown with the passing years to a stature larger than any of his people had ever attained before him. But his own young were already larger than he by several finger widths, and the youngest was only four years old. In the years since the Woman died, he had seen many changes in his people, and he wondered often about them.

She could have explained these things to him, now that he was so much more fluent at Man-talk. Indeed, her son could probably give him much information, he felt, though he was hesitant to trouble that busy man. Ko knew about responsibility, for he kept an alert eye on all the families of his kind, no matter how distant their habitats or how independent their members.

He was not, of course, the leader of his people. That

was a thing that he had tried over and over to explain to Eric, when the man visited him. The macaque had no leaders and needed none. Each of them was bright and alert, inventive and brave. The few exceptions had fallen victim to jaguars and ocelots over the years, and those remaining had had old weaknesses removed from their heritage.

But Ko felt bound by his old sense of responsibility. There had been a time when he was the only one of his people who could speak in the Man-talk. There had been a time when he had met with the Woman and the Doctor, before the great sickness, on behalf of his people. He found himself unable to relinquish the welfare of his kind into their own hands.

He moved through the jungle, from the river to the deep forest, from the village to the old compound, where young macaque often played in the huts, pretending to be men. He did not interfere with anyone or argue policy with those who, by virtue of their age and wisdom, considered themselves advisers to their own families. But he knew what was happening, from the deserted village of the Butterfly People, almost two days travel to the south, to the hidden shelters of the Cochona, many days' journey deeper still into the vast forest between the headwaters of the biggest stream flowing into the Rio Negro and the great river itself.

He had gone, from time to time, on that long journey to gaze on the tremendous bulk of water that Eric called the Amazon. Other men, very few and unorganized, lived along its banks or up the tributaries feeding into it.

He had seen them, without being seen, and he thought often of the difference between such representatives of Man and those he knew in the village.

The group in the village he knew were well protected inside their fence-wall. They hunted and fished and frolicked in the forest and along the bank of the Rio Negro, but they went always accompanied by armed men and women, and no lurking Cochona had yet succeeded in surprising them. Though a few Metal People had been killed over the years, nobody had ever been taken captive successfully, for Ko made it his business to know when someone had been seized. The routine for getting word to the village was swift and effective. Help arrived for the beleaguered people so quickly that even the Cochona, masters of quick jungle travel and magical disappearance, had not been able to spirit away a single member of the Metal People.

Now Ko sat on a high branch. From its elevation, he could see a glint of the river on his right, beyond the peccary forest. The macaque were beginning to relish meat, and they tended the beasts for their own benefit as well as that of the Metal People. On his left, he could look over a vast green stretch of treetops, with here and there a giant standing above its neighbors.

Ahead he glimpsed a shiny spot that was something in the village, and when he turned completely around, he could imagine he saw the remnant of the compound off to the east. His whole world was there, and when he sat just so he felt that he was in control of it. He worried more than he had ever mentioned, either to the men who still visited him or to Kree or his other mates.

For he had gone, within the past days, to the wild reaches where the Cochona lived. He had rested high in a tree and watched them moving like insects in the village below. They were unusually animated, he was certain, as if they had plans afoot. Though they always went armed, they seemed even more busy with making darts and mending bows and blowpipes than usual.

The women were mixing ashes and grease, and that made a tremor of alarm run through Ko's entire body. They painted themselves with those terrible designs that turned them from slim, brown-skinned human beings to frightening demons only when they intended to go to war.

There were other tribes, across the stream on which the Cochona village had been built, and it was possible that they might be the target of this new venture. But Ko had a feeling, deep in his bones, that they intended, yet again, to come against the group that had been the first and only one to defeat them, time after time: the Metal People.

He now was trying to decide if he should warn the villagers or hold his peace until he was more certain of the enemy's intentions. But he was finding that as he grew older, his instincts were more and more reliable. He seemed to be able to tell when danger approached, even if it was only a hungry jaguar that moved toward his family.

Now all his instincts told him to go at once and warn Eric and the Metal People that danger was coming soon.

Very soon.

He dropped to a lower level and moved through the branches, his hands unerring on vine and limb, his toes and tail stabilizing him from leap to leap. He passed Kree, and she came after him, her newest infant clinging tightly to her fur as she hurried. Together they went to tell Man their warning, and Ko hoped that he was right. And then he realized what that meant, and he hoped just as devoutly that he was wrong.

*   *   *   *   *

If there had not been the constant danger of attack, Eric would have felt that his present life was perfect. He was busy from dawn to dark with interesting and useful tasks, ranging from teaching the three-year-old twins to handle their small spears and bows to sitting for hours with the leaders of the village, working out problems among fishermen wanting the same spot for setting nets or among women who coveted the same garden spot.

When he tired of those things, he could take off into the forest with Moses, and the two would range from their favorite haunts along the river to the distant stream, with its complex of caves. There they kept a store of weapons, constantly added to and tended, to ensure they did not deteriorate.

He had wondered, before his children had been born, how it would be to be a father. Now he couldn't imagine being without Bonnie's Link and Mark, or Tasla's small Juli. There were more, too, for Bonnie had a one-year-old daughter called Jan, and Tasla had just produced a dark-haired son that they had decided to name Norman, in memory of the child's grandfather.

When his three older children and Moses' youngest two got together, their fathers often took to the woods in self-defense. Better young lungs had never been exercised.

It was the thought of the children that drove Eric to keep strengthening the fence. He thought often of the secure world in which he had grown up, the "civilization" of which his kind had been so proud. But it was gone, and only the fence stood between his own people and those who would kill them, if there was a chance of it. Outside its linked layer, he had planted thorn trees, and in the two and a half years since they had been put into place, the plants had grown to respectable dimensions. Anyone approaching the wire would be pretty well shredded by the time he came within reach of the fence. And there a worse shock awaited any attacker.

Cash and Tom had worked together, uniting the generator from the compound with a pair of boilers, one from the old system and another cannibalized from the launch that had brought Alberto Gunter back upriver. The village children were given the task of keeping tremendous piles of wood ready at hand, for fueling the steam-powered generator. Every time a child went into the forest, he or she returned with an armload of wood.

Eric should have felt secure, but he kept thinking of the child, long years ago, that would have been carried away by the Cochona if the macaque had not been alert and the Indios had not been nearby. Somehow, as long as the savages lived in the forest and harbored their fanatical hatred of the Metal People, he knew he would never feel that his family was entirely safe.

There came a hail from the eastward lookout, one of the youngsters who climbed high by turns and watched the forest and the trails and the river. "Ko!" was the word, in a delighted tone. The young ones loved the macaque devotedly, though many of the older Indios still regarded them with caution, feeling that nature had somehow been twisted in their creation.

Eric climbed down from the roof of the hut he shared with his family and went to meet his old friend. But he knew, as soon as he saw the macaque, that something was wrong. The shape of the shoulders, the nervous twitching of the tail said that Ko was having one of his premonitions of danger.

Eric thought of what his father used to say about hunches . . . and then he laughed. He had known too many times when his own life and those of his people had been saved by the macaque's ability to foretell danger. Some things worked, no matter if they could or couldn't be reliably reproduced in the laboratory.

As he ran toward Ko, he found himself chuckling at the thought of what might have happened in a laboratory if the Cochona had attacked in strength. A lot of researchers would have been turned into believers, he suspected. It took, he had decided, a really strong incentive to bring out the gift the macaque now possessed.

"Er'c!" shouted the macaque, as he raced through the

gate, followed by Kree and a baby that was holding onto her for dear life.

"Chona! I go. I see them make weapon ready. I see women make face paint. I feel danger, come soon. Come ver' soon, but not today or tomorr'w, maybe."

Eric stopped in his tracks, feeling a great sadness settle over him. Would there never be an end to this? His people had never gone into the forest of the Cochona to retaliate. They had attended to their own business, peacefully when they were not being attacked. What would stop this repeated danger and death?

Moses appeared from his own tasks and stood beside Eric as they greeted the macaque. Eric could feel the anger of the Indio, as well as his own, so well did they know each other and so closely had they related over the past years.

Porter came up from the river, where he had been mending his fishing canoe. "What now?" he called.

"Cochona. Again." Eric felt rage build inside him. Again, he found himself trying to think of something to eliminate that danger from their lives.

And then he had it. He turned to Moses and caught Porter by the elbow. "I know!" he shouted, and Ko started back, startled at his vehemence.

"We must attack them. At home, in their own place, where nobody has ever gone before, except for Ko, here. He can show us the way!"

He turned to the teen-aged boy in the nearest watch-tree. "Blow your horn!" Eric yelled. "Bring all the hunters and fishermen home. We're going to attack the

Cochona for a change!"

Bonnie came from the hut, followed by Tasla. "We're what?" Bonnie asked, her blue eyes worried. "Did I hear you correctly?"

"You did," said Steve Porter. "You did, and it's about time we did just that!"

Eric grinned at the ex-pilot. He knew that Porter would love this adventure, though the rest of them would endure it. It was wild and daring and unheard of. That was why it just might work.

* * * * *

The Armadillo People had numbered perhaps eighty souls when the plague struck them. That had cut their numbers drastically, though by the time Nathan Whitlock died they had built up again to about fifty members of the village, most of them children.

Whitlock's death had left the Indios and the whites alike feeling orphaned, and only the busy lives they led had kept them from grieving too much. The addition of the Butterfly People to their roster had brought the village a greater population than it had ever had, for the plague had not been carried to the Butterfly People, across the many miles of jungle.

So it was that when the proposal to attack the Cochona was put to the combined group, their leaders looked about them and saw that they had ample manpower for attacking their deadly enemies on their own ground. And though they knew that Whitlock might well have been opposed to the plan, they also knew that they must do what was best for themselves.

Tulunga was now very old, too feeble to go with the war party. Still, he was in the middle of all the planning and preparations. He had thought for years that the only way in which his people might be able to stop the depredations of the Cochona might be just such a foray, though his people were too peaceable to entertain such a thought at the time he proposed it.

When Eric had brought the matter before the combined council of the Metal People, the old man had listened intently to his talk without translation now, for Eric had learned the dialect so well that anyone would have thought he had been born an Indio. When the young man paused, Tulunga got to his feet, with some effort, and held his hands high.

"It is good!" he shouted. "It is the only way. The Cochona will pick us off, one by one, as they have done for years, until we are too weak to take this step. I believe that we should do this, and soon."

Kolambe's successor, Yochoi, rose quietly. "I, too, think this is a good plan. I have thought that perhaps the monkey-men might help us. Is that possible?"

Eric looked thoughtful. "I have already asked Ko to guide us. I will ask him if his people might also help us to harry the Cochona, once we attack them. It may be that they could distract our enemies while we fight them on the ground."

Now Halloran rose from his seat, his red hair showing a lot of gray in the sunlight. "Remember," he said, his tone terribly earnest, "that these are human beings. They are a part of the tiny remnant left in odd crannies of the world like this, all that can ever hope to keep our kind alive. Their genes are valuable, to them and to us, no matter what their manners and their habits may be.

"I urge you . . . keep alive any you can. Bring back with you all the captives you can catch, particularly women and children. We are like the Indians of North America now. We need new blood, a mixing of heritages, in order to keep our species strong. Cochona may be fierce, but that is a characteristic that should be helpful to our descendants in ages to come. We are not the last, thank God, of our people. We may be the beginning of a new and better kind. Remember this!"

He, too, now spoke the dialect flawlessly. Tulunga heard his words with wonder, and he grasped the concept, though he had not heard some of the English words before that had no equivalent in his own tongue. The word "genes" sounded strange to his ears, but he realized that this must be something that came down from parents to children, making every generation strong.

With urgent speed, the attack was organized. The macaque agreed to send some young adults with the group led by Ko, and if they saw the opportunity they would attack as well as they could from the trees.

The planning and readying for the expedition did not take long. On the day after Eric voiced his plan, supplies and warriors were prepared to march out. And they went after dark, as dangerous as that was in the jungle, for they knew that if the Cochona were getting ready to attack them, it was likely that lookouts were already in place in the surrounding forest, keeping an eye on their comings and goings.

The old shaman stood at the end of the fence, where each armed man or woman climbed silently and slid into the jungle without a sound. Anyone watching the gate would, he knew, feel sure that all was quiet for the night.

Eric left last, following Moses over the wire. Tulunga looked up at his shadow against the stars. He said nothing, but he was thinking that his people were very fortunate to have joined the numbers of such a strong leader. Eric's thinking was straight. His word was true.

What more could anyone want in a leader? When this was done, Tulunga intended to propose that Eric be made chief of the combined peoples in the village. He knew the ways of both the white men and the Indios. With such a chieftain, the combined tribes could hope to stand, if those other wild Indios beyond the river ever decided to try their strength against them.

The last of the warriors was out of sight in the forest, which loomed dark and forbidding against the sky and the feeble rays of the waning moon. Tulunga felt himself shiver . . . with dread or excitement? Both, he thought, as he pulled the thorn back into place against the fence and made his way to the hut where his granddaughter and her family kept his home.

The air from the river was damp, and as he moved along in his G-string and sandals, he shivered again.

What would the next days bring to the Metal People?
He would have given much for some word from his voices, but they were silent. Had they gone altogether to
Kaliche, leaving their former listener alone and without
comfort in the danger of the world?

He could only shake his head and go to find his kin.
When all was said and done, prophecy was a vague and
undependable thing, warning of matters about which he
could do nothing. He felt that his years of accumulated
experience at dealing with people was of far more value
to him now, than all the decades of listening to those
voices in his spirit.

* * * * *

Ko moved through the upper layer of the jungle,
hearing behind him the sounds of those who followed
him. Twenty young macaque had agreed to go and help
the men with their expedition against the Cochona. All
of them had lost friends or relatives to the blowpipes or
the arrows of the Cruel People, for when they traveled
about the forest they sometimes came into areas where
those ash-marked people hunted. To the Cochona, anything was prey fit for their cookpots.

But something troubled Ko. He had seen men kill
each other many times and in many terrible ways. He
had known when the Woman died, and her friend with
her. Often he had wondered, in that part of his mind
that seemed to grow more and more dominant as time
passed, why it was that macaque had no need to kill their

own kind, no matter how bitter the quarrel, and Man seemed always to be finding ways to destroy his own.

This attack made sense. His mind accepted the need. And yet something inside him resisted the thought of killing thinking beings. It was not like eating a bird that you caught in the treetops or a peccary that you tended for food. Those were creatures incapable of deep thinking, as well as of dread, he was almost sure. The Cochona were different. As cruel as they were, they were still beings who used their minds, no matter how ferociously.

* * * * *

There was no need for caution. The jungle was a cacophony of squawks and shrieks, hoots and honks and rasping cries from the many creatures hunting there by night. The occasional tribe of spider monkeys they passed stirred little as the macaque sped by them. Ko knew that even if the Cochona detected the presence of his group, they would not realize that these were not mere beasts in the jungle. They would not understand that here was a kind that could comprehend its own danger and react against it rationally.

He wondered how far the men had come. It was slow, walking on two feet through the thick growth below the highways of the monkeys. But if he got his group into place well before the arrival of the men, he could go back and guide them by the most secret ways he had found, as they approached their enemies.

Well before dawn, the macaque were scattered in the

largest of the trees around the huddle of shelters that was the Cochona village. They had armed themselves with sticks and nuts and other missiles they could find handily. Ko left them there, well satisfied with his deployment, and hurried back toward the river.

The men had come much farther than he would have thought. He dropped from a tree at Eric's feet and stared up at the man.

"Macaque in place," he said. "Now you go this way. I show. You watch tree!" He sprang again into the branches, this time remaining low enough for his followers to see, and he found a way through the interlocked growths of branch and vine. The freshness of the morning, for once, did not intoxicate his senses. He was worried about the thing he was about to do. What did it feel like to kill Man?

Before dark on the second day, he had his group of warriors hidden near the Cochona enclave. His own people were waiting patiently—that was one of the major differences he could see between his own kind and the native monkeys. The wild primates were terribly impatient, with easily distracted minds. His own could wait for days or weeks or even months for the time to become right for anything they were determined to do.

The day waned. Ko went high and observed the Cochona village, finding the natives still busy with their preparations for war. There were as many warriors visible as there had been before, and he descended and reported to Eric that it was almost certain no party had yet been sent out against the Metal People.

Eric looked down at him and took his hand. "We will attack in the night," he said. "That is not a normal thing among the Cochona, Tulunga told me, and it should shake them up a great deal. Will your people be ready?"

"Be r'dy."

It seemed a very long time that he waited in his tree-top, listening for Eric's whistle. It was almost a relief when it came shrilling through the night-cries of the jungle, and he could shake out his cramped muscles and send his own screech among the many others, warning his fellows that the time had come.

He saw the line of shadows go darting into the midst of the random array of thatch-roofed huts. Fire burst from roofs, as torches were flung into the inflammable material, and Cochona boiled out of them like ants from a disturbed hill. Ko shrieked again and dropped lower, aiming a stick at the head of a tall Cochona who had emerged into the glare and was staring about, stupid with sleep.

The man dropped as the missile struck him broadside. Then Ko was caught up in a fury like none he had ever dreamed could exist. He saw through a red mist, as the flames below leaped higher and higher, and the men locked in combat. Ko smelled blood, and the sharp odor drove him almost mad.

He found himself on the ground, his teeth sunk in the calf of a rank-smelling leg, his hands busy with two stones he had picked up as he dropped. The man struggled, struck hard at Ko's head and back, but the skin and bones of a macaque were tough, and he hardly felt the blows.

Around him, he could hear grunts and cries and groans, and his feet moved over men as his own victim dropped senseless, his face a blur of blood. Ko caught up a club dropped by a dying Cochona, and with it he struck and struck and struck again, raining blows among the naked bodies of the Cochona, and sometimes even hitting one of the Metal People by mistake. Eric's paler skin gleamed reddish in the light of the fires, and Ko took up his place beside him, taking the direction of the man's attacks as his own.

But he found himself still filled with a mad fury, biting and hitting and wrapping his sinuous tail about necks to strangle their owners. He lost track of his own people, never even wondering how they were reacting to this terrible activity in which they found themselves.

The fires burned low, and shadows were darker about him as he fought. He leaped over bodies onto other bodies, on whose backs he clung, biting at their necks. The world was a whirl of blood-scent and smoke and the acrid odors of sweat and death. When at last he felt hands take him from behind, he tried to whirl, to sink his strong teeth into this new enemy, and it was only with difficulty that he stopped himself. This was Eric.

"Ko, it's over. It's all over. You can stop fighting now." The voice was as deep as ever, but the tone was raw and rasping, as if Eric might have shouted all through the battle. "We have killed many. Too many. The women and children have run away into the forest, and we must find them and take them back with us to the village. If they want, later, they can return here, but we have to try to teach them the things they need to know. Will you . . . can you help us locate them?"

The macaque looked about him. Dawn had lit the sky, and the tops of the tallest trees were glinting with sunlight. The huts of the Cochona lay as drifts of ash about them, and among them lay bodies of men . . . and one of a macaque.

Ko made a soft sound in his throat and sprang to the side of the still form, whose tail lay limply in the dust, and whose eyes gazed up at him, unseeing and glazed with death. He crouched beside Keecho, mourning softly deep in his throat.

Eric came to his side and squatted there. He reached a comforting hand. "You are hurt yourself. Let us tend your wounds, my friend. We have already taken the other injured into the shade of the forest, for the sun will be brutal here in another hour. We will bury the dead when we have tended to the wounded."

Ko took the man's hand as he had, years ago, that of the younger man that Eric had been. He sat still under the ministrations of the uninjured. Three of his group were there, also being tended. He glanced up, his small eyes frantic.

"How many macaque? Wh're r'st?"

"Only one was killed." That was Porter, who was binding his shoulder with a long strip of stuff that smelled like medicine. "These three were hurt, along with you. The rest had the sense to stay in the trees and throw things, instead of getting down into the middle of the mess along with people so much bigger than they are." He tied off the bandage and stood looking down at his patient.

"You will do, for now. Go find your people and check to see if any of them got hit with arrows or darts from blowguns. Though I must admit there was a lot less of that sort of fighting than I expected. We hit them too hard and too unexpectedly, I think. They never had time to get many of their weapons, and most of those burned up in the huts."

Ko nodded and limped away to find his own kind. He was puzzled at the cheerful note in the man's voice. Even Eric sounded somehow satisfied and at ease with himself and the night's work. But Ko knew that his own stomach was queasy and his heart sore.

He had killed men. Perhaps many men. And it had made him sick and unhappy, filled with visions of blood and dying human beings; his nostrils were clogged with the stink of death.

He wondered how many of his own people felt as he did. For the moment, he felt that he never wanted to see another Man as long as he lived, though he knew that would change, once he was himself again. And yet—and yet he had a strong feeling that it would be best for the ways of Man and macaque to go apart for a time. For, perhaps, a very long time, while the two kinds found their individual ways toward living in this new world that El Malo had brought to the jungle.

17

Once the adrenaiine in his system had subsided, Eric found himself deathly tired. The thought of his children, now safe from this group of wild Indios, did little to lift his mood, as he moved among the ruins of the Cochona village.

The dead had been buried in the shade of the forest. Their bodies had not been burned, as was the custom, their bones not powdered nor drunk by their descendants, to give them a kind of immortality. The omission of this ceremony had bothered even his own tribe of Metal People, and the remnant of the Cochona, now glowering from their position in the shadow of a great mesh of buttress roots, seemed to be horrified.

He had talked with Tulunga, before setting out, about this very thing. Though Nathan Whitlock had preached against it as long as he lived, many of his converts had slipped away into the jungle with the bodies of their dead, instead of burying them in the neat churchyard behind the mission. But Tulunga had understood many things that a man born and reared in the jungle should not have been able to comprehend.

"If they drink the death-potion, some part of the cruelty and the determination of those who died will come to them through it. They will be hard enough for us to teach, even without that. We should bring them here as a conquered and captive people, subdued and afraid. Perhaps even then we may not be able to make them entirely a part of our people, but at least we will have terrified them so that it may last for generations."

Those had been the shaman's words, and Eric thought he had heard some faint echo of other words, spoken by no human tongue, in them. Now, watching the prisoners covertly from the corner of his eye, he realized that the disruption of their lives, the negation of their ritual had had a tremendous effect on the Cochona.

Even the warriors who had been captured were no longer the defiant and arrogant creatures they had been a few hours before. Their heads hung on their chests. Their erect shoulders slumped wearily, as if there could no longer be a reason for pride. Tulunga had, once again, been right on the mark with his advice.

Eric found himself, for the thousandth time, wishing that he could talk with his father. Norman had been not only a highly educated man, but also a good one, with a deep understanding of his own kind and insatiable curiosity, unalloyed with chauvinism, about others.

No one else could have worked with animals who were in the process of becoming humane, except those who could accept the fact that Man was not the premier achievement of nature.

Gunter, for instance, had already been having trouble with the idea, when his world came crashing down about his ears and necessitated a complete change in him. Others would probably have left the project before long, when it became obvious that the macaque were no longer beasts of the jungle, but thinking beings, in some ways superior to their creators.

Norman Littlefield might have been able to explain to his son why he felt suddenly dirty and evil. Why the smell of blood, already corrupt in the dirt at his feet, threatened to send him, retching, into the trees. With all the intensity of a five-year-old, Eric wanted his parents to comfort him, to make him feel innocent and clean again.

He sighed and looked about the circle of faces that had gathered around him. "Are all the prisoners secured?" he asked.

"They are well tied. They can walk, but they cannot run, and they cannot reach to untie each other," said Moses. "Come. It is time to go home. Our people will be worried about us."

"Where are the macaque?" Eric stared up into the treetops, where a group of shadowy shapes huddled along a set of fanned branches. He lifted his hand and gestured for one to come down.

Ko dropped to the ground. His fur was rough with dried blood, his body patched with bandages, and even his tail, his pride and joy, drooped. Eric went to his knees and put out his arms. Ko went into them and they gave a fierce hug.

When Eric stood again, Ko stepped back and looked up at him. "Er'c, we know long-time. Y'r moth'r know. Fath'r, too. They . . . make . . . macaque be think, be talk-people. We feel much f'r you, f'r them. We know Metal People, too, and we r'spect them. But macaque . . . macaque not kill'rs."

The small being sighed deeply, trying to put his deepest feelings into the tongue of Man. He started again.

"Time come we must, we fight. We kill. Today, I kill Chona. Many, I think. I go mad with blood. I fight even fr'nds. Oth'rs do, too, some of them. We all sick. We all ashamed. We all hate what we do last night, what we see today. We not kill'rs, Er'c. Man be kill'r for long-long. Woman tell us, long-time ago, about Man. He f'rget, between time, how it is to kill.

"Macaque not f'rget. Not ev'r f'rget. Smell of blood, smell of death, feel of ang'r, feel of stick cr'sh skull . . . those nev'r go away. So macaque must."

Eric stared down, puzzled. "Must what, Ko?"

"Go away. Now. F'r long-time, maybe. Macaque must think. Must put all thing togeth'r, make sense of them. Make feel bett'r inside. Learn to live with be kill'r for now, nev'r again, maybe. Good-bye, Er'c." He turned and leaped for a low branch, hauling himself into the tree quickly. "Be back, sometime."

"Ko!" cried Eric. "Must you go?"

"Must go!" came the reply. "We come again when can. But f'r now, we go deep in jungle. Go think. Go cry v'ry loud, wh're Man not hear us."

The macaque in the treetop stared down sadly, and their arms rose in a gesture of farewell. Ko turned into the branches, and in a moment the last of the hairy bodies were out of sight amid the lush foliage.

Moses touched Eric's shoulder. "We go, too," he said. "You talk with Tulunga when we are at home. He will help you to understand. Tulunga knows much, and his voices tell him more."

"I thought Kaliche had taken over as shaman," said Eric, shouldering a Cochona boy and absent-mindedly cuddling the still sobbing young one to his chest.

"Kaliche learns now. Advises when he can, goes to Tulunga when he needs help. The voices have come to him, but Tulunga heard them for many years. He knows what they would say, I think."

* * * * *

It was a much larger group that returned through the thick forest ways to the village beside the river. Ten women, fifteen children, three men of fighting age, and four ancient ones had been taken captive. They were coffled together at intervals, along a length of tough fiber rope. Too far apart to reach each other, they were separated, also, by watchful warriors. Eric came last of all, watching everything.

Nights were difficult, for all the captives had to be bound hand and foot. The Cochona did not take captivity lightly and even the children tried to escape again and again. At last Eric agreed that they, too, must be tied.

When the fence of the village again came into view, it was a welcome sight to everyone, even the weary Cochona, whose wrists and ankles were sore from the rubbing of the cords and whose feet were raw from thorns and splinters picked up in the forest.

Halloran, who had been prevented with difficulty from going on the expedition, came through the gate to greet them, followed by the wives and children of those who had gone. Bonnie and Tasla ran to hug Eric, and the children swarmed about underfoot, hugging anyone they could reach.

The Cochona, Eric saw once he disentangled himself from his family, were staring with bewilderment at this open expression of affection. Did they never show love for their families, then? Eric wondered. No wonder they were so fierce and cruel, if that were true.

Tulunga greeted each of his people as they came through the gate. When Eric passed, last of all, he put out a withered hand and stopped him.

"You need to talk?" he asked the younger man. "I think you need time of quiet now. Come to my house. I have deep ears—what goes in does not come out again."

Eric nodded, feeling something inside him begin to unknot. "Yes, Tulunga, I will come, after I speak to my family. I do need to talk to someone, and you are the one, next to my father, who can help me most."

He turned into his own house, which he had added to from time to time as children came. Bonnie and Tasla had a meal ready and the children quieted. Home. He smiled and entered.

There was comfort in the feel of his own place and his own people. He took the time to play with the youngsters, to cuddle tiny Norman, and to talk quietly with his wives. But all the while, he knew that he was going, when the fire burned low, to talk with Tulunga.

What would he do without that ancient man? He shivered at the thought.

* * * * *

When he came at last to the old shaman's hut, he found the ancient one sitting in darkness, staring into the night as if it spoke to him.

"Eric," he said. "Sit. They speak to me, those voices, even now. They tell me that my time is very short, but yours will be long. You will be the chief of these people, my own and the Armadillo People, and the Cochona and your own white ones. You think quickly, and you act with speed. You understand all of us, better than we Indios could ever understand your kind.

"When I die and Kaliche stands alone to speak to and to hear those who have told me what will happen in the world, you will be at his side, helping him to know what is best for all the Metal People. And you will help him to understand those monkey-people, who are so strange to us.

"I will not see another moon, but you will live for many hands of years, keeping our people safe and helping them to grow. And you will not need me, for I have told you all that I know."

The old man sighed, and Eric reached to take his hand. It was chilled, as if death already touched it, and as Eric sat talking with Tulunga, he felt a hollow feeling of loss already.

18

The planet turned, still, and days followed nights. Few counted them into years, for most of the living creatures left in the world were animals. The small enclaves of humankind struggled in a world grown alien to all their experience, and, having lost the technology that had made them strong, even those tiny groups suffered losses from their numbers. Mankind was now only a subspecies among many, instead of the Lord of the Universe that he had always considered himself to be.

The virus that had killed the major part of the human race had altered not only the balance of life forms but also the genetic makeup of every kind it touched. The throngs of dogs left to starve in the cities devastated by the plague thinned to a few . . . but those few grew and grew, until the second generation of their offspring were the size of small horses.

Other species changed drastically, birds growing too large to fly, wild animals becoming bigger with each generation until even the lowly armadillo attained the size of a Land Rover. In every hemisphere, mankind found itself surrounded by predators of gigantic size and augmented ferocity. Those, too, took their toll.

But the stimulus that the viral strain seemed to have given the human reproductive capacity took up the slack as time went by. Women gave birth to twins and triplets. There were almost no sterile people left . . . only those incapacitated by disease or accident lacked for children.

The small communities sprinkled over the globe in likely and unlikely places began to increase in population, bit by bit. The wild kinds of humanity, most of them untouched by the plague, did not increase, however, and continued to dwindle as they had for generations.

Along the coastlines of North America, little groups clung to life, beginning to grow enough to hold their place in the altered ecosphere. In the heart of Africa, a few tribes grew strong again and looked with acquisitive eyes at their neighbors. In Australia, the Bushmen wandered the deserted streets of Sydney from time to time, marveling at the ruined wonder of the place, while on distant grasslands a few whites still held on.

South America, touched more devastatingly than anyone would have dreamed by the plague, seemed deserted. The cities, lacking sanitation for their swarming and starving remnants of population, had gone under at *once. Even the towns along the rivers and in the mountains had been touched by the hand of El Malo.*

But in the area between the Rio Negro and the Amazon, the Metal People thrived and grew stronger. Attacks by the wild Indios from across the Negro had succeeded in doing nothing except decimate the attackers. The combined tribes of the Metal People, under their tall, fair-haired leader, increased in numbers from year to year, and many small groups left, from time to time, to form their own communities up or down the river.

In the years since the catastrophe, all had changed, and yet human nature, of all the matters known to its possessors, had not.

* * * * *

Eric moved silently through the giant ferns, instinctively avoiding anything that would have crackled underfoot. He was thinking of the armadillo in the clearing he had just passed. The thing had been tremendous—the size of a small horse, at least.

The changes in size among the wild creatures had taken place swiftly, and yet he had been so busy that it had not really caught his full attention. All the animals in this part of the jungle were much larger than those of his youth. Only the reptiles seemed to have escaped the genetic effects of El Malo.

That more than anything else, he thought, had been the thing that made the Cochona remain a part of the combined peoples who had made Eric their chief. When parrots the size of helicopters flew over, or agoutis large enough to root up an entire garden spot with a single swipe became the normal thing, life in the jungle had become much different and more dangerous than ever before. The Cochona might have been fierce, but they were not mad.

Even when the wild ones from beyond the Negro had occasionally attacked, soon after the melding of the tribes, the captured Cochona had stood aside from the battle. They had not helped their cousins, but they had not fought against them either. And when it had become obvious that the jaguars were now of appalling size, the Cochona had bowed their proud heads and become Metal People, abandoning their former ways entirely. Nobody sane would want to face those huge cats in the deep jungles without anyone to call upon for aid.

Eric had lost many of his own people, even with the combined strengths of all the tribes that had joined together. Moses' second son, Kalit, had been killed beside the walls of the village—Eric still shuddered at the scene he recalled too clearly. The jaguar had swaggered out of the forest as the young man approached the gate, carrying a small deer that he had killed.

Kalit was a bright one. He flung the deer carcass at the predator and sprang for the wall, but the big beast had swatted him flat, ignoring the animal meat, and had bitten him in two before the Metal People could get the gates open and their weapons into play. That was when they began leaving a guard on duty with one of the rifles and some of the precious ammunition. The measure had saved many others, for the beasts learned that this was the place to lie in wait for their human prey.

Eric's hair was gray now, and his body was more reluctant to perform as it had when he was young. Aches were common, and painful, when he pushed himself too hard.

He went high into a tree, staring down through the tangle of branches and leaves. Below him, a toucan the size of a parasol preened itself in the shade. He moved higher to reach a point from which he could stare out over the tops of the trees toward the distant wall that marked the other side of the Rio Negro.

He would never again see the world beyond that wall, he knew. For a moment he wondered what his life might have been like if he had been able to study law, to live in the civilized world he had left all those years before. He sighed and began to descend. It had died, and he no longer cared. His life was full of responsibility and work and affection, and he was content.

He leaped lightly onto the mulchy ground and moved away toward the compound and his people. However long he might live, whatever he might do, here he was of more use and more importance than he could possibly ever have achieved in the world from which his people had come.

The battles he had fought would never have been dreamed of in that world. The needs of this primitive society, which he learned to meet anew every day and every year, might well have been scorned in that sophisticated context. He had performed appendectomies under the direction of Halloran, as long as the doctor lived, and without that help after his death from a heart attack. More of his patients lived than died, which was, perhaps, as much as any physician could hope for.

His children were grown now, healthy, with families of their own. Juli, in particular, seemed to have inherited Norman's ability to assess and fulfill a need in one swift glance. She would, Eric hoped, assume his duties when he became too old to do his work.

A child ran from the forest, followed by a teen-aged boy. "Grampa!" she cried, darting toward his waiting arms.

What more, indeed, could life offer than this?

*   *   *   *   *

Beyond the Rio Negro, the jungle also was changing, though the men living there did not understand why. Kerito, who had been shaman of the Toli Cochona for many rains, looked for signs, made up tales to explain the strangeness that had come upon the land, and wondered.

His people lived as they always had, and though the days when white men intruded upon their country had almost receded to a time of myth, they held in their hearts an anger that had never died. It was not directed particularly toward the whites—the Cochona had always preyed upon their fellows, back into the mists of time. They now lacked anyone with whom to make war, and that more than anything was destroying them.

Kerito knew their feelings, for he shared them. The cache of shrunken heads that the tribe had collected had not grown since he was a young man. The craft of removing skin from skull, and treating it to make a tiny, grimacing minikin of what once had been the head of a man or woman, was all but lost.

The battle fires that always had lived in the hearts of his people were burning away their own spirits, lacking victims more suitable. Kerito had sent scouts into the ever dangerous jungle depths, looking for Indios who might serve. But there seemed to be no one left on his side of the river, except for his own kind.

There were, however, beyond the black river, villages of people. Many of them were pale people, the sort that his tribe had hated and feared when he was young. White heads with yellow hair, shrunk and finished as trophies, would put new life into those of his tribe who now seemed to be growing despondent.

New blood, spilled in the act of war, might well strengthen them to deal with the terrible animals that grew more ferocious every season. The very act of putting together groups of warriors for a raid seemed desirable, for the tribe was shrinking, growing listless, as if it were unable to cope with this new world in which it must live.

Kerito was too old himself to scout the forest, something he had never denied. But if he were to keep his people from sinking into apathy and death, he would have to drive his aching bones once more through the network of faint paths to the river's edge. He must observe those beyond it, in the fastness of their villages, and decide if a raid could be made with some hope of success. It was better, he decided, to die in battle than wither away like fruit upon a vine whose stem had been cut.

He took no one with him. If the raid were impossible, he wanted no disappointment, so he had to go alone, taking his thick staff and his blowgun, along with enough poisoned darts to give him some chance of survival if he were faced with danger. The parrot that he had tamed would ride his shoulder, squawking from time to time to note others of its kind. The presence of men would make it set up a din that would warn him long before they could see him, allowing him time to hide.

He had no idea if those beyond the river ever scouted his side. They seemed a strange breed, he remembered from earlier observations, mixed kinds whose colors ranged from palest tan to deepest bronze and mahogany. They had no pride of kin, he thought, that required keeping their blood untainted by that of alien people.

The trek was difficult for his stiff legs, and he had to hide several times. Once an armadillo, larger than the hut in which Kerito lived, sent him scurrying, and he was grateful that such huge creatures ate only roots and insects and small animals.

He came to the river's edge at last and hid behind a thick clump of vines that had overgrown a leaning bush. Downstream, almost hidden by a bend in the watercourse, he could see the fishing nets that had been draped to dry over a row of posts. The village was beyond, and he crept along, keeping always inside the dim shadow of the trees, until he was directly across the stream.

It was a large village, well prepared against attack. He could see down a cleared passage to a stout fence that walled it from the jungle. The people moving about the huts looked strong and well fed, and the children were lively as they splashed in a pool at the edge of the river.

He moved along the river again, downstream for a day and a night on foot, until he was opposite another village. This was less forbidding than the first. A possibility, he thought. Then, turning in his tracks, he moved upstream, reclimbing the rocky ledges he had come down, moving deeper into the jungle when the ledges were too much for his aged legs.

A day's journey took him within sight of still another village, this one looking more promising. It was newer than either of the others, he could tell, for the thatch of the roofs was not discolored by sun and rain. There was no wall on the jungle side, and the approach by the river was clear of obstruction. An attack in canoes, by night, could be made.

He watched as two children ran down the slope to the water, carrying a pot between them, which they filled with water and took away, slopping wet dollops as they moved. There were reeds on either side of the main approach to the village—a good place for men with blowguns to pick off any resistance.

This was the place. This was the target. Now all that remained was for him to prepare his people for war, to build the fires in their hearts again to the fury that became the Toli Cochona. With the blood of these mixed-race people, he might renew the spirits of those who depended upon him.

When the time came, his tribe would strike here! The parrot, as if reading his thought, squawked and flapped its wings, and others of its kind in the branches overhead took up the sound like a war-cry.

* * * * *

Juli moved through the jungle with the ease and speed of one of the cats, her blowgun ready at hand in a loop of her G-string, a small bow and a bundle of arrows over her shoulder. Though her ears and eyes were alert for any sign of danger, her mind was busy with other things.

Her father was going to die—that was the matter that concerned her most. The thought of trying to lead the Metal People after his death troubled her greatly, for she relied on his advice, as well as that of her Uncle Moses, for many of her decisions.

There came a crushing sound ahead of her, and she slid behind a tree and readied her bow. It sounded like—yes, it was—one of the giant peccaries, bumbling its way through the heavy growth, pausing from time to time to root under a fallen tree or around a clump of stilt roots. Juli crept past on the other side of the clutter and moved onward.

Things were about to change. Always, when that happened, Kaliche, now the old shaman of her people, heard voices that told him something of things to come. He had not the gift of his uncle, the fabled Tulunga, but often his warnings had given her time to rally the people and ready them against attacks from across the river or to move them to her father's escarpment to avoid unusually high floodwaters. And Kaliche had spoken with her just three days ago.

"Go and find the monkey-people," he told her. "Bring one here, if one will come. It has been a long while since Ko visited us. I hope he is still alive, and that his people can find it in themselves to work closely with us again. The time has come, I think, for the great ocelots and jaguars grow more numerous every season. The time is coming soon when we will become their prey, even more than we have been already. The macaque, too, will need allies against those terrible enemies. Go, Juli, and ask Ko, if he still lives, or one of his kind, to come to the village and talk with Moses and Eric."

That had told her that the shaman expected her father, at least, and possibly Moses, too, to die soon. She felt her throat tighten as she moved along a path worn by the pads of some small beast, going always toward the big forest that lay between the river and the sacred waterfall.

From time to time, she paused and gave a shrill call. The howlers and spider monkeys, high above her in the canopy, chattered and grunted, but the reply for which she waited had not yet come. Again she stopped and cupped her hands about her mouth.

"Macaque! Ko! Come and talk!"

She sighed and moved forward, slipping through great drifts of fern and clumps of vine-covered bushes. She was entering the edge of the area of tremendous trees, and soon she found herself walking easily beneath the dark layers of leaves and branches above her. The twilit reaches sometimes glinted with a scarlet fungus or a tiny flower on an almost invisible stalk, but she kept her eyes sweeping from low to high, checking the branches far overhead for a blur that might be the body of a macaque.

A toucan lurched from a bough and swept heavily above her, its big body almost too bulky for its wings. She could remember when she was a child, and the birds had been much smaller, even the parrots that now were the size of tents, with beaks that could disembowel an animal or a man.

A soft snarl jerked her to a halt again. She was up among the stilt roots of the nearest tree before she had time to think, climbing past the sprawl of bracing onto the tree trunk itself. The rough bark gave her purchase, and she inched upward until she reached the first branch that would hold her weight.

She sat there, her heart thudding heavily, her breath easing itself. Below, on the mulchy ground beneath her perch, sat an ocelot, almost invisible as its dark spots and streaks blended with the uneven coloration of the leaves and shadows. It was not the medium-sized beast that she had seen as a child. In the years that had brought her to middle age, the cats had grown huge. Now they were a deadly peril to everything that walked in the forest on the lower level. This one seemed intent on waiting her out, for it made itself comfortable in the scurf of dead leaves and rotted wood that floored the forest and gazed upward steadily.

Juli shivered. She was safe. She could, if she had to, travel through the trees, as her father had taught her, but still she felt it strange that any beast should seem so confident when hunting for humankind. In her youth, even the jaguar had gone cautiously when humans were nearby.

The day moved slowly. After a long time, she knew there was no point in trying to wait out the carnivore, and she rose and climbed higher, searching always for heavy branches lying in the direction in which she must go. She made her way from tree to tree, testing holds and trying every limb for rot before entrusting her weight to it. This was a very slow way to travel, and she hated the wasted time.

After what seemed hours of careful inching along, avoiding tree snakes and scorpions, she knew that she was clear of the lurking cat. Down she came, still cautiously, until she stood again on the forest floor.

As she eased her aching arms and legs, a voice said, "You come find macaque? I take you."

She whirled, her hand going instinctively to her blowgun, but it was only a monkey-man who stood there, his dark eyes surveying her, his lips drawn back in the toothy grin of his kind. She sighed and relaxed.

"Does Ko still live?" she asked, as she fell in behind the creature, who walked this awkward path to spare her the rigors of travel through the trees.

The dark-furred head turned. "Ko? Live, yes-yes. V'ry old, now. Can h'rdly walk. But wise. Teach all young, teach old, too. If macaque have lead'r at all, it be Ko."

"I would like to talk with him, if it can be done. There is word from the village that he . . . and all your kind . . . should hear."

The macaque nodded and moved on, but the long, sinuous tail curled and twitched, and Juli suspected that the little creature's stoic attitude might be betrayed by the evident unease of its tail. She said nothing more, following him silently between the towering tree boles, into yet deeper forest, until the shadow at ground level belied the day and the sun, still high and invisible above the treetops.

They came out at last into a small area that was cleared of any growth and of all deadfall. It was hidden closely on all sides, of course, and the layered branches roofed it so tightly that Juli felt certain that even a heavy rainfall would only drip through in spots. Although she had not heard any cry from her guide, she found a group of macaque waiting for her there.

Ko was there as well. Though she had not seen the macaque since she was a small child, Juli knew that the bent shape with gray tipping every hair on his body had to be the patriarch of his people. All his children and his grandchildren, as well as those of his brothers and sisters of the first altered generation, had now developed into much larger creatures than he, but his authority was evident as he sat among his family.

Juli moved toward him and sank into a squatting position among his kindred. "Ko?" she asked. "I see you."

The macaque gave its chittering laugh. "Long since Ko hear those w'rd. Think much about Hairless People, but y'r go, v'ry busy time, now too old to go and see old fr'nd."

"I hope not," she answered. "I, too, have grown old. Now I help lead the Metal People, as much as they are led at all. I have come from Kaliche, who is the successor to Tulunga. Do you remember the ancient man who heard voices in his heart?"

"Memb'r Tulunga v'ry good," said Ko. "Wise man. He know, I think, why macaque go away into for'st alone, aft'r fight Chona. Er'c . . . he not know. He hurt, I think. Too bad."

He gave a very manlike sigh and stared up at her with button-bright eyes. "What br'ng you into jungle aft'r macaque, eh?"

"Kaliche sent me to tell you that his voices have spoken to him. He has not the gift that Tulunga had . . . not so strong a one . . . but they do tell him when danger is coming. And now he thinks we are all in great danger from the big cats. He thinks they will hunt us all, Man and macaque alike, and he believes that we should unite against them. This will not, he told me to say, be like killing thinking people."

Ko laughed silently for a long time, his narrow shoulders shaking, his tail quirking with mirth. At last he coughed himself still, and one of the youngsters in the group brought him a nut husk filled with water.

"Wond'r when Metal People learn that. Wond'r when they send aft'r macaque," he gasped. "I know f'r many season that those cat get too big f'r fur. I know f'r long-long that something must be done, but too old to w'rry. Now is time. I go with you. See Er'c. See Moses. Make plan, like old days."

Juli took his small hand in both her own. "We must go soon," she told him. "My father will die soon. And Kaliche thinks Moses will go, too. They are very old, and both have been sick all through the rains."

Ko shook his furry head. "All old," he said. "But most are dead. I r'memb'r long-long. Macaque not live long like man. Er'c old, but Ko old'r. Much old'r. Die soon. Maybe do good thing before dying, eh?"

He grunted and shook himself. A young macaque female came to take his hand and pull him up, and another took his other side to help steady him.

"We go through for'st. Can't climb tree now. Go slow, but we get there."

Juli nodded. Together, the group of macaque and the woman turned back through the jungle, slowly but steadily making their way toward the village beside the river.

19

The Downstream People had been busy with their work. The fish had grown larger as the years passed, and now fishermen and -women worked in teams, for easier and safer handling of their catches. The pirarucu, huge to begin with, were now monstrous and often ate the persons who had intended eating them.

Strangely, the anaconda had not increased in size. Link, who now led the Downstream People, felt certain that the serpent had been so slow in the beginning that greater length and weight would make it too inefficient to live.

The piranha had no such problem. The little demons were now the size of small dolphins and made the deeper parts of the river hazardous for anything attempting to swim it. The only good thing about that was the fact that the shallows were now safe, for the vicious fish were too large to navigate in their old habitat.

When he had left the village where his father led the Metal People, Link had taken his followers downstream to a bluff overlooking the Rio Negro. It was well above the level of even the worst flooding, and behind it was lush jungle, in which game and birds flourished. So, also, did jaguar and ocelot, armadillo and agouti, the latter of which had grown to tremendous size, and the cats were now huge enough to form a real peril to anyone hunting or traveling in the forest.

It was the children who made the discovery that freed them from the worst dangers of the predators. Link's small Bonnie and her brothers, playing near the palisade that shielded the village from the forest, had found a half-grown armadillo, whose size was that of a large dog of the old days. They had tamed the creature, carrying insects and scraps of meat and root vegetables to it, and it had responded well.

As it matured, growing to vast size, it remained tame, and the children began riding on it. A dozen at a time could take their seats along the ridged armor of the back, and their shouts of laughter echoed through the village for months before it occurred to their elders that here was a resource that could not only, perhaps, help them with the predations of the cats, which were not foolish enough to attack those mail-clad giants, but also be useful if the wild people should attack again from across the river.

The young people were sent out to scour the jungle for

more of the armored infants. Those that were caught adapted readily to their new lives, enjoying food that they didn't have to scavenge for, though they kept bumping irritably against the palisade that shut them into their pen in the forest. Only the fact that the butts of the logs were buried deeply kept the creatures from digging out.

Link took time from his constant overseeing of repairs, his hunting, his children's training, to work with the shell-clad beasts. He found them exasperatingly stupid.

Their attention spans were incredibly short, and their appetites were incredibly large. It was impossible to guide one by kicking its armored sides or to spur it on by beating with a stick. Nothing penetrated the shell, and little got through to its tiny brain. He found it necessary to invent a system of reins with flaps that could be shut over one eye or the other, thus turning the beast toward the side from which it still could see. Total blackout brought it to a standstill.

There was another peril as well. When the things ran, which they did when startled and at great speed, anyone riding on the rough-shelled backs tended to fall off at once. Link and his wife Kendra had only to see one of the children take a bad tumble to put their minds to the problem.

His other wife, Sula, was a mistress of plant uses. She had a glue made of the sap of a certain vine, which she boiled with animal claws, hooves, and hides. The stuff would stick anything to anything, seemingly permanently.

When Kendra decided that the only thing to do was to put handles onto the shells of the armadillos for the children to hold onto, Link thought at once of Sula's glue. And it worked. The handles, formed of carved bone, seemed to become part of the beasts onto which they were stuck, and no young ones fell again.

The village continued to grow, as did their ungainly beasts. When at last Link traveled upriver with his families to visit his parents and half sisters and brothers, he waxed enthusiastic about the riding animals, the "Dillos," his people had trained.

Eric listened intently, nodding from time to time. It seemed strange to Link to see a white thatch of hair where his father's pale blond curls had been. The wrinkles grew deeper every time he saw the old man, and even Moses, who had seemed indestructible, had faded to a shadow of himself. The two sat together most of the time now, speaking little, though Link knew that they understood each other so well that words were no longer necessary.

Bonnie was frail, her blue eyes faded but still full of spunk. She looked after her husband and Tasla with quick efficiency, nursing her co-wife in her last illness with the tenderness of a sister. Link found himself thinking that he might have to say good-bye to his mother even before he did to his father. She seemed to grow smaller every time he saw her.

"Can you make those creatures stand, if a cat makes a dash at them?" Eric asked, interrupting his thought. "Or if some wild Indios come shouting and shooting arrows at them?"

Link laughed. "I don't think they would know anything was happening until it was all over. If then. They
take forever to catch onto an idea, and even then it
doesn't sink in deep or last long."

Eric looked over at Moses. In the shade of the porch
that had been Nathan Whitlock's, Moses almost
appeared as he always had. His dark skin was only lightly
lined, and his hair was still pitch black. But Link knew
that if the old man should get up and walk the length of
the porch, his breath would come hard, and his limbs
would grow weak.

The thought saddened him, and all the while that he
remained in the village he found himself staying very
close to his people, feeling that every time he saw them
might be the last. As he pushed his canoe off the rickety
dock, leaving for home again, he looked up into his
father's blue eyes.

"Things are going to change," said Eric to his son.
"Kaliche says so. My bones tell me so, and Moses agrees.
Juli will come back from the forest soon, and perhaps the
macaque will come with her. We will beat out the code
on the big drum if that happens. You need to take coun-
sel with your sister." He reached down to take Link's
hand with a grip that was still strong.

"Train some of those armadillos for us, will you? I'm
going to send out hunters to find some for us, but you
have a lead on us in the training. Can you imagine charg-
ing a band of Cochona, riding on living tanks and shooting as we go?" His eyes flashed with enthusiasm, and

Link recalled suddenly the strong young man who had been his father, the man who had learned to use the Indio weapons as well as any warrior. Who had attacked without caution, according to the old tale, the Cochona in their own place and broken their wild spirits, adding the remnants of the tribe to his own people.

"We'll get some ready. I can send them up the inland paths . . . nobody and nothing is going to mess with them or their riders, be it jaguar or Cochona, believe me. They look like . . . like walking houses. Those creatures are *big*."

He pushed off with his paddle, and the first canoeload of his children moved smoothly into the current. Behind him, Sula and more children came in turn.

He twisted to look back at the dock. Three fragile shapes stood there, waving. They were thin, they were old, and they were none too well or strong, but he knew that those three, his father, his mother, and Moses, were among the wisest people he would ever meet in all his life.

He turned back to the river and dug his paddle deeply. His youngest daughter, Chilla, giggled up at him from the bottom of the craft, and he smiled in return, though his mind was busy.

He would, indeed, ready some of the riding animals and send them up to the village. Four were all but ready now, and he could send his oldest son and daughter and a half-dozen other young people with them.

Not only Kaliche felt that change was in the air, Link thought. He himself had a chill along his bones, a feeling in his gut that not only change, but danger, was on its way.

*   *   *   *   *

The night had been restless for Mark. He found himself twisting on his palm mat until he disturbed his wife. He rose and moved out onto the porch of his high-stilted house. Below his dock, just at the end of his path, the river moved sluggishly, low as was usual for that time of the year.

He gave a reassuring whistle to let the lookouts know it was only he. Then he wandered down the path in the moonlight, staring downstream toward the other villages. Sometimes he found himself very lonely for his twin in Downstream Village, as well as for his parents and kin. This seemed to be a night for sleeplessness, for thinking about old times . . . he came to a halt, frozen, listening.

Something was moving on the river. He had heard a splash that was not that of a fish or of the water moving over the scattered stones at its edges. A paddle splash, distinguishable only by an ear accustomed to the sound.

He dropped off the edge of the dock onto the smooth rock at the level of the river. Lying flat on the stone, he stared up the moonlit expanse of ripples and wavelets, trying to silhouette anything on its surface against the bluff on the farther side of the stream. After a long moment, he caught the flash of moonlight on the surface of a paddle, the quick blip of motion across the light-colored stone beyond the water.

There were no other villages upriver . . . not villages of those he called his own kind. Only the wild Cochona surviving on the other side lived in that direction. Before Steve Porter disappeared for the last time downriver in a canoe, he had made a map of all the settlements he had found before running out of fuel for his chopper, and not one of them was on the Rio Negro.

Mark slid backward under the dock, then rose on the other side and ran, stooping, toward the small plaza of the village he had helped to build. He gave the low whistle that meant trouble was on the way, at the same time clicking his fingers in the code that brought every watcher out of his tree to wake the sleepers in the huts.

They had been lucky in the ten years since he had brought this group upstream. Only the overgrown predators had threatened his people. But he had known that a time would come when men might pose a danger. His father, his uncle Moses, and his sister Juli had agreed with him, every time he went down to see his kindred. His plan had been worked out years before.

Now his people rallied as if they had done this every night of their lives. The children sped for the heavy growth along the river, where they hid, holding the big gourds carved out for carrying water. If fire was used against their homes, they would douse every blaze they could reach without endangering themselves.

The heavily pregnant women went with them to supervise and to watch over the smallest. The other men and women armed themselves with whatever weapons they found themselves most apt at using, and he knew that the poison for darts and arrows was kept fresh. The daily hunts required that, and it was very useful now.

Each warrior paired him or her self with another, with whom he was used to hunting or fishing, and they took their planned stations. Some went into the trees and disappeared into the heavy foliage. Some went under the huts and became invisible in the shadows. All were indistinguishable in the tenuous light, and the village seemed to sleep peacefully beneath the full moon.

Mark was in his own position behind the wall that enclosed the school. It had been built to keep the children in during the hours devoted to teaching them the few matters from the old world that the adults considered important for them to know. Left in an unenclosed yard, the small ones tended to melt into the forest instead of return to the classroom.

Now Mark was glad of the stone-and-mud construction. A line of bowmen was sheltered behind it on all sides. No Cochona would be able to come at the enclosure without drawing fire, for the trees that shaded the area were inside the wall. Those outside had been cut away after an anaconda had dropped into the midst of a game of Spear-your-enemy.

Chiya, Mark's wife, was safely waiting at the river's edge with their young ones. Her baby was due within weeks, and he was glad of it. She was too daring, entirely, for his peace of mind. He shook away the thought, straining his ears after any sound that might indicate that the enemy had landed and was approaching the village.

The water rippled quietly, low in the banks of the river. The light breeze touched leaf to leaf, making a whisper of sound that might conceal . . . what?

He leaned forward, staring through a crevice in the wall. A shadow had flicked across the path, dark against the pale dust. Another followed it.

He hissed between his teeth, softly, softly, warning his people to get ready. Then there came a shattering screech, and the wild people charged among the huts, shooting arrows into the windows and doors. Someone came dashing from the river with a fire arrow and a torch, and the thatch of Mark's own house blazed up.

He aimed his blowpipe and puffed a feathered dart into the chest of a warrior who had just turned to urge the others onward. The man gave a startled grunt . . . and then the plaza was filled with arrows and darts and spears.

The firelight from his roof outlined the enemy all too well, and the Cochona understood that immediately. They tried to retreat behind the huts, but those who hid under them filled their legs with darts, whose poison quickly paralyzed the muscles of the attackers. Some tried to go into the forest, but those in the trees cut them down from above.

There came a rasping cry, and the rest of the wild ones hurried back toward the river. Mark had a terrible thought, and his heart thudded into his stomach. They would run into the children and the pregnant women if they straggled to the water instead of following the hard path!

He vaulted over the wall and ran at full speed toward the reeds and brush where his family hid. Behind him, he could hear others coming, too, for the danger was obvious. The weak spot in his plan—the invisible weak spot that might cause disaster to his own—was now glaringly plain.

There came a chorus of yells from the river. A child's cry, a woman's shout reached his ears as he plunged into the cover. He slowed, taking care that anyone he killed should be an enemy. His people fanned out on either side, going cautiously.

He heard vicious "whick-whicks" as arrows sped through the reeds and bushes, but he could not tell from which direction they might have come or where they had been aimed. Nothing zipped through the growth near him, he was certain.

He lay flat and wriggled forward, taking his chances with water snakes and poisonous insects. Ahead he heard a whimper . . . an infant, he was sure. He flowed over the ground faster than he had ever gone before, and he touched, at last, a child-sized leg. Warm. It jerked.

"Who?" came a small scared voice.

He sighed with relief. It was his older son, Eric. "Your father," he whispered. "Where is your mother?"

"O-over there," came the reply. "She shot at those men. I did, too. We all brought our bows and blowpipes. They tried to come through here, and we shot them."

A cold knot formed in his stomach. "Chiya?" he

called softly.

An arrow "whicked" through the leaves above his head, and he pushed his son flat, lying on top of him. Steps crashed through the brush to one side of their position, and in an instant a heavy body splashed into the river.

He rose, stooping, and put his foot on his son. "Stay there!" he hissed. "Flat. We're here, now. Don't shoot anymore. You might hit one of us!"

Then he was running through the clutter, passing a woman or a child from time to time and knowing that they were alive and seemed unhurt, though he did not pause to see more closely. He was near the water. Out on the river he could hear the thrashing of swimmers, and he stopped on the shore and listened hard.

Somewhere they had their boats hidden. Would they go on downstream to hit Juli's village, or would they drop down to Downstream Village, knowing it to be newer and less well defended, as his own was?

He knelt at the water's edge, sorting out the flashing of ripples from the gleams of wet skin and movements against the current. They were going down, all right. The boats must have been beached on the spit just below the village. They were going to hit his twin, probably tonight.

He whistled a shrill note that rang above the normal sounds of the night-bound forest. He could hear a chirping reply almost at once, and he knew that old Ekla was making her decrepit way to the dhangi, the great drum that was one of the three connecting the villages through their roaring messages.

He crept forward, listening for any betraying splash as the Cochona gained their boats. When he came out into the smooth glare of moonlight on water, he could see six dark blots against the silver water . . . canoes, on their way downriver.

Even as he thought of that, the bone-shaking roar of the dhangi boomed out over the forest, the river, making the very ground beneath his feet seem to quiver with its vibrations. BOOM! BOOM-BOOM! BOOM! The coded signal echoed from the other side of the river, and he knew its warning was even now rousing his sister and her people from their sleep.

Mark stepped back and moved along the riverbank, pulling hidden children from their hiding places, helping heavy-bellied women gain their feet. "Chiya!" he called. "Bani! Eloro! Fenyi!"

Young Eric wriggled out of the reeds and ran ahead of him. "Mama!" he called.

A quiet voice said, "Here," and something in the tone struck terror to Mark's heart. He had never heard his Chiya sound like that, as if all the life were running out of her, leaving no energy and no strength.

He plunged into the undergrowth, crashing and smashing the thick stalks and leafy fronds beneath his feet. He could see something between the moon-washed reeds, and he moved toward it, hearing his son following.

He stepped on something smooth that cracked beneath his foot.

"My bow!" came the quick protest. "You broke it!"

He dropped to his knees beside his wife. It was too dark, there in the shadows, to see anything except her dark outline. "Are you all right?" he asked, reaching for her hand.

"We drove them away from the children," she said, still in that controlled voice. "They would have come right through the smallest ones if we had not had our weapons. We made them sting, those Cochona. You will find dead ones in the water if they have not drifted on down the stream."

"I thought of that too late," Mark said. "When I realized that they would retreat right over your position, I almost panicked. But you and the children did very well. The small bows for hunting birds can bring down men, too, if the poison is strong."

"Which it was. I brought a pot with me, and as we waited I dipped all the darts and the arrow points." Her breath caught in her throat, and she stifled a groan.

"You are wounded!" he said. He stooped to lift her, but she gasped a protest.

"Where?" He squatted again, and ran his hands over her body. Her belly was moving strangely, heaving itself up into ridges and then relaxing again.

"If I am wounded, it is not the Cochona's doing," she chuckled, letting out her breath in another gasp. "Your child has decided that it is time to be born . . . and a less convenient time it could not have chosen. I am close to birth. Help me to walk—it is better so."

"Oh." He felt his entire being relax. He had been too

certain that she had been pierced by one of the Cochona arrows. This was life, not death, and he welcomed her weight on his arm as she heaved herself upright and began to walk with determination through the dragging reeds, making for the path below the dock.

The dhangi was still shaking the world with its bellows of warning, but Mark seemed not to hear it at all. He was thinking hard as he helped his wife up the bank and into the hands of the other women. Ekla left her whanging away at the drum and came last, chirping with excitement.

As she led Chiya away to the hospital hut, Mark turned to Kole, his best friend and adviser. "They will hit either First Village or Downstream Village," he said. "Do you agree?"

Kole nodded, his teeth flashing in the moonlight. "I agree. They will be warned, but the Cochona will also know that they do not go against unsuspecting prey. That will change their tactics, I think. Should we go behind . . . take them by surprise?"

Mark smiled for the first time that night. "Just what I was thinking. If we follow in our own canoes—taking our nets—and bind up all the Cochona boats as soon as we find where they have left them, that will leave them afoot on the wrong side of the river. We can catch them, and, if we are lucky, maybe even convert a few to our own ways."

He whistled again, and the warriors of the village left those tasks that could be left and circled around him. "We go to the aid of our people downstream. Who will go with us?" he asked.

There was a quiet murmur among the warriors for a few seconds. He did not rush things, for he knew that many of these men and women had families that needed attention, wounded needing treatment, or homes that had suffered badly in the attack. Those who could go would go, and those who could not would help the families of the ones going downstream.

When they sorted themselves out, some fifteen were ready to follow Mark and Kole, and they quickly slid their hidden canoes out of the concealing growth high on the riverbank. When his small flotilla set out, it was again armed to the teeth, for the older children had scavenged even among the dead, retrieving arrows and darts, renewing their poison, and filling the pouches and quivers of their fathers, mothers, brothers, and sisters. Wherever the Cochona stopped now, they would find themselves flanked by angry and determined warriors who intended to avenge themselves upon those who had disturbed their peace and wounded their people.

20

The moon had grown full. Juli slept until the light moved to fall across her face through the unshuttered window, but she had never been able to sleep in moonlight. She woke and rose, knowing that she would have a hard time resting again that night.

She went onto the veranda, her accustomed ears not even hearing the cacophony rising from the forest around the perimeter of the fence. She did hear her father's rasping breaths, as he slept, and she listened intently for a moment, hearing the difficulty with which each one seemed to be drawn.

She realized that Ko had seemed saddened by the shadow of death that hung about her father, because the macaque was far older than either Moses or Eric, in terms of survival within their respective species.

The moon turned the little plaza to a place of silver and black shadow, and she stepped from the veranda into the dust, moving toward the dock. Sometimes the ripple of the water soothed her on wakeful nights, when she remembered her two husbands, now dead, and their children, who had not survived infancy. Something seemed set against her, she thought, denying her the comfort of a family of her own. And now she was going to lose her father; Moses, who was almost a father to her, and both her mothers, too, were growing fragile. There was no doubt in her mind that the time was very near.

A small dark shape moved across the lighted space, and she recognized Ko by his stiff-legged walk. She went to meet him, and he took her hand as they strolled toward the water.

The river was low; the season of heaviest rains was only weeks ahead. The voices of stones usually deep underwater chattered away, and Juli found herself relaxing. As she turned to speak to the macaque, a clamor rose above the forest, seeming to echo down the narrow corridor that was the river. The dhangi . . . from upstream. Mark!

Juli shouted with all her strength, "Up! Danger! The drum!"

Ko slipped from beside her to meet a group of his own kind who had dropped from the trees inside the fence as soon as the dhangi spoke. The Metal People were pouring from their huts, weapons already in hand, making for their pre-planned posts. Juli felt a surge of pride as she saw her lieutenants gather before her.

"If Mark has warned us, it means that there is danger

on the river. Anyone coming through the forest would take a day to travel the distance, and he could send a canoe down to tell us of their coming. So we must concentrate our attention upon the riverside and the dock. Put up the barriers that block off the shallow banks, you three. Get the children together and give them their tools. They will hide in the walled area around the spring behind the church. See that ten are told to guard them, Osholo."

As she spoke, those indicated moved swiftly to attend to their tasks. They had rehearsed for a long time the response they would make to any attack from across the river, and now it was almost with enthusiasm that they put into practice the years of preparation.

Eric was on the porch, and his old rifle leaned against a post. He had saved ammunition, cleaning the mold from the lead points, keeping the brass cartridge cases free of corrosion, bright against any need. When she stepped up beside him, he turned to her with a smile.

"So we have a chance for action, before we old ones go. I would have chosen this way, if it were not for the losses among you youngsters. And a good thing I kept this weapon ready, too. . . . I couldn't draw a bow if my life depended on it, nowadays. And I haven't the wind for a blowgun either, though Moses can still beat most of the young warriors with the thing."

She leaned against the railing, watching the glint of moon on ripples below the dock. "Who are you calling a youngster?" she teased. "When you have a daughter who is almost forty years old, she is no child, I can tell you. And you are not old—sixty is no great age!"

"It wasn't, in the old days," he sighed. "But the life we have led for the past years is enough to make an old man out of anyone. And whatever it is that is happening inside me is out to get me, and don't you forget it."

Juli lifted her hand, as the old woman who had been assigned to their own dhangi came across the plaza, her club in hand. Nodding, Luti turned and went into the shadow of the biggest tree in the compound. After a moment, the sonorous voice of their own drum passed the warning down the river to Link's village downstream.

Anyone on the river would certainly hear that warning and would be, in turn, cautioned against reckless attack. That would make them more dangerous still, but she could not leave the Downstream People in ignorance, and the voice of the upstream drum did not carry so far, as they had determined by repeated testing.

"Kindle the big torch," said her father. "Canoes come fast, even when the water is low. The second warning sounded fifteen minutes ago. They will be here soon, if they don't run afoul of the rocks in the shallows."

Juli leaped over the rail and ran toward the dock, taking with her the torch that Osholo handed her as she passed him. The heavy bow was in its place, held by hooks beneath the planking of the dock, and she pulled it free as she reached it.

She went to the very end of the pier and drew the bow, blessing her wiry strength as she did so. The long years of training were paying off even more now than in the past. The kindled arrow she had set on the string whizzed into the spangled light of the river and struck a post set into the rock formation just upstream. The pitch-soaked cord wrapped tightly around its top flared at once into brilliant flame, lighting the river to a sullen red.

Smelling the acrid smoke of the thing, Juli pitched her kindling torch into the water, and walked away amid the angry hissing as it was quenched. The post would burn for hours, backlighting anyone trying to approach from the river.

She went quickly to the hut that concealed and sheltered the boiler and generator. It had been some time since she had tested the thing, and she said a small prayer as she fanned the blaze already set in the firebox and closed the valves that would build the steam necessary for generating the electricity to charge the fence. She wanted no subtle warrior attacking her forces from the rear.

Her father and Moses were standing together at the light barrier set between the village and the water. Each was armed, and beyond them she could see Bonnie, who held her old revolver in a hand that seemed too frail to sustain its weight. She knew that her mother Tasla was fretting in her place among the children at the well, wanting to help her own but unable even to stand. Then Juli shut away the thought, for she could see dark shapes on the water.

One . . . two . . . three . . . it looked like six canoes, only now coming around the bend above the falls.

Those manning them were skilled at their work, she realized, and must have scouted out the river from the forest on its other side. They were ready for the waterfall and shot it on its lower side, coming through upright, though pretty full of water. But they were trying to angle for the shore, warned by the big torch waiting in mid-stream.

The first canoe made the bank, and the figures inside it bailed out into the thick growth edging the river. Juli heard something rustle in the trees along the water's edge, and a shrill cry told her that the macaque were moving upriver.

She pushed through the barrier with a group of war-riors and rushed upstream toward the spot where the canoe had beached. She cursed her aging legs, which now were painful when forced to too much speed, but she moved quickly, nevertheless. She had had no time to plan strategy with the monkey-people, but it seemed that Ko and his peers had done a lot of thinking in the years they had kept so much apart from Man. Now the dark-furred creatures were dropping from branches onto the Cochona in the ferns and reeds. Cries reached her ears, and they were not those of macaque.

She shouted as her people fell upon the canoes now drawing near the shore. Her spear caught a slender dark shape in the chest, and it fell into the water and was washed past her legs as she waded out into the deeper part of the stream.

She found herself yelling, splashing through the red-dening ripples. A macaque leaped over her head onto the big man ahead of her. She ducked aside, thrusting at another, smaller shape behind him. A canoe swept past her, and she tried to turn to keep it in view, but her foot slid on a rolling limb, sunk beneath the surface, and she fell.

Something pushed her down, and her lungs filled with water. She struggled upward, clinging to an anonymous leg near at hand. As her head broke through the surface, she began coughing, water pouring from her nose. She heaved desperately to gain her feet, caught again at the person beside her. . . .

And saw a Cochona, marked with black stripes aslant his face and body. A knife, coming at her low and swiftly, caught her in the stomach, and she bent forward, as the Cochona fell beneath the club of a snarling macaque.

She tried to gasp her thanks, to call out to her people, but the remaining fluid in her chest choked off her voice. Pain caught at her midriff, making her gasp, warring with the near-drowning for dominance. She stared up at the round moon, which seemed to peer sadly down the slot through which the river ran. She had given it all she had. She could find no regret in her heart, as she thought of those who had gone ahead of her . . . two husbands, four sons, and a daughter . . . she would see them again, perhaps, beyond the darkness.

And then it was very, very dark indeed.

* * * * *

The voice of the dhangi woke Link from a troubled dream. Even as he rose from the mat he shared with his wives, they, too, were springing to their feet, rummaging about for their weapons. He could hear outside the feet of the watch running toward the huts that circled with his about the plaza.

He took the heavy bow, the blowpipe, the long knife that his father had given him long ago, when he showed an aptitude for that weapon. It slid into the worn sheath, and he thought briefly of his father's words: "A good friend gave it to me. I give it to you, and may it serve you well."

Then he was on his veranda, out among the warriors who were speeding for their posts about the perimeter of the thorn fence they had planted in an arc toward the jungle. But he knew that it was from the river that the problem would come. The dhangi would not have been sounded because of a problem with animals, no matter how large and fierce, and an enemy from landward would not have required that kind of warning.

These foes would be men, and the only enemies his people now had lived beyond the Rio Negro. The old Cochona had been assimilated into his own tribe, and it was impossible to say which of the people he knew in the three villages were the children of those, but their fierce cousins were unchanged by the years, or by El Malo.

His people had known for years that, in time, those beyond the river would build up their numbers and their ferocity to the point where they would attack. War was the principal thing in their lives—or it had been through all their history—and once they reached a point at which they could sustain it again, that would be their goal.

Even as he thought, he was running to the small cove

that curved toward the village. It was edged by a rocky barrier, with only one narrow opening through which they could take their canoes. He had chosen this spot partly because of that barrier—it had seemed such a natural defense, if ever an attack should come. Now he was profoundly happy that he had done that.

Behind him he heard the snuffling grunts of the Dillos that were being led from their pen into the plaza. He grinned as he dropped to the little beach edging the cove and leaped from stone to stone, followed by a half-dozen of his best warriors. The Cochona would have more than one surprise if they came this far.

He slipped into the water, concealing himself among the current-rounded stones of the barrier. He could not see even one of his companions, so well did their dark heads blend with the water and the rock. Even his sun-bleached crop would not show, for the moon was silvering the water and the stones indiscriminately.

He turned to stare back at the village. The shapes of the Dillos were huge in the glare of moonlight, which was so bright that there had been no need even for torches to light their preparations. Dark figures clung to the ridged backs of the beasts, and he knew that any Cochona who got into the village would have nightmares forever . . . if he survived.

Link waited . . . and waited. The shallows were treacherous this time of year, and he thought that any attacking force might have encountered enough resistance upriver to make it very cautious as it approached his village.

And then he realized that something was happening on the other shore of the stream. Black shapes moved canoes down to the water. Had the Cochona sent their attacking force in two parts, one to come down the river, doing what damage it could, while the other came through the forest to canoes that must have been put into place long before?

He hissed between his teeth, and the sound, he knew, carried no farther than the nearest of his fellows. Tensing, he watched three canoes slip into the water, but they did not approach. They would wait for whoever was coming down the river, he suspected.

And then there came the grate of a canoe against rock as something upstream came nearer. His people would meet two groups, a fresh one from across the river, and the initial one, or what remained of it, coming down the stream from the attacks on the other two villages.

He gritted his teeth and put his knife between them. Then he could see, between two concealing stones, a line of canoes rush into sight and dart toward the cove. The Cochona had scouted well from across the Negro . . . they knew where the break was in the barrier, and they headed for it with sure accuracy.

Link submerged as the first came through. He shot up again and thrust the tough blade of the knife through the bottom of the log canoe, jerking it free as he rolled the craft over. The water was suddenly full of struggling Cochona. He could hear yells and gasps, and he knew that his companions were upsetting the vessels as quickly as they could.

A slippery shape grappled with him, and they went under together. Link rolled onto his back, pushing the body of the other man away with his feet. His hand came up, and the knife met resistance. He tasted blood, as he surfaced and drew a great breath.

"Ashore!" he yelled, swimming strongly for the glimmer of the beach.

Every one of the canoes was overturned, the Cochona now being a milling group of swimmers trying to reach the shore before a strong resistance could be organized. That was the weakest part of their nature and their culture—they had lived so long without the need to plan ahead, not only for seasons or years but for decades, that such forethought seemed like magic to them. Link's father had taught him and his siblings all that he had learned about the Cochona from those who had been integrated into the tribe of Metal People. It had taken those newcomers a generation to learn the value of such careful planning, Eric had said.

Now Link blessed his father and Moses, Bonnie and Tasla, and all those who had remembered the ways of the white men so well. The education they had insisted that all the children, not just their own, must have was serving the tribe well now, as it had for years.

He crawled onto the beach and stood, waving his own people into position as they gained the shore. They disappeared into the shadows, and he dropped also as a dart, waterlogged but still deadly, zinged past his head. He slid backward through the growth edging the beach, and he could hear his people moving, too. He grinned again.

As the first wave of Cochona found their feet and made for cover, the heavy feet of the Dillos pounded down the slope to the water. Link, lying under a shelf of rock, saw one of the huge animals clamber down, clumsy because of its bulk, and stand guarding the beach. Ten others lined the shore, and every one was ridden by at least four warriors, whose bows and blowguns were busy.

The smell of blood filled the heavy night air. Link climbed the tail of the nearest Dillo and stood precariously, hooking his foot into one of the glued-on handles. From that elevation, he saw motion upriver.

Not another wave of Cochona! His people were holding their own, and the Dillos were causing terrible consternation among the enemy, but if another fresh group should come ashore upstream and attack from the rear, he knew that his defenders would be stretched perilously thin. The pregnant women, the very old and infirm, and the children would have to bring their weapons into play, and the thought of that filled him with pain.

The loss of grown men and women—of the elderly, even, though it was their advice and long experience that made life easier for the tribe—could be borne. The loss of the small ones was far more serious, for they were the future of the tribe, the slender thread on which the survival of his kind depended.

He roared a warning and leaped from the Dillo onto a big Cochona who seemed to be trying to rally his fellows in the shadow of the shoreline boulders. A shout from upstream greeted him as he rose from the body of his victim, wiping the knife with his hand and washing away the blood in the river.

Then he recognized the voice, and he sighed, deeply, feeling himself relax. It was Mark, his twin. And that meant that Upstream Village had dealt well with the attack. The middle village must have, too, or the relief group would have stopped there to help.

Now the Cochona were breaking for the river, crawling over the stones and plunging into the deep water beyond them. It was a foolhardy thing . . . but so had been the entire attack plan. The river was deep there, and the piranha patrolled it from shallows to shallows.

Even as he thought that, Link heard a scream, and the water, flowing so smoothly that it looked like silver cloth, was thrashed into foam, droplets sparkling as they flew upward. The first four Cochona to make it to the river disappeared quickly, and Link knew that the smell of their blood would bring every piranha in the area to that spot.

The Cochona who had gained the barrier now hung there, watching with horror the end of their fellows. To swim for the distant bank in order to go home through the forest would be death . . . certain death. What lay behind them would also be death, Link knew they were thinking, but not, perhaps, as terrible a death as the one lying before them.

They turned, dropping their weapons, and stared dumbly at those who now approached them over the stones. The canoes on the river lined up and came through the slot, which was too shallow for the passage of the piranha, and the newcomers came ashore in time to help with the captives.

"I was certain you were more Cochona, coming to help this bunch," said Link, hugging his brother. "You were a welcome sight, believe me."

"I think you could have handled it," said Mark, staring at the Dillos, which were now placidly grubbing along the shoreline, ignoring the milling group of Cochona and the villagers alike.

"I want some of those creatures. We can catch them, if you will help us train them. Father told me, a bit ago, that you were going to help them with the project. I want in on it. That can make things much safer for anybody who goes out foraging for plants or hunting. Wow!" He stood staring with admiration at the immense animals. "Just like the tanks Father used to talk about!"

"They're all in good shape, then . . . upstream?" asked Link. "I didn't have time to worry when I heard the drum, but it's catching up with me now."

"Father and Mother and Moses and Tasla are fine," said Mark. "But . . . we lost Juli."

Link felt his heart thud, and sickness filled his stomach. His little sister Juli! She had been one of the close-knit group that was formed by all the older children of Eric and Bonnie and Tasla and Moses and his wives. Almost a small tribe within a tribe.

"How?" he asked, turning to look upriver as if he might somehow see his sister again there.

"Fighting . . . how else?" said Mark. "She didn't suffer, at least not for more than a moment. The macaque who killed her attacker got her out of the water immediately, and two more took her to the hospital, but she was already gone. Old Ko cried. . . ."

"The macaque? Ko? You mean the whole bunch has come back?" It seemed incredible, after all the years that had passed, but Link found himself warmed by the thought.

"I think, perhaps, for good. I didn't wait for long at the village, but Ko was talking with Father and Moses, and all the rest of his family was listening and nodding and talking among themselves.

"It seemed to me that they had been wanting to come back as a group for some time, but they just hadn't gotten around to it. When Juli went to find them, they were more than glad to come with her to talk it over." Mark sighed and put his arm over his brother's shoulders.

"I wish . . ." he began. And then he fell silent, feeling his twin wishing, too, with all his might, that this attack had never happened, that their losses, and even those of the Cochona, had not occurred.

"There are just too few of us to go around killing each other," said Link softly.

"We have all these warriors. It's probably the bulk of the males from the families across the river. So, when we can, we just might go and see if we can round up the rest of them and bring them back. We civilized one batch. Why not these as well?" asked Mark.

It sounded sensible to Link, but he turned to check his people. A number had been killed or wounded, he knew. Until he found out who had been killed, how all the injured were, he would never be able to rest.

Followed by his twin, he made his way through the deepening shadows, for the moon was sinking behind the forest now, to learn the worst. Once that was done, he might think of tomorrow, but for now he was too weary, too dispirited, too hurt by the loss of Juli to think further than the next few hours.

Behind him, Mark said, "Father asked that we both come upriver as soon as we can. I think—he thinks—he's going to die, Link. He wants to talk to us before he goes. Can you make it now, tonight?"

Link sank onto a length of log that served as a stool for those tending the poultry. This night had been a disaster from its beginning, and it was never, it seemed, going to end.

21

Kaliche oversaw the laying of the funeral pyres. The ritual that Nathan Whitlock had feared and despised had been revived among those of his people who had relinquished it as long as the old missionary lived. Many, of course, had never changed that ancient method of disposing of the dead, though they pretended to for the sake of the old man they revered.

Among Kaliche's own people, before the merging, the ritual had been filled with awe and love and hope, and as it was continued in this new tribe those elements had become stronger and stronger. The white people had insisted upon some changes, but those seemed minor, and now even they took part without hesitation.

He was happy to have something to do other than watch the pain of old Eric's family. They had come from upstream and down to speak with him for a last time, and Kaliche knew that would be a sad thing for all of them. Eleven children survived the old man, from both his old wives and the younger one they had insisted that he take when they became too old to conceive. There was a large group of people gathered at the old mission house now.

Even as he thought that, one of the macaque came and touched his elbow. "Er'c ask f'r Kaliche. You come?" The bright eyes stared up at him pleadingly, and the shaman sighed and set a last billet of wood on the last of the pyres. Fourteen of his people had died in the attack, and they would accompany Juli and her father into the fire.

He followed the waddling walk of the macaque across the plaza into the shadow of the veranda. Lato, one of the twins that Tasla had borne to Eric, sat on the step, her youngest child on her knee, her adult children standing about her uncertainly, looking ill at ease.

Kaliche touched the woman's graying hair. "Send the young ones away," he said, his tone quiet. "They can do nothing here, and it makes them sad."

She looked up, and he could see that she was near to tears, though she controlled them, as all the Metal People learned to do before they reached their adulthood. "Yes," she said. "You are right. Go about your work, my children. I will stay here and wait for all of us."

Kaliche smiled down at her, though he knew that the mourning marks of ash around his eyes and down his nose made his face look ferocious. He went across the porch and into the wide central hallway, where Link and Mark were standing, just outside the door of the big bedroom where their parents had slept for all of their lives.

Ko was sitting on a cushion on the floor, his small face still, his tail curled tightly around his feet, which were tucked up against him as if to ward off some danger that only he could see. The macaque rose when he saw Kaliche and came to take his hand.

"You come," the small being said. "Er'c want speak to you. To all who knew the old ones, the old ways. Come into r'm now. Boys come, too." He gestured commandingly, and the two middle-aged men, who had been reduced to youngsters by this ancient of his kind, shrugged wryly and followed them into the chamber.

The blinds, woven of bamboo and providing a sort of cool shadow to the room, were drawn. The harsh light from outside reflected from the bare ground of the plaza and again from the whitewashed ceiling, and even in the dimness Eric's face stood out strongly, his blue eyes wide, and his cheekbones sharp under his skin.

"Kaliche," he said, extending his hand.

As the shaman took the bony fingers, he saw that Tasla occupied the other side of the bed, her shape so shrunken that she hardly showed as a presence at all. Bonnie stood at the head of the bed frame, a palmetto fan in her hand, with which she kept a draft of air moving over the sick.

"I am about to lose them both," she said, her tone infinitely sad.

"Don't talk about that now," commanded Eric. "I

have things to say, to our children and our friends. I have been thinking, since Juli died, very hard about our lives here, the world out there, whatever is left. About everything. It seems that things come very clear when you are standing on the very edge of life, about to go over to the other side. There are matters you need to know, to be thinking about. I wish Tulunga were here! He could put things so well. . . ."

Eric's voice trailed off for a moment, and his hand relaxed a bit in Kaliche's. The shaman thought for a moment that the old man was gone, but Eric gave a deep sigh and released Kaliche's fingers. Eric's eyes were brighter than they had seemed for a long time, and he seemed to be looking inside himself, remembering.

"We have tried to keep all the important things alive. My mother and father, Halloran and Porter and Tom Butler and Cash all taught me—us—things they knew that can't be learned anyplace else. If you let the teachings die away, there is no way to get them back again.

"Keep the school. Teach the young ones all we taught you," he said to his seven oldest children, who stood at the foot of the bed. "You have all learned to speak English, and this is good. Keep reading and rewriting the books, as they crumble. Keep the ability to do mathematics, if nothing else, for that gives the ability for logical and analytical thought. Check the old laboratory from time to time. There are things there that might be useful one day, if they are kept in order and free of rust and mold." He gasped for breath, coughed, and lay still for a long moment. "Never forget to keep learning from the jungle and the Indios who are left out there. It is a treasury—if we only know how to use it fully.

"There is so much still to do. Our numbers are too few to let us explore, trying to find those who Steve Porter located so long ago. His maps are in my metal case. If they begin to be illegible, copy them, again and again. One day my great-grandchildren may want to find more of our kind."

He reached blindly, and Ko came forward and took his hand. "Ko, your people are my pride. My parents and those distant, ancient Frenchmen did well when they made your kind and nurtured it. You are good people. Perhaps, at times, better than those who made you what you are. You have good heads and kind hearts, and nobody can ask more than that."

Eric stared up at Kaliche. "Do you think the time has come?" he asked the shaman.

For an instant, Kaliche thought he was asking if the time had come for the man's death, but then he remembered a conversation that had been lost among past years, and he smiled. "I think, indeed, the time has come," said Kaliche.

He took from about his neck the thong on which the old amulet hung. He thought of Tulunga, who had worn the thing for so long, whose spirit, surely, had gone into it, along with those of generations of his predecessors.

He understood with sudden clarity just what it was that Eric was asking him to do. The macaque no longer depended upon or even needed humankind. But they had come when called, and this was a kindness on their part that he wondered if his own sort would reciprocate. Perhaps this symbolic gift would seal the bond of that strange friendship between their two peoples.

"I give this to you, Ko of the macaque, to bestow upon any of your people who show that they deserve it, when the time comes. And when that person's time has passed, he will give it to the one who succeeds me among the Metal People. We will pass it from hand to hand, Man to macaque, as long as our kinds endure. Those who think deeply, care for others, try new things . . . all are deserving of honor. But the one who holds this has more. It is the holy thing of the Metal People, who give it into your hands for safekeeping, and no matter how our kinds live in time to come, it will seal us together."

The macaque took the thong in his dark-furred hands and slipped it about his neck. He lifted the amulet, and it gleamed dully in the tenuous light of the room. He turned to Eric . . . but Eric had gone to join his parents and his daughter. His eyes were open, but he no longer lived behind them.

Bonnie touched Tasla's forehead. She looked up at her assembled children. "She, too," she breathed. "They have gone together. And that—" she almost sobbed the last words— "is good."

Kaliche turned blindly toward the door. He nodded to the other children, who waited in the shadows of the trees in the garden, and then he hurried toward the pyres, as if only there might he find help.

* * * * *

The night sky glowed red, reflecting the blazes below it. The village of the Metal People was silent except for the roar of the flames. Even the creatures of the forest were quiet in the trees and the undergrowth, as if they, too, knew that the world was changed.

The people watched the pyres as they dwindled to ash. They raked fragments of bone back into the coals again and again until everything was reduced to the smallest possible trace.

When dawn lit the river, they raked out the bone fragments and poured them from each of the two pyres into an ancient stone pot. Kaliche sang a plaintive chant as he took up his stone pestle and ground the ashes further to dust, and all the people stood in a circle and sang with him, counterpoint to his chant.

When he was done, he poured the white powder into a finely woven basket and held it out. Bonnie, first of all, approached him and touched her fingers to the ash. She marked it in a cross on her forehead, showing that the wisdom and the strength of those who were gone were still preserved in the people they left behind them. Moses followed her, his face a mask of grief.

One by one the rest of the villagers from all the three villages filed past, touching the ash, marking their foreheads, some of the older ones touching that fingertip to their tongues before making the sign. Kaliche chanted steadily, his old hands firm on the basket, his voice strong and sure. When the last, smallest child had passed him, he poured the ash back into the stone pot and buried it in the grave prepared for it in the little cemetery, where many such minute grave marks made slight mounds in the turf.

He turned toward the forest and made off in the direction of the waterfall where he had met Eric for the first time. He heard footsteps behind him, and when he glanced back, he saw Moses following him. It was fitting that they go together to the spot where their people had joined forces, he thought.

When at last they reached the waterfall, and that took a full two days, for both men were now old and their steps were not as quick and sure as they had been in days gone by, Kaliche sat under the fall, facing outward through the veil of water, while Moses went back into the caverns and out of his sight.

A voice, speaking to his heart—one last time, perhaps—demanded to be heard. Kaliche closed his eyes and listened to the words in his spirit.

EPILOGUE

The mist was cool on his face. The stone was wet and slick beneath his body, but those things meant nothing. He saw the world—the world out there beyond the forest, beyond the river and the bigger river at its end. The message came, in part, as pictures this time, and it took his breath away as he seemed to fly, birdlike, above it all, moving swiftly toward the immense span of water that he knew must be the ocean that Eric had told him about.

"The world goes on," said the voice in his mind. "Man has returned to a humble station and is a new thing now, becoming something that has not been seen before. Beyond the seas, a few survive. But that is not the most important thing. They have a new chance to grow, which is the vital part of living.

"The animals have changed and now grow wise, some

of them. The plants grow and die and grow again, and their fruits feed birds and animals and insects. The great cycle goes on and on and on.

"Your small band has begun to learn a great lesson, perhaps the last and the best for your kind. You are learning to work together in peace, without killing those whom you consider your enemies, without fearing those who are different in body and in spirit from your own kind. There is a light, kindled here in the jungles of the south, which may, in time to come, cast a glow in places you have never seen or dreamed of."

*   *   *   *   *

The voice went still, but he flew onward, and in his spirit-picture he saw great herds of beasts moving over wide spans of grass where no forest grew. He saw jagged peaks, which must have been mountains, and great chasms cut into the skin of the world. He went higher and higher, and then he understood the thing he saw, and he smiled and opened his eyes.

As if he had heard the movements of those eyelids, Moses came from the cave and stood beside him. "Is all well?" he asked.

Kaliche nodded and put out his hand for help in rising. "All is well with the world," he said. "Our kind has lived for many lives of men, here in the jungles, prospering as long as the white men were not here. Now they are still here, but they are friends, not enemies. Together, we will make a new sort of life, a fresh kind of civilization that may, in time, spread to the empty reaches beyond the forest and the Great Waters. We have the chance to start again, threading together many sorts of lives, many kinds of skills and talents. The world will go forward, and our kind will change and grow, and in time we will stand as tall as the great animals and as bright as the morning sun."

And that, he realized, was far more true than he or Eric had dreamed it might be, when they said good-bye. The people were strong, and they were learning to be kindly and helpful to other sorts.

As generations passed, perhaps they would go out of the jungles, across the seas, find others of their kind to help and to teach these new ways they were learning. In time, there might be, once again, a world tenanted with humankind.

Kaliche sighed and stared up at the stars that were beginning to break through the evening clouds. Then he moved toward the village and the small and warm and vital affairs of his people.

ABOUT THE AUTHORS

Ardath Mayhar operates a small bookstore in Texas with her husband. She has published poetry, numerous short stories, and novels, and is represented in many horror, Western, and fantasy anthologies. Among the novels she has had published are *The World Ends in Hickory Hollow*, *Warlock's Gift*, *Makra Choria*, *Seekers of Shar Nuhn*, and *Trail of the Seahawks*. Her book *Medicine Walk* was named "Remarkable Juvenile Literature" by the Parents' Choice Foundation, just one of many honors she has received for her writing.

A Vietnam War veteran, Ron Fortier is currently writing a comics adaptation of RAMBO for Blackthorne Comics and a completely revamped POPEYE for Ocean Comics. He first teamed up with Ardath Mayhar when they wrote *Trail of the Seahawks* for TSR. Fortier resides in Somersworth, New Hampshire, with his wife and five children.

New Characters. New Adventure.

THE AVATAR TRILOGY
Richard Awlinson

Shadowdale

Stripped of their powers and banished from their planes because of some missing tablets, the gods seek an unlikely group of adventurers and their magic-user, a young woman recently infused with god-level magical abilities.

Tantras

Convicted for the murder of Elminster, the heroes flee in search of evidence to clear themselves, and to find the missing Tablets of Fate, the artifacts needed for the gods to return to their planes...or for others to take their places....

Waterdeep

The search continues to the largest city in the Realms, where the characters believe the last tablet is hidden. However, one of the heroes has cast his lot with the evil gods, and his denizens await the others at every turn.

FORGOTTEN REALMS is a trademark owned by TSR, Inc. ©1989 TSR, Inc. All Rights Reserved.

THE MARTIAN WARS TRILOGY
M.S. Murdock

Rebellion 2456: Buck Rogers joins NEO, a group of freedom fighters dedicated to ridding Earth of the Martian megacorporation RAM. NEO's goal is to gain enough of a following to destroy RAM's Earth Space Station. The outcome of that mission will determine the success of Earth's rebellion. Available in May 1989.

Hammer of Mars: Ignoring RAM threats and riding on the wave of NEO's recent victory, Buck Rogers travels to Venus to strike an alliance. Furious, RAM makes good on its threats and sends its massive armada against a defenseless Earth. Available in August 1989.

Armageddon Off Vesta: Martian troops speed to Earth in unprecedented numbers. Earth's survival depends on Buck's negotiations with Venus. But even as Venus considers offering aid to Earth, Mercury is poised to attack Venus. Relations among the inner planets have never been worse! Available in October 1989.

BUCK ROGERS IS A TRADEMARK USED UNDER LICENSE FROM THE DILLE FAMILY TRUST.
©1989 THE DILLE FAMILY TRUST. ALL RIGHTS RESERVED.